Also by Cathryn Grant

Cathryn Grant

THE SUBURBAN ABYSS

A Novel

D2C Perspectives

FOR MY PARENTS, who nurtured my love of reading, fed me with crime stories, and provided me with a front row seat in suburbia, where my attention was immediately drawn to the dark end of the street.

One

A HAMMER POUNDING on fresh wood is a beautiful
sound if you're remodeling your home or building a gazebo.
But the sharp burst of iron against a hard surface at seven-
fifty on a Saturday morning in October could make a man
consider taking that hammer to someone's skull.

Brian pressed his thumb into the clay, forming an
indentation that would become an eye socket. He stroked his
fingertip across the cheek of the figure he was creating. It was
so firm — youthful flesh — not like his own skin that was
looser than it had been even two or three years ago. His
wasn't papery and dry like an old man's, but it certainly wasn't
as taut as it had been in his early thirties. At least the rest of
him was in good shape.

He pressed gently to deepen the eye socket. Working in his
small studio on Saturday mornings used to be one of the
highlights of his week. Now, his fence was backed by a wall
of plywood. Twenty feet beyond that they were digging the

foundation for the new medical center and underground parking garage.

The worst part was, the hammering wasn't even the start of construction. Once they finished digging there would be the slamming of pile drivers and the screeching of metal on metal as beams were bolted together right behind his fence. The temporary wall designed to *protect* his property would be useless in protecting his ears and his sanity. Earlier in the week, the grinding of earthmovers had started before he left for work. In just a few days, they'd managed to open a yawning pit in the earth, thirty-five feet deep and a block wide. They could bulldoze all five houses in his cul-de-sac and the debris would only fill a small corner of that canyon.

The pounding of iron on wood that pierced the soft tissue of his brain this morning was the sound of the Neighborhood Disturbance Coordinator hanging signs. He knew this because the evening before he'd carried his pre-dinner martini down the front path, past the softly gurgling fountain, toward the mouth of the cul-de-sac. She'd been dragging painted sheets of plywood out of the back of her car. She'd leaned them against the chain link fence and crawled into the open hatchback, then climbed out. She'd opened the front passenger door, bent over, and patted the floor. He'd guessed she was missing either hammer or nails to hang her signs. She'd left them leaning against the fence and driven away. He'd considered taking them, but decided that was overtly aggressive.

Now she was nailing the first sign to a post, informing neighbors how to contact her if the construction workers broke the *good neighbor guidelines*. The guidelines included not starting work until eight in the morning, not driving heavy equipment on non-designated streets, or doing something untoward, such as urinating against the few curbside trees that hadn't been torn out to dig the pit.

He laughed. The woman's title was absurd on so many levels. The collection of words itself was meaningless — Neighborhood Disturbance Coordinator. He couldn't believe that was actually a job. Not a real job where you produced something tangible, children qualified to move on to the fourth grade, in his case. What did she do all week besides hang signs, disturbing the neighborhood in the process? He supposed she answered phone calls, responded to emails, wrote meaningless words for brochures and community updates. That last bit was what she'd emphasized when she spoke to Brian and his neighbors about her role in the construction of the new medical center. It would be a three-story building with two levels of underground parking, replacing the rustic, one-story complex that had sat on the opposite side of the fence for nearly twenty-five years.

The thing that irked him most about her title was the assumption that there would be such a level of disturbance that a full time position was required to manage it. Despite all the assurances that the expanded clinic would be a good neighbor, he knew they would be anything but that. First they'd finish scraping out that huge pit. Between November and January, a skeleton would emerge, extending into the sky. Glass and steel would be wrapped around the frame and the neighborhood could look forward to the blinding glare of reflected sun rather than the gently moving branches of the eucalyptus trees that used to line the property.

They were trapped. Powerless against government control. Two of the homeowners in the adjacent streets had tried to sell their houses once the city made the final decision to approve construction. But it had been too late. The nature of the project had to be disclosed, and once potential buyers saw the artist's sketch, their interest turned to other neighborhoods. It was outrageous that a group of five city officials possessed the power to control the quality of life and the financial future of nearly thirty families. And Brian.

He used to be a family, like the others. Now that Jennifer was gone, taking their son with her, Brian was a family of one. He'd come to terms with losing them, and he'd come to terms with being alone, but he still felt fragile, easily upset, and this was too much.

His backyard, made larger than average by its placement near the curve of the cul-de-sac, had a large expanse of lawn, a flower garden, and the pottery studio he'd built himself. The studio housed his potter's wheel, a small kiln, and wood shelving covering two walls where he kept clay, tools, and the half-finished results of his efforts to sculpt the human form. He'd more or less abandoned the potter's wheel and the throwing of bowls and vases once he'd learned that creating human beings out of clay was far more satisfying.

The hammering had stopped. His irritable, ironic side wanted to hurry through the house and out the front door to catch the DC, as he liked to call the woman with a decently curvy figure and pale blue eyes, to tell her he had been disturbed and wanted to file a complaint. The Neighborhood Disturbance Coordinator was disturbing him and he wanted to know how she planned to manage that. She wouldn't even laugh. She'd stare at him with those eyes the color of faded blue jeans, her lashes long and dark with mascara.

He sprayed the sculpture with a light dusting of water and wrapped it in a thin cloth and a sheet of plastic. He wiped his hands on a damp towel. He stood and thumped across the wood floor, down the single step to the gravel path, and closed the door behind him. He inserted the padlock in the hook and snapped it shut. The air was crisp and cool. Sometimes when he was in the studio, where it tended to get muggy from the figures all covered with wet cloths and plastic to keep the clay moist, he forgot that he no longer lived in the tropical atmosphere of south Florida where he'd spent the first nine years of his life. That climate had seeped into his malleable bones and half-formed psyche where it remained even now. Florida was filled with enticing creatures — snakes and gators and colorful birds. Much more interesting than the dull gray squirrels and the brown and black birds, the occasional blue jay, of the San Francisco Bay area. Even after all these years, he missed it — the variety and the heavy presence of hot humid air, the tropical storms that made the weather a living being.

He took a few steps along the gravel path leading to the patio. An earthworm writhed on the stones, its body already losing moisture. He couldn't bear to watch any creature suffer, sometimes he even ached for flies caught between the screen and the window. The worm had no way to escape, unable to scurry off the path, forced to wriggle and twist, hoping for the best, like life itself. He picked it up between his thumb and forefinger and carried it to a shaded part of the lawn near the foundation of the studio where dirt was exposed.

He went inside and walked quickly through the house, not bothering to close the doors behind him, hoping he hadn't missed his chance to catch the DC before she hopped into her white Prius and silently exited the neighborhood.

She stood in the center of the street, admiring her sign. It was painted dark orange with black lettering, as garish as its message.

"Hey!"

She turned and watched him jog to the corner. She smiled. "Good morning. What can I do for you, Mr. Abrams?"

"There's not supposed to be any noise before eight on Saturdays."

"That's right."

"You were hammering."

She increased the intensity of her smile, her expression filled with condescension.

She treated them like whining children, not homeowners held captive by a government whim, people with justified anger. Their lives had been invaded, the promise of suburbia destroyed, not just during the noise and dirt and crumbled curbs and blocked sidewalks of construction, but forever. This would last forever. And no one who lived outside the five block area surrounding the site seemed to grasp that fact.

"It was only ten to eight and you were making noise."

She lifted her shoulders and let out a dramatic sigh. "The restriction applies to construction work."

What did she think she was, a teenager and he was her father, telling her she'd missed her curfew by ten minutes? He waved his arm toward the chain link fence backed with green canvas mesh. "This is the construction site and you were hammering. It disturbed the neighborhood. You're breaking your own guideline. Whom do I report it to?"

"Please don't be childish."

"I'm not. That's a legitimate question. We were told no noise before 8 a.m. on Saturdays and you're making noise. I want to know where I report it. Oh, wait. You're the Disturbance Coordinator, I guess I tell you."

She giggled. "Oh. I get it. You're teasing me."

He was sure his mouth dropped open, but she didn't seem to notice.

"Are you flirting with me?" she said.

His sarcasm had glided over her black sweater and forest green slacks as if it was a barely perceptible breeze. Not only was she completely oblivious to the anger simmering behind his eyes, she thought he was hitting on her? First of all, her face was so elaborately made up there was nothing appealing about her. Second of all, she was a clueless bitch, or maybe that was the first thing. Third of all, he didn't think he could be interested in another woman ever again, not after how things had ended with him and Jennifer.

Although if he *was* ever interested in another woman, it would be someone like Claire Simpson. His anger subsided just thinking about her. Delicate, angelic Claire, with her long, dark, curly hair, and no phony makeup. There was something about Claire that made him want to protect her. Twice a week — Tuesday and Thursday evenings — he watched Claire's son while she was in class. It made him feel good that she leaned on him. He wished he could do more, he wanted to do more, but she didn't want protection, or someone to confide in, just a neighborly friendship. At least he knew she needed him.

The Disturbance Coordinator grinned. He didn't know why she got under his skin. It wasn't her fault his peaceful existence, the friendly neighborhood, his sustenance since the dissolution of his family, had been gutted. She had a silly job to do and she was nothing more than a clerk, someone put in place to listen and smile and calm people by giving them non-answers until they realized they were helpless and went away, defeated into inaction. But her very title enraged him, and her lack of sympathy grated, because anyone who stood where she was standing and looked at the fencing and saw the breadth of the construction site and its proximity to his house should be outraged.

If he could succeed in getting her to acknowledge how his life was being destroyed, he could go back in the house and pour a final cup of coffee, satisfied that he'd won, even though it was pathetically obvious that he'd lost everything.

"Do you live around here?"

Her lips closed over her teeth and he saw that he'd put her on the defensive.

"No."

"Where do you live?"

"I don't think that's an appropriate topic of conversation," she said.

"Why not? You know where I live."

"Well of course, because I'm…"

"I don't have to know the street name. Is it an apartment? A condo? A house?"

"I own a condominium."

He nodded. "For how long?"

"A year." She took a step back. She slid her fingers into pockets that looked too tight to be of much use. She looped her thumbs over the edges, making it look as if her fingers had been sliced off and all that remained were thumbs and the backs of her wrists. The way they were bent forward, it looked as if there were no bones in her hands. He forced himself to look away.

"Can you walk to work? Are there any parks nearby? Do you live near a downtown area, a coffee shop, a movie theater?"

"Why all the questions? I really should be getting to the office, Mr. Abrams." She took a few more steps away from him.

He wondered what she'd do if a car turned onto Fairview, if she'd take it as an opportunity to turn and run, or if she'd be forced to move back closer to where he stood. "I'm curious," he said.

She slid her fingers out of her pockets. He felt a strange sense of relief to see that her hands were intact, even though he'd known they were, hadn't believed the illusion for a moment. It was just a momentary flash, but still, it had been unnerving.

"I'm here to ensure the relationship between the construction company, the medical foundation, and the neighborhood is a mutually beneficial one. Discussing my personal life isn't relevant."

Only a moment ago she'd giggled foolishly, then this corporate speak flooded her brain as if she'd flipped a switch. "There's nothing mutually beneficial," he said. "I'm asking about your home because I imagine an upscale condo with trees that were already halfway to maturity before they were planted. I picture a courtyard with a fountain and flowering shrubs, a local grocery store, and a few nearby cafes and restaurants. I wonder how it would be for you if someone bulldozed that quaint downtown neighborhood and constructed a hotel chain, or an employment office where rough characters loitered. I… I… I can't even think of an appropriate disruption to your life to make you recognize how we've been violated."

"I live in a condo near the 280 freeway. That's the way the world is, Mr. Abrams. Suburbia is a relic of the twentieth century. It's more efficient to have mixed use neighborhoods and to ensure people are within walking and public transportation distance of the services they need. Medical care is the number one service most people will need in their lifetimes. Especially in an area like this where nearly twenty percent of the residents are retired and headed to old age."

A squirrel leaped from the tree a few yards away onto the branch above her. The DC jerked her head up and looked to see what had caused the sudden movement. Blonde hair splashed across her arm. She turned back and tossed her hair over her shoulder as if she was challenging him to argue with her. The squirrel chattered, ran along the branch, down the trunk, and darted across the street. Her speech about the state of suburban life sounded like something she wrote for one of her brochures. Between the unreal color of her hair and her automated words, she seemed not quite human. She couldn't begin to understand how any of them felt, and she really didn't care.

He wanted to keep trying to press his point, to force her to understand. If they would at least acknowledge what they were doing to his neighborhood, he might feel better, but they acted as if the residents were stupid for being upset. "You win," he said.

He turned and headed back around the corner. He walked up his front path, a series of flat stones he'd laid himself, interwoven with thin strips of grass that he clipped with sheers every other week. He didn't hear her drive away, but of course he wouldn't, the hybrid was soundless, failing to give any warning when it was on the move, putting your life in danger.

Two

CLAIRE RAN THE brush through her hair. It caught on the tight curls and she winced. Tears rushed to her eyes. She should have been more thorough, threading the conditioner all the way along the strands. She couldn't bring herself to cut it, although life would be easier if she did.

Her dark, curly hair, reaching to the small of her back, brought second looks. It gave the impression she was beautiful even thought she was not. Her lips were too thin, her nose too pointed. She was skinny. Her legs and arms looked like they belonged to a child rather than a twenty-eight year-old woman. But she had this spectacular head of hair and that compensated for everything.

Not that she was trying to look good, trying to attract a guy. Far from it. The only male that mattered was Joey, raising him to be smart and kind and good. All the things his father was not — he whom she preferred to keep nameless, even in her own thoughts. It was better for Joey and better for her.

The only place his name should appear in her life was on the deed to the house. And someday, she would erase it from there as well. A home bought and paid for with her own money, a place free of his touch. She could almost see it through her tear-filled eyes.

She blinked, pulled the hairs out of the brush, and set it on the bathroom counter. She threaded her fingers along her scalp, spreading them evenly. She slid them through her hair, gently moving her hands down her shoulders, along the sides of her breasts, past her ribs. It was the guaranteed way to remove the tangles. Yanking the brush accomplished nothing except breaking some hairs and ripping out others by the roots. It was a good lesson for life, go slowly and gently and the tangles had a way of working themselves out. Except sometimes they didn't.

The curls were more defined when she used her fingers as a comb rather than cruel metal spokes protruding from a wooden handle. Maybe she didn't really need a hairbrush. For a moment she considered dropping it in the trash, but at some point, she'd feel the need for it again. She had to stop this habit of tossing things so eagerly, then paying the price, literally, with money she didn't have, purchasing replacements. Keeping her house and closets and drawers nearly empty, filled with only the most necessary and frequently used items, was admirable, but she couldn't get rid of everything.

She liked the serenity of her home, the clean, knickknack-free surfaces, the minimum required pieces of furniture. The spaciousness calmed her, molded her mind into an equally spacious and uncluttered place. It was difficult to understand how people lived with sheds and garages and basements and attics crammed with things from the past, how they maintained closets stuffed with clothing they hadn't worn in a decade, boxes overflowing with memories. The past was gone, it was best to move on and not spend time moping over it.

She went into the living room and peeled the sheet off the hide-a-bed mattress. She folded it in a loose, uneven rectangle and set it on top of the comforter and top sheet that were already folded on the floor. A photograph of California redwood trees, taken from close to the base so the trunks were enormous and the tops seemed to rise forever into narrow points, hung on the wall above the hide-a-bed. She felt the trees looking down on her as she lifted the mattress and pushed it back into the frame and stuffed the cushions into place. The redwoods seemed to whisper that the world could be trusted, the earth was reliable, even if human beings were not quite as predictable.

The room felt abnormally large once the bed was folded back into a two-person sofa. The photo of the redwoods was the sole piece of art. The only other furniture was a nondescript coffee table she pulled back into place near the sofa, an oak rocking chair in the corner near the sliding glass door, and the TV on a low stand. She stuffed the bedding into the drawer beneath the TV.

She walked down the hall to Joey's room. The door to the bedroom across from his stood open, a yawning mouth with nothing inside but a small cupboard from IKEA that held her clothes and a wood chair in the opposite corner. It had been an office, but all the computer equipment, the desk and bookcases, the sports memorabilia and framed awards were gone now. She didn't miss any of it. She preferred using her laptop, sitting with Joey at the kitchen table, doing their homework together. At the end of the hall was the master bedroom, the door closed. Inside was the king-sized bed, stripped bare. Her antique dresser with the marble top was gone, sold on eBay since he hadn't wanted it. Even though she hadn't opened that door in two years, she could still sense the hollow, subtle echo of a room without window coverings.

She knocked on Joey's door. "Are you ready? I want to get there before it's too crowded."

The door swung open. Joey jumped toward her, bumping his shoulder against the lower edge of her ribs. It amazed her that she could look at him each morning and be shocked at his height, the dissolving of his soft, round cheeks into something more angular, the slight thickening of his eyebrows and lashes, no longer downy toddler hair. She glanced at the hems of his jeans. They still brushed the tops of his athletic shoes, he hadn't grown last night after all.

"Did you call Kevin's mom? Can he come with us?"

"No, he still has a cold."

Joey's grin collapsed. "Then can I bring my skateboard?"

"You know you can't." She bent her knees slightly and put her face close so that her nose touched the tip of his. "Why do you ask me every week? You're a very persistent boy." Joey laughed. "You might change your mind." He ducked around her and ran down the hall, made a sharp turn into the entryway, and burst out of the front door. Like she did many Saturdays, she wondered how much longer he'd be excited to go to the Farmers' Market with her. At what age did boys find it embarrassing to be with their mothers? The mothers of his friends who had older sons said it varied, sometimes ten, sometimes not until eleven or twelve. Every so often, a boy rejected the public presence of his mother when he was only eight. Joey was seven. She had another year for sure, most likely more.

It wasn't that she was one of those women who wanted to trap her son in perpetual childhood, afraid to let him grow up, wanting to keep him dependent. She loved this age, loved his adult-like questions and observations of life mixed with constant optimism and all the excitement and curiosity and lack of cynicism. But she also loved that he was excited to go to the Farmers' Market with her, even without his best friend for more interesting company.

She went into the kitchen and grabbed her orange crocheted shopping bags. After she locked the front door, she turned and glanced across the cul-de-sac. Brian stood on his front porch. Even in the shadow of the overhang, his blonde hair looked pale, cut close on the sides, but longish on top.

He waved. Claire lifted her fistful of bags in the air and flapped them in his direction.

She should invite him to join them. He'd gone to the Farmers' Market with her and Joey several times before, more or less forced into it when they happened to leave their houses at the same time, headed toward the small downtown area. It was awkward when they met up, but once they got going, things shifted and the walk was pleasant. She didn't want to give him the wrong impression by offering a formal invitation. From time to time, Joey insisted that Brian wanted to kiss her. She didn't believe it, didn't get any vibes to that effect, but Joey wouldn't let up. It was better to be overly cautious. She wanted to keep good relationships with all her neighbors, but especially with Brian. Without his help, she wouldn't be able to finish college. Hopefully he'd be agreeable to continue watching Joey once she got into law school. Every time she thought of it, a shiver ran across her shoulders. A life of independence was getting closer every day, years of fantasizing would be a reality by the time she was thirty-three.

Brian stepped off his porch and walked to the edge of the yard. His gentle face was made even kinder by his hesitant expression, as if he couldn't quite find the energy to lift his lips into a full smile. He wore jeans that looked new and an untucked, baggy green t-shirt that made him look leaner than usual.

"Are you joining us?" She had no idea why the words

slipped out when her intention was always to carefully avoid giving the wrong signal to the wrong man.

With his hands shoved in his pockets, Joey gave her a flash of Joe-the-man, coming in the not-too-distant future. His face remained smooth, already learning to conceal his feelings, but she knew she'd hear complaints later, downgraded quickly to whining about Brian sticking himself in where he didn't belong, segueing into an explanation of how weird Brian was — too eager, too nice, too everything. Too interested in Claire was what it all boiled down to. It made her smile that her son was so protective. On the other hand, it didn't make her so happy that he was aware of adult relationships at the age of seven. Shouldn't he be a little more oblivious? She wasn't sure why he'd interpreted Brian's casual friendliness as something more. And yet, why did she have rules about not sending the wrong message if she wasn't, on some level, concerned that Brian had gotten the wrong message?

As he walked down his front path, Brian placed a foot on each stepping stone, not speaking as he appeared to concentrate far more than necessary on each step forward. When he reached the end, he looked up. "I might. I hadn't thought about it."

Joey kicked the fence post in the corner of the yard next to theirs. He inched along the sidewalk, making it clear he was eager to get going, more eager to make sure Brian's ambivalence shifted to *no*.

Claire knew she should urge Brian to accept, now that she'd made the initial offer, but between Joey's obvious irritation and her own annoyance at herself for breaking her rule, she hoped Brian would inform her he'd dedicated the morning to sculpting, or yard work, or grading spelling tests. She said nothing, hoping that if no second offer was forthcoming, he'd decide against it.

"I think that sounds great. I'll grab a carrier and lock up." He turned and walked back up the path, taking the same deliberate care in placing his feet at the center of each stone.

"Why'd you invite him?" Joey asked.

"I don't really know."

"Then un-invite him."

"We can't do that."

"Why not?"

"It's rude."

"He'll want to look at every single thing. And he'll hog you."

She laughed, but stopped herself before she spoke. Joey was right about Brian's shopping habits. When he'd gone to the market with them before, he insisted on stopping at every stand. He couldn't make a purchase without inspecting each vegetable. Green beans were chosen bean by bean, rather than grabbed in handfuls. She admired his patience, his attention to making sure he was getting the best quality, but it was draining, and kind of ridiculous.

"Can I get popcorn?"

"We'll see."

"Please?"

"We're not even there yet. Let's see how it goes."

"I know I'll want popcorn."

Brian emerged from his house, closed the door, and turned the key in the deadbolt.

"I bet he doesn't step on the cracks coming back either," Joey said.

"What?"

"The cracks. Don't step on the cracks or you'll break your mother's back. He walks on the stones so he doesn't step on the spaces in between."

She had no idea where Joey had heard that rhyme. Did kids still say that? It seemed like something from the distant past, something kids said when they played without adult supervision, walked to school with other children instead of arriving in carpools. Silly rhymes like that annoyed her — an attempt to make a child anxious about something as natural as walking to school.

Watching Brian, she wanted to laugh. Joey was right, Brian moved awkwardly over the stepping stones, as if the placement of each foot was cause for significant concern. She wasn't sure if he was avoiding the spaces between the stones, or simply wary of turning his ankle if he placed his foot off-center.

"Can I please bring my skateboard?"

"You know the answer."

Joey climbed the fence rails and stood on the top one. The sun glistened on his hair, trimmed into a buzz cut, which he'd asked for but she'd learned to love because it showed off his dark brown eyes.

Joey swayed then steadied himself. "Why not?"

"Come on, Joey." She put her hands around his waist and lifted him down. "There are too many people, too much potential for an accident. We'll go to the park after gymnastics. Okay?"

He let go of the fence. "And popcorn. I'll eat just a little there and we can take it to the park. Can we go to Morgan, so I can climb that tree?"

"Sure. Morgan is perfect." She liked the Farmers' Market for the fruit and vegetables and didn't really want to spend money on the glazed, overly-sweetened popcorn sold by the pound. A pound. Who needed a pound of popped corn drenched in syrup and butter? It tarnished the whole idea of the market selling fresh, local produce. They had to add things designed to entice kids. But then, Joey might not be as willing to walk downtown without the lure of popcorn and grilled sausages, fries and ice cream bars. She wished she could make him as excited about fresh fruit, but that was probably unrealistic.

Brian crossed the cul-de-sac, his two carriers stuffed under his right arm. "Thanks for inviting me. I haven't been to the market in months."

"Not true," Joey said. "You went with us the weekend after

school started."

Brian laughed. "Are you sure?"

"Yup."

Brian stopped walking. He closed his eyes as if he had to visualize a calendar. After a moment, he opened his eyes. "So I did."

They walked to the corner and turned onto Fairview.

Now that Joey had pointed it out, Claire couldn't help watching Brian's footsteps. She was relieved to see that he seemed unconcerned about where they landed in relationship to the squares of the sidewalk. For some reason, this made her feel annoyed at Joey. He emphasized Brian's quirks, as if he was determined to remove the man from their lives. But Brian was a nice guy, so willing to offer help. She never felt she was imposing. He never made her feel like she was too dependent. Joey could never explain specifically what bothered him about Brian. Why was being *too nice* a reason to avoid someone?

"Did you hear the hammering this morning?" Brian said.

"No."

"The Neighborhood Disturbance Coordinator was pounding a sign on the post near the construction site." He waved his arm behind him, swinging it wildly.

Claire ducked. It was silly, there was no danger of him hitting her, yet his gesture was full of force, as if he was trying to fling something at the temporary fence separating his yard from the construction site.

"Who's the Neighborhood Disturbance Coordinator?"

"You know, that woman from the medical foundation who spoke at some of the community meetings."

"Oh, right."

"It's kind of ironic, pounding a nail into a sign, disturbing a perfect Saturday morning, when your whole reason for existence is making sure the neighborhood isn't disturbed."

Claire laughed.

"How can you be so casual about all of this? There's a pit the size of Alaska twenty feet from my fence. That thing could swallow every one of our houses and you'd never even know we were here. The noise and the dirt will be atrocious, and when it's done, we'll be left with a monstrosity glaring at us."

He stopped in front of an adobe house. It had been built in the thirties and was set far back from the sidewalk, the expansive front yard dotted with apricot trees, echoing a time when houses had land around them. Behind the fence, a dog whose build and coloring said he could be dangerous, but whose demeanor said otherwise, reclined on a wood platform in front of a good-sized dog house. Claire smiled at the dog. She wiggled her fingers at him. She always waved at him, wanting to pet him, scratch between his ears. "We've already talked about it a hundred times. Why do you keep going on about it?"

"I guess I'm having trouble processing it," Brian said.

She edged forward. Brian remained rooted near the

platform where the dog reclined. It stared at them, clearly not alarmed by their presence. That's what was so strange about Joey's objections to Brian. He almost made her feel as if he was wary around Brian. Yet she felt comfortable around him, and the dog was equally unconcerned, despite the increased volume in Brian's voice, his violent gestures, and his proximity to the dog's territory. Joey's complaints must be rooted in fear that she'd start dating Brian. Well he could stop worrying, dating anyone was the last thing that was going to happen.

"Let's keep going," she said. She started walking.

After a moment she heard the soft tap of Brian's elfin-looking shoes with slim rubber soles and a zipper running up the top.

"Our property value is gutted," Brian said. "We've been robbed of our privacy, our peace of mind. I look over the fence and I'm staring down into this abyss."

"Don't be dramatic," Claire said. "If it was an abyss, you wouldn't be able to see the bottom." She laughed. "It *is* a rather large hole. I didn't know it would be so huge."

"It's outrageous that they can just come in and do whatever they want."

"We knew there was a medical center there when we bought our homes."

"The Reynes didn't know."

"Okay, so one family who's been here forever. And Mrs. Bennett was here before it was built. Do we really have to talk about this? Again?"

"I just wish we could have stopped it. We should have fought harder. It's even worse than I imagined. That woman, the Disturbance Coordinator, acts as if it's a minor inconvenience, a tree trimming machine grinding branches for a few hours, one day out of your life."

Claire walked faster. Maybe this was what Joey meant when he said Brian was *too everything*. He got so wound up. Part of her understood why he was upset. The planned three-story building was awfully close to his house, while she had the buffer of the cul-de-sac. The angle of her roof line would prevent her from seeing the building from her front windows. But to be honest, she didn't really care. All that mattered was finishing college, getting into law school, making enough money to escape the house that she'd moved into as a happy bride and was now trapped in, a near-prisoner of Joey's father. Still, Brian needed to let go. He needed to realize that it was too late. The neighbors had mounted a vigorous campaign against it and they'd lost. It was time to move forward. It wasn't the end of the world. It wasn't an *abyss*, for God's sake. "The noise will be awful for a while. But once it's complete, things will be fine and we'll get used to it."

"I won't. The Reynes won't."

"I know you're upset, but it gets old, complaining about the same thing over and over. I know you're closer to it, but you have to move past it. Think about the good aspects."

"There aren't any."

"It will be a huge help to me, if I can get transferred to

that facility. I won't have to depend on you to pick up Joey from after school care. I'll save on gas, stress, everything."

"I'm happy to help."

Joey had slowed his pace. She could tell he was listening.

"You're being short-sighted," Brian said. "You'll get a better commute, but you won't be working as a receptionist forever, and you won't have a young child forever. Then when you want to sell your house, you'll get less for it. And you won't ever look out your window and see trees and a glimpse of the foothills. You'll see a huge, glaring building blocking the sky."

"I can't see the foothills. Anyway, it doesn't matter. It's a done deal and you need to let it go."

"I can't."

She glanced up at him. He was a tall man, yet he managed to match his pace to hers. His jaw was tight and for a moment, she thought she saw him grinding his teeth, but maybe he was only swallowing. She looked forward. It amazed her that someone could be so upset, could talk nearly every day about how much he hated something about which he could do absolutely nothing.

Sure the noise and dirt would be irritating for a few months, but the building was only three stories tall. And even though the pit for the foundation looked like it went precariously close to Brian's property line, there would be space between. They'd plant mature trees, it was all there in the sketches they'd been shown, in the adorable model with tiny people and cars that had been on display in the lobby of city hall. Brian was blowing it out of proportion, turning it into a story of David and Goliath, except David had used up all his stones and the giant corporation had won. Big deal. The people with power and audacity always won.

Three

MICHELLE REYNES SLAMMED the knife blade through the carrot. She had a splitting headache and she needed to be lying in her bedroom, the drapes pulled, a pillow under her neck, ice on her temple, not standing here making stew. But she'd already defrosted the chuck roast, it had to be cooked today.

She was hacking the knife through the carrots to let them and the cutting board and her husband down the hall in the office, the whole world, know how angry she was. It didn't make for uniform carrot slices. The disks were fatter on one side, some of them not even full circles — a chunk that slivered off into nothing. She'd pay the price when she was eating the stew, hating each poorly cut carrot as she put it into her mouth, but right now, wielding the knife without care was far more satisfying.

The inside of her hand was sore from gripping the handle too tightly. She set the knife on the counter and turned her hand over. The palm was red, streaked with white creases where the skin had folded inside her clenched fist.

She pressed her palms against her apron, a silly gift Gerard had given her years ago, burgundy with a design of grape leaves, her name machine-embroidered in white thread across the chest — *Michelle Reynes — Chef Extraordinaire*. She didn't even know why she wore the thing, it was embarrassing. Most women didn't even wear aprons anymore. Although perhaps that was an exaggeration, another example of catastrophic thinking, as her son the shrink reminded her more often than necessary. Two of her daughters-in-law didn't wear aprons. But then, they didn't do a lot of cooking. Easily a third of their meals came from the prepared foods section of the supermarket, and a quarter of them came from restaurants. She had no idea whether or not Ellen wore an apron, since she and David lived in New York and Michelle had never visited their home. Her sons and their wives always came to her home, which was as it should be in most cases, but an occasional invite would be nice. At least one chance to see their loft, instead of relying on photographs and video clips posted to the Internet.

She went to the freezer and pulled out a flexible ice pack. She wrapped it in a clean linen towel and placed it against her temple. It did nothing to constrict the dilated blood vessels pressing against hyper-sensitive nerves, but the numbing of her skin provided some relief. For a few moments, when cold first touched the heat of her temple, she had a moment of clarity. It was as if the migraine prevented her from thinking straight, sending her thoughts on a dismal trail of negative commentary about her sons' wives. She should look at the positive side, she was blessed to have such admirable sons. She and Gerard, mostly her, had done an excellent job raising them. An engineer, a psychologist, and a ... she was never exactly sure what David did. Something related to computers. Whenever he opened his mouth a flow of gibberish came out — software, hardware, Java, OS, apps, bugs. There was more, but those were the only words that made sense. Although she wasn't sure what OS was and Java always made her think of coffee.

Blood pulsed through her cranial vessels. She pulled out the coffee pot, filled the tank with water, and scooped in the grounds, adding another half scoop for extra caffeine. It would relieve the headache enough to allow her to finish preparing the stew. Once their meal was in the slow cooker, she'd go to bed with her medication. The migraine would be gone by dinnertime.

When the coffee machine beeped its readiness, Gerard appeared in the kitchen doorway as if the sound summoned him from whatever he was doing on the computer with the office door closed. Why did a machine that was cheered as making life better and easier eat up endless hours simply to keep functioning?

"Coffee smells good."

"I have a migraine."

"Sorry. Are you going to lie down?"

"After I drink this and finish the stew."

"Is there enough for me to have a cup?" He grinned. Despite his eyebrows sprinkled with gray and gray-streaked hair, when he smiled, he looked the same as he had forty years ago, the same magnetism filling his dark blue eyes, penetrating even from behind his glasses.

There wasn't enough coffee, but it had been selfish of her to make it without asking if he wanted any. On the other hand, if he was in the mood for coffee, why hadn't he suggested it? Better yet, made it himself? Sometimes she wondered if he didn't know what he wanted unless she came up with the idea first, as if he was living through her, his brain a passenger on the back of hers. His commercial real estate career had been successful by any standard. He surely hadn't needed her in order to think, to function. But since he'd retired, he drifted around the house, keeping the yard as lush as always, slipping in and out of his study, reading and playing chess online. Still, sometimes he didn't seem to know his own mind until she took action. "I only made enough for myself, but I can spare half a cup. I probably won't drink it all anyway."

He kissed her earlobe. "Thanks, babe."

Using one hand as she continued to hold the ice pack to the side of her head, she opened the cabinet and took out too smallish mugs, filled hers two thirds full and his a little less than half. She handed it to him.

"Are we going to sit at the table and drink it, or do you want to go into the living room?" He lifted the mug to his nostrils. Steam fogged his glasses. He pulled them out from the bridge of his nose until they cleared.

"I'm going to finish cutting the vegetables."

"Oh. Can I sit here and watch?"

She shrugged. Really? Watch? Twenty years ago, that question would have meant something entirely different. She glanced at him. He winked. Her shoulders relaxed and the throbbing in her head slowed its pace. That was almost worse — the rapid beat of a snare drum giving way to the slower, heavier beat of tympani.

Still, if he noticed the irony in what he'd said, why was there no hint of sadness around his smile? They hadn't made love in two months, and before that, it had been six or seven weeks, and before that, she couldn't recall. Of course things slowed down with age. But they didn't have to come to a complete stop. She was only sixty-two. Her body ached for him the way it always had. The touch of his fingertips on her hip before they fell into a deep sleep melted her insides. She wondered whether he had similar sensations. If he did, he hid them carefully, buried so deep there was no flicker in his eyes, in the sound of his breathing.

"Why don't I hold the ice on your head while you chop?" he said.

"That's awkward."

"It will go faster."

"Okay."

"Why the migraine?"

"Who ever knows why."

"I hope you don't start having them every day when the construction ramps up."

Her thoughts exactly. The migraines were usually an indecipherable combination of a few triggering foods, the weather, mild dehydration, and her own tension. It was her own tension that promised more migraines as they continued digging deep into the earth, machines rumbling thirty or forty feet from her kitchen, even closer than that to her bedroom. Tears flooded her eyes. They'd lived an admirable, well-thought-out life. These were supposed to be the years full of rewards. They'd raised wonderful sons. Soon they'd have the pleasure of grandchildren, countless family gatherings to look forward too, many more years in their home that had been adequate for the three boys, and then remodeled to provide contemporary features — a bona fide dining room and the great room opening onto an expanded back patio for respectable parties. The medical facility was destroying it all, turning their property into a shack in an alley, surrounded by high-rise buildings.

She was being childish, but it wasn't fair that some people had everything go their way in life, and others were invaded by outside forces. Disease, loved ones stolen by mental illness — *Paul.* Hadn't she had enough suffering for one lifetime? Tears pooled in her eyes. "Why did this have to happen to us?"

He pressed the pack more firmly against her temple.

She pulled away. "I know it's pointless to talk about, but I can't help it."

"We did everything we could."

"So now we just give up and take it? We worked our whole lives for this?"

"We should have tried to sell when we first heard about it. When we could have gotten away with not disclosing it."

"I feel like my life is getting sucked into that hole."

He set the ice pack on the counter and put his arm around her shoulder.

She hacked at the last carrot with such force, he dropped his arm away from her and stepped to the side. "Careful."

"Why should I be careful? What's the point?"

"You'll cut your finger."

"The pain can't be any worse than what's in my head."

"Do you want to go rest and I'll finish?"

"You don't know what needs to be done."

"You can tell me."

She poked her elbow at him and he backed away. "That will take longer than doing it myself."

"I don't like it when you're upset," he said.

"You better get used to it."

"Please don't be like that."

"I love this house! They've destroyed it."

"No they haven't."

"I don't understand how you can just accept it. Let them walk all over us, gut our property value and our privacy and our peace all in one sweep." She put a bowl under the edge of the cutting board and pushed the carrots on top of the cubed potatoes. All that was left was the meat and adding broth and spices. The onions and garlic were already browned and waiting in the crock pot. "It's immoral what they've done to us."

"You spend too much time talking to Brian. He gets you too wound up. There's nothing moral or immoral about it."

"I don't need anyone to get me wound up about it."

"Please calm down."

"Since when are you so accepting? You were furious last summer. What changed? Your *so-what* attitude makes me angrier."

"You're going to make your headache worse. It's not that I don't care, I just know when I've lost, and there's nothing I can do. Construction is starting. The government does what it wants."

She ripped the paper off the chuck roast and dumped it onto the ceramic cutting board. She took a thinner, sharper knife out of the block and began slicing the meat into bite-sized strips. Of course she couldn't do anything about it, but how was that supposed to make her feel better? It was incomprehensible that he could talk so casually about making the best of it. The injustice burned in her stomach every single day. The only time she forgot about it was when she got busy with her sculptures, creating precious polymer clay kittens and puppies, turtles and frogs. Even that pleasure would be taken from her, because the noise of the trucks and equipment would be non-stop from dawn to dusk, six days a week for nearly a year. And it wasn't the kind of thing that you could survive by knowing there was an end point, because when it was finished, all she'd have would be the glare of too much glass and hundreds of medical personnel and patients looking down into her backyard.

She turned, careful to keep her hands on the cutting board so she didn't inadvertently touch something and get uncooked fat tinged with blood on the counter or her apron. Gerard had slipped out of the room. He was probably back in the office, the door closed again. Sometimes she wondered what he did on the computer. Exchanging emails with her sons and a few friends was enjoyable, and *YouTube* clips of animal antics and small children was a relaxing way to pass time, but that certainly didn't consume more than thirty minutes a day. Gerard spent hours at a time. If he was a different man, she'd worry he was looking at porn or gambling, hanging out in salacious chat rooms. No, Gerard was too careful with their money, and he was comfortable with his body as it down-shifted over the years. She was not so pleased with the transformation of her flesh. She was still petite, her weight hadn't changed much — a hundred and three pounds — but she sometimes felt she was turning into a small, soft pillow.

She didn't like to consider that Gerard's behavior might be abnormal. The thought of a sudden shift, a pulling away, would be too much like her brother. The memory of Paul's rapid deterioration had remained like a sharp stone at the base of her skull for over forty years. The loss of her best friend, her only sibling, and the one person who understood her when she was a child, had never faded like they said it would.

Gerard's retreat to the office, his absorption with the computer, reminded her of that, although she couldn't say why. There weren't any computers back then, so what was it? If she had to give an answer, she'd guess it was the distance, a closing down of the connections between them, cords fraying and finally pulling apart. Not a sudden breaking of the bonds, just a wearing out as one person retreated into a world that only existed inside his own head. She knew it was paranoia, drawing parallels where none existed, but she couldn't seem to stop herself. She was always inspecting Gerard, and her sons, for signs of mental illness.

The pain behind her left eye was burrowing deeper. If she didn't get some medication into her system soon, she'd be useless until the next morning. She sliced through the remaining meat quickly. Her control of the knife was efficient as her anger cooled, pushed to the background by the stabbing pain. It would boil over again soon enough, but she felt somewhat relieved to be free of it, for now.

Four

RIGHT ON SCHEDULE at eight o'clock the grinding of trucks and earth movers roared through the cul-de-sac. Another beautiful autumn Saturday stripped of its tranquility. Claire filled her coffee mug and tugged the cord to open the blinds. She placed a silent bet on which of her neighbors would be the first to drop by, complaining about the particles of dirt caught on the breeze, the sound of metal digging into the earth, groaning mechanical arms lifting rock and soil, moving it to huge trucks that lumbered out through the opening in the fence.

The medical center would be a very modern building, sleek and glossy. It was much better looking than the cinder block backs of the grocery, sporting goods, and discount clothing stores that backed up to Billings Avenue across from the medical center. Everyone needed to face reality — it wasn't as if they lived in a gated community or a lush enclave of winding streets and long driveways, homes hidden by trees and walled gardens. Theirs was an eclectic neighborhood. The downtown, trying hard to be charming, was less than six blocks away, along with a super-sized discount store. A six-lane thoroughfare was three blocks in the opposite direction, lined by an endless stream of strip malls, car dealerships, and suburban blandness. No, the medical center would be a jewel.

Her money was on Michelle leading the charge with complaints today. Although Brian was beside himself, he was depressed more than angry. Michelle was filled with rage, as if the world had conspired to destroy her retirement years. Claire knew she should be more compassionate. Both of their homes backed up to the site. The building would emerge from the pit mere yards from their property lines.

It was still another spectacular weekend with a lingering whisper of summer. Soon it would be cold and rainy. She wanted to head out to the Farmers' Market, but Joey wanted to watch the earthmovers. She'd better get dressed and wake him, he'd be disappointed if he missed any part of it. She went down the hall and opened his bedroom door. He was already out of bed and dressed in jeans and his faded, too-small *Exploratorium* t-shirt.

"Did they start yet?"

She shook her head. "I think they just got here. I only heard the trucks a minute ago. Let me get dressed before you go out there."

"I can go by myself. They have a fence, nothing can happen to me."

He was right, as he often was. "Okay. I'll take a quick shower and be out there in a few minutes. But we're not spending all day watching bulldozers."

"I know. Gymnastics this afternoon." He climbed on the bed and bounced.

"Joey."

He took a few more bounces before free-falling onto his back.

"Eat some breakfast first. There's oatmeal on the stove. I just made it, so it's still hot."

"You're trying to make sure I don't go out there before you're ready."

She laughed. "I'm not. Eat something. And I don't mean cheese crackers or peanuts."

CLAIRE WON HER bet with herself.

Michelle Reynes stood on the apron of her driveway, yelling at Gerard on the front porch. "I can't stay in this house. It's so loud I can't hear myself think!" She tilted her head back, staring at — nothing. No trucks were visible over the plywood wall.

Claire's flip-flops slapped the blacktop as she crossed the street. A pebble flew up and caught between the rubber and her foot. She stopped, steadied her coffee cup in one hand, and brushed away the pebble. She rubbed where the stone had poked at the most tender part of her arch. She walked the rest of the way across the street. "Hi."

Michelle's eyes watered. The edges of her lower lids were red. "We should call every single person on that planning commission and the city council and insist that they come over and listen to this."

Claire glanced toward the corner of the cul-de-sac. "Did you see Joey?"

Michelle stared at her as if Claire had spoken in a language Michelle couldn't comprehend.

Claire turned and walked to the corner. A few yards away, Joey stood in front of the chain-link fence. He was peering through one of several holes cut in the mesh backing that allowed passersby to view the construction.

"See anything interesting?"

"Come look." He moved to the right to make room for her.

The bulldozer was at an incline, moving like an obese man, making its way down the ramp it had carved in the earth, careful not to let its weight carry it too fast, causing it to lose control, and possibly topple over the edge.

She backed away so Joey could resume watching. "I'll be talking to Mrs. Reynes, okay?"

He nodded.

She walked to the corner, dragging her heels slightly in order to steady her hand so she could sip her coffee as she went. She wasn't sure why she wanted to talk to Michelle. It would be nothing but a continuation of the lament that had echoed the same phrases and themes for the past fifteen months. The injustice, the outrage, the destruction of her life. Some days, she thought Michelle was close to the breaking point.

Michelle was a frail-looking woman, despite her large, soft breasts and a fleshy belly, prominent through the form-fitting knit dresses she wore most of the time. The dresses, cut a few inches above her knees, revealed slim legs and narrow ankles. Her arms were equally thin with delicate wrists and fingers. Pale hair, not quite blonde or brown, hung to the base of her neck and constantly fell across her face. She patiently tucked it behind her ears. Claire thought she must place it behind her ears fifteen times an hour. It would save her a lot of effort if she held it with a hair band. The dress she wore today was black with a collar that fit closely around her neck. She looked good in black, it reduced the lackluster quality of her hair. She still had her head tipped back as if she was trying to see past her side gate and over the wood barricade behind her back fence.

"What are you looking at?" Claire said.

"The skyline that will disappear soon."

"I don't think it will completely disappear."

Michelle lowered her chin and looked at Claire. She raised her hand to tuck her hair behind her ear and realized it was already there. She rubbed the edge of her ear.

"Gerard and I were eating eggs on the back patio when the noise started."

Claire nodded. She sipped her coffee. It was cooling fast.

She took a long swallow.

"That barricade is a joke. It doesn't block out anything, not the dirt, certainly. I think it amplifies the noise. And it looks hideous."

"It will be harder on your side of the street, until it's done."

"It will *never* be done."

"Nine months," Claire said. She knew what Michelle meant by never, but she couldn't help correcting her. There was something about Michelle's single-note, non-stop stream of complaints that made Claire want to argue. Michelle and Brian acted as if the apocalypse was at their doorsteps. It was a three-story medical center, not a football stadium or multiplex with sixteen theaters. She hated it when people exaggerated, made something monumental that wasn't, as if their concerns were the only ones that mattered.

"As long as it takes to form a baby," Michelle said.

Claire laughed. "You're right." Maybe Michelle would change the subject now. If not, it might be best to go into the house and stay there for nine months. Although as Michelle had said, since it would never really be done, the anger wouldn't subside in nine months. "You know, there's a couple on Fleming Way whose daughter is in Joey's class. She has some kidney problems and needs dialysis a couple of times a week. They're really excited that this facility will be so close. It will save a lot of wear and tear, and make her illness seem less intrusive, not such a major part of her life.

Michelle crossed her arms and glanced at her front porch.

Gerard had gone inside. As if to punctuate the crossing of her arms, fingers white from gripping her elbows, the earthmover ground into a lower gear. From where they stood, the shuddering of the makeshift plywood wall was apparent. Claire wondered what it sounded like from the Reynes' backyard. It might seem as if the boards were going to collapse right into their garden. She could imagine the motes of dirt flying through the air, clinging to flower petals, turning them dingy.

The truck stopped and began to back up, signaling the change in direction with an insistent beep. Michelle squeezed her eyes closed. She uncrossed her arms and put her hands over her face.

Claire touched her shoulder. "Do you want to come over for a cup of coffee?"

Michelle remained motionless for several seconds. Finally she uncovered her face, tucked her hair behind her ears, and looked at her front porch. Gerard hadn't returned. She nodded.

Claire stepped off the curb and Michelle followed. "Aren't you going to put on shoes?"

Michelle looked at her feet as if she'd forgotten she wasn't wearing any. She curled her toes and spread them slightly. A ring on the second toe of her left foot slipped closer to the base. "Do you mind me coming in barefoot?"

"No, I thought it would hurt, walking across the blacktop."

Claire studied the toe ring. Michelle was a glamorous woman

for a sixty-two-year-old. The toe ring didn't look at all silly because her feet were smooth, her toenails cherry red.

Michelle shook her head. "I'm tough."

Whenever Claire saw Michelle working in the front garden, she was barefoot, walking across grass, standing in the dirt, padding down the concrete path and around to the driveway. It shouldn't surprise her Michelle's feet were tough enough to walk across the blacktop. Although it was a little funny to think of Michelle as tough in general, since she was completely unglued by the construction. *Fragile* was a more appropriate description.

Claire opened her front door. Inside, she kicked off her flip-flops and went into the living room. The soft pile of the gray carpet was comforting on the soles of her feet. She dragged the rocking chair close to the coffee table. "Have a seat, I'll make a fresh pot of coffee. It'll only take a second."

Michelle settled on the rocking chair. Claire unlocked the sliding glass door and slid it open.

"When are you going to get some new furniture in this place?"

Claire shrugged. "We don't need anything else."

"It looks empty. Doesn't it make you depressed? Blank walls? Nothing but the sofa and TV?"

"And the rocking chair. The coffee table."

"How can you have people over?"

"With work and school, there's not much time for that. And Joey's friends don't care."

As she walked into the kitchen, she wondered it if had been a mistake to open the living room door. The noise from the construction site would be louder and the whole purpose of the coffee invite was to get Michelle out of her environment. Oh well, too late now. She dumped the damp filter and grounds into the trash and re-filled the pot. While it did its work, she took two pink mugs out of the cabinet and put the sugar and a pitcher with a bit of milk on a tray. She picked up her other mug and poured the remains of the coffee down the drain.

When she returned to the living room, Michelle had closed the door. "It was cold in here."

Claire put the tray on the table.

"Where's Joey?" Michelle said.

"He's watching the bulldozer."

"Where?"

"Around the corner. On Fairview."

"You let him stay there by himself?"

"Why not?" Claire handed a mug to Michelle. "The fence is over eight feet tall, and it's very sturdy. There's no way in."

"I didn't mean the danger of the construction, although there is that, too. You never know with little boys. I raised three of them."

Claire smiled. She knew Michelle had raised three boys. Why did she find it necessary to announce that fact, and with such a condescending tone?

"He could scale that fence before you could cross the

street."

"He wouldn't do that."

"You have no idea what a boy that age will do. You don't know until they do it. My boys climbed on the roof, locked themselves in the garage, kicked a soccer ball into the back of a garbage truck, and dug a tunnel that ended up caving in half the back yard. Those were the things two of them did before the third one came along and gave them more ideas."

It sounded to Claire as if the Reynes boys had been out of control.

"I suppose one boy on his own won't think of as many ways to injure himself or someone else, it does multiply the more of them there are. They feed off each other. But you must already know that from watching Joe with his friends."

Claire sat on the couch and sipped her coffee. As it slid down her throat, too hot, she realized she didn't want any more. She'd already had three cups. She set her mug on the tray.

"Anyway, I wasn't only talking about him getting so interested in what's going on with those trucks that he forgets himself and climbs the fence, I was talking about a small boy standing on Fairview alone. There are creeps ..."

"There are other people out there," Claire said. "People going to the Farmers' Market, jogging and stuff."

"You never know." Michelle set her mug on the tray. She picked up the sugar bowl and tipped it over, tapping the side to dump more into the mug. Claire thought it was a risky move — Michelle could end up with half a cup of sugar if it all let loose at once.

"I think older people are worriers," Claire said. "I don't mean you're old, just ... Brian's that way too. Joey said when he's staying there, Brian walks him across the cul-de-sac if he needs to get something from our house."

"You should worry *more*."

"Worrying is pointless. I don't want Joey growing up afraid and anxious."

"Caution is a good thing."

"And have him turn out like Brian? He's like an old lady. No offense."

"None taken," Michelle said. "But I think you should be more careful. You'd never forgive yourself if something happened to him."

Claire stood and walked to the door. She slid it open. She definitely regretted inviting Michelle over. She liked her well enough when Michelle talked about gardening, or her clay figurines, even when she reminisced about her boys. But when she got into this lecturing tone, it was irritating. She didn't need a second mother. If she wanted advice, she'd call her own mother. And that comment about not forgiving herself. Michelle made it sound as if she was predicting Joey would be hurt, or worse. It sounded threatening. Even if it wasn't a threat or a prediction, there was a hint that she had foresight, or wanted Claire to think she had the power to predict. Well no one had that. Michelle was just an extreme worrier.

"He'll be fine. He's smart and he knows how to be careful."

Michelle leaned back in the chair, lifting her heels off the floor, rocking slowly. "You take too much for granted. Letting Brian watch him, for example. Are you sure that's a good idea? It sounds like you have doubts about him."

"He's over-protective, that's all."

"There's something strange about him."

"Like what?"

Michelle rocked the chair harder. "I don't know."

"Well that's not very helpful."

"Don't you feel it? That he stares at you too long, or that you wonder if he's watching you from inside his house?"

"That's crazy."

Michelle planted her feet firmly on the floor and abruptly stopped the movement of the chair. "I just wonder why you allow him to spend so much time with your son when you're off going to school. Is that really necessary?"

"Yes."

"Why?"

"I've told you before. I need a better job. A career. I don't want to live in a house that I can't pay for."

"Your ex owes it to you."

"Well I don't want it." The words hissed out of her throat. She coughed.

"There's no shame in taking what's rightfully yours."

"I'm not going to be dependent on a man. Any man. Ever

again."

"You're dependent on Brian."

"That's different."

"How?"

Claire wasn't sure if she was on the verge of shouting or crying. "Why are you doing this?"

"I just think you should be more careful. Put your child first. He won't be little forever. Before you know it, they grow up and they're gone."

So that's what this was about. Michelle and her empty nest. Well it wouldn't be that way for Claire. She and Joey spent plenty of time together. And she was going to have a great career on top of it. Everything was fine. Michelle was just trying to drag someone else into her own misery.

"It's a little cold with the door open," Michelle said.

"I like the fresh air. And it's warm out. It's supposed to get into the high seventies today. Can you believe it? Even though I've lived in California all my life, I'm still amazed. When you see videos of the weather in other states, it makes you feel like you live on a different planet, you know?"

"It's cold when the breeze comes into the house."

Claire moved so she blocked the opening. She inched the door along the track until the gap was only a few inches wide. There was no way she was shutting it. The room was stuffy, the whole house was, closed up all week. When you spent your day in a climate-controlled office, you wanted natural air. Michelle couldn't possibly understand that.

Michelle put her mug on the tray and stood. "I should get back and see what Gerard is up to you. And you should check on your son."

Claire glanced at the mug. Michelle hadn't taken more than two or three sips after dumping in all that sugar. Nice. She wasted half of Claire's sugar bowl and now it would get thrown away.

Michelle walked through the entryway to the front door. Claire followed. At the door, Michelle turned. "I'm not trying to be critical. Or tell you what to do. But there will be more strangers around with all this construction. A lot of coming and going and curiosity-seekers. And you don't know what might prompt him to walk around the block to the gate where the trucks go in and out. I know they're supposed to watch, but they're not going to watch with the same care you would. That's all I'm saying." She opened the door. "Thank you for the coffee. I don't mean to rush out, but I think I'll run down to the Farmers' Market."

"Thanks for the advice," Claire said. "I won't disregard it." She smiled to show it wasn't going to become a burr in their casual, occasional friendship. She really did like Michelle. She supposed it was natural for people who were done raising their children to want to give advice, but Michelle sounded so ominous, as if Brian was some kind of monster masquerading as a schoolteacher. She had to trust someone. Otherwise, what was left of her life?

Without Brian's help, college was out of the question. Her

parents lived too far away. Her few friends had marriages and children and jobs of their own. It wasn't as if Michelle had ever offered to watch Joey. Claire had hinted at the idea — once. Michelle had stared blankly, almost as if she hadn't heard Claire speaking.

She needed Brian. She hated it, but she did. In some ways, she'd put him in a box of not mattering, so needing him was okay, less risky. Maybe she *was* using him, but he hadn't complained. He was a little unusual, too nervous. Too lonely and needy and wanting something from her that she couldn't identify. But until he complained or spoke up, things were fine. You couldn't second-guess everything, or you'd drive yourself mad.

Five

BRIAN LOVED THE feel of a hammer, the solid fit of the iron head on a sleek oak handle. Nowadays, they rarely used that perfectly designed tool. Nail *guns* were preferred. Rapid-fire instruments that required no human effort. Ugly contraptions lacking finesse, sending the nail in securely but not always with the head well seated. It said a lot that they called them guns.

He had no idea why he was thinking of hammers and nail guns. He supposed the non-stop construction was sending his thoughts to the topic of tools, but he would hear neither nail guns nor hammers in the steady racket over the next four or five months. There probably wasn't a single piece of wood in the entire building. Steel and concrete. And glass of course. Reflective glass that would allow the occupants to look out on the nearby houses but prevent any neighbors from seeing inside. That in itself was a perfect illustration of how unjust the whole situation was.

Today, it was quiet. A Sunday. Would he find himself living for Sundays? Once the project was complete, Sunday was the one day they'd be free of the steady flow of cars and delivery trucks in and out of the parking lot.

His plan for the morning was to email the Neighborhood Disturbance Coordinator. Even though it would accomplish nothing, it didn't hurt to keep making noise. If she were irritated enough, she'd pass his comments up the management chain. The rational side of his mind told him he was wasting energy and time, but the other side whispered — *you never know*. He couldn't simply roll over and let them think they weren't having any impact. Their very existence was a disturbance.

After a leisurely shower, he brewed a cup of black tea and toasted a slice of whole grain bread, drizzling honey across the surface. He stared out the window of his dining area at the cul-de-sac, lifeless at seven on a Sunday morning, but already promising another day echoing summer, he went into the bedroom that served as an office and woke up his computer.

A photograph of the Himalayas filled the screen. He gazed at it for a moment, then closed his eyes, visualizing a trip he'd never taken. Someday. That was one of the best aspects of being an elementary school teacher — his free summers allowed him to travel anywhere he chose. So far, he'd thought about going to the Grand Canyon, possibly returning to Florida for a visit. He wanted to venture even further but without a companion by his side, his desire took on the consistency of overcooked pasta.

He grabbed his mug. It was a tannish color streaked with dark red glaze. His hand shook. He lifted it to his lips and let the tea burn across his tongue. That was better. He swallowed. It hurt, but it brought all of his thoughts back to the present moment and the morning's project.

There was no need to look up the NDC's email address. His computer had captured it. This was his second message. He would send one every Sunday, recapping the outrages of the previous week. Soon, he'd increase his communications to twice a week, perhaps daily at some point. Maybe he'd send one daily starting with today's message. That would be decided later.

His first email had been a bit tongue in cheek, following up on their conversation that Saturday morning. He'd pointed out that her title was absurd. The word itself admitted they expected disturbances or they wouldn't need someone to coordinate them. And their expectation of disturbances meant they knew they were disrupting the lives of people who had no say in the matter. In the email, he'd speculated whether her role was a permanent one — a target for complaints from here on out, traffic, bright lights in the parking lot shining into neighbors' homes at night, discarded medical waste appearing in the gutters around their neighborhood. He knew that last part was unlikely, but not completely outside the realm of possibility.

He left the *To* line blank for now. It was best to think carefully through the message before adding the address so you didn't inadvertently send it before it was ready. Leaving out the addressee was a safeguard he'd learned after one horrible incident a year ago.

He'd written a scathing indictment of the mother of one of his students — a woman who refused to teach her son to accept responsibility. Every missed homework assignment had been the result of "extenuating" circumstances, every outburst in class was some other child's fault. In eloquent language, Brian had described the mother's clothing — belonging to a teenager, her voice — childish, her parenting skills — doing only what was convenient for her, also like a teenager. A capricious hand that ruled the universe had auto-completed the email address and he'd clicked send before giving the message a final check. The mail had gone to a close friend of the woman's, another parent with whom he occasionally exchanged email regarding her son's educational status. What a firestorm that caused. Nothing he'd written was inaccurate, but of course, no one wanted to hear the truth. The Vice Principal had monitored Brian's classroom and his parent-teacher conferences for three months after that incident. He'd been required to cc the Vice Principal on all his correspondence for the remainder of the year.

He stared at the subject line. He typed *Trucks on Saturday*. That would do for now, he could always change it when he was done if something better came to mind.

He lifted his fingers off the keyboard and took a sip of tea. The temperature was bearable. Still, he didn't regret the earlier torment, the rawness on his tongue and lips. The email would flow much more smoothly now that he'd locked the demons in the back of his mind where they belonged. Every corner of his head felt clear, soothed by the flavor of the tea and the heat.

Without pausing, his fingers flew across the keys, expert at connecting his thoughts with the tips of his fingers as a single unit after years of typing lesson plans, exams, and end-of-the-year student assessments. When he was finished, he re-read the email. It was brief. He made some edits. He thought about adding a fourth paragraph but decided against it. Going on too long, especially with this only his second communiqué, might make him look like a crank. He read the email out loud to enjoy the flow of words off his tongue.

It was explicitly promised to the residents of the Cherry Orchard neighborhood that construction on the new medical facility would never begin before eight o'clock in the morning on Saturdays. As if to deliberately exhibit who is in charge here, the trucks were roaring and their back-up alarms beeping at three minutes before eight on Saturday, October thirteenth. It's estimated those alarms, with their high-pitched tone, operate at 97-112 decibels, which is well above the range that causes damage to the human ear. If they have concerns about hearing loss, neighbors need sufficient time to leave their homes before the trucks arrive.

This complaint should be included in the public record, and as an act of good faith and in an effort to show courtesy to the surrounding residents, work next Saturday should not begin until eight-thirty a.m. This infraction would be forgivable only if the construction crew is operating in a different time zone and believed it was actually three minutes to nine, Mountain Time, when they began work.

He was especially proud of the last line. A touch of humor to show that he wasn't a nut case, that he was a good-natured man with a serious concern. He proofed it one more time. He entered the email address, not even a name — disturbance@bamf.org. He clicked send. For the next few minutes, he read through the messages in his in-box. There was a string of jokes from his younger sister, who seemed to think it was her mission in life, since his had gone awry, to cheer him up with silly cartoons, stupid jokes, and sappy poems that warned him of doom if he didn't share them with twelve friends. "Ha," he said. "My life already went through doom and came out the other side." He clicked delete on her poem about the meaning of the colors of fall leaves. He laughed at her jokes and replied, telling her about his week and asking about her children.

There were three other emails, two from fellow teachers, and one from his tennis partner. He responded to them while he drank the rest of the tea, now edging toward lukewarm tinged with cold because he'd forgotten all about it while he composed the message to the Disturbance Coordinator.

It was only seven-thirty-five. He washed his mug, dried it, and put it in the cabinet. He should work on his latest sculpture, but he wasn't in the mood — too wound up after brooding over the outrage just beyond the fence. He hadn't been out to his workroom for several days now. It was unlikely he'd be working on his sculpture any more on Saturdays, that mind-numbing beeping made it impossible, so Sundays, or evenings, were all that remained. He'd work on it tomorrow evening. Definitely tomorrow. His latest piece was giving him as much trouble as all his previous efforts. He wasn't good enough yet to sculpt faces that looked like the real person — maybe some day. It might be time to take another class.

It was time to feed Antony and Cleopatra. He opened the door to the other spare bedroom. When he'd first taken ownership of the house, the bedroom had a window looking out on a small fenced area in the side yard, a fertile patch of ground filled with a good-sized vegetable garden. He'd hired a guy to remove the window, plaster over the space, and had the house re-painted. The contractor hadn't liked the windowless room. He said it would decrease the value of the property. Brian gently reminded him that this was his property and he could do as he pleased with its *value*.

The room was then transformed into an environment for Antony and Cleopatra.

He opened the door and flicked the switch. The recessed lights came on, providing a soft glow. He walked into the room and closed the door behind him. The space was empty except for four large terrariums and a humidifier he used when the air got too dry. The tank on the left housed Antony. Cleopatra was on the right. The two smaller tanks were for their feedings.

He approached Antony first. Antony was a thirteen year-old Burmese Python, ten feet long. He had beige skin decorated with coffee-colored markings that darkened almost to black at the edges. Cleopatra was two years younger and twelve feet in length. She was also a Burmese Python, an albino — a gorgeous creamy white with pale yellow markings.

Brian removed the terrarium cover and squatted slightly to get into proper position to lift Cleopatra. She weighed about ninety pounds. He'd been advised he should have help when he handled her, but he was strong, knew what he was doing. It wasn't a problem. He took her out of her cage and placed her across his shoulders. He went back to the computer and spent some time surfing the web while she enjoyed his affection. She lifted her upper body, looking around the office, studying the photographs on the wall, then turned her head to look out the window. Cleopatra was his favorite. She was the strongest, the biggest, and the most dangerous. He liked her coloring and she seemed to have a special psychic connection with him that Antony did not. He would never admit that to Antony, or anyone else, if they happened to find out about his pets. It wasn't right to favor one over the other, but he couldn't help it.

He'd acquired Antony and Cleopatra after his mother died. Living alone in a three-bedroom house had spooked him. He was only twenty-seven years old and somewhat lost, eating alone at a table that seated six, walking through too many rooms, empty of life. He'd felt he needed a pet. In his apartment, he'd kept two rats, each in its own cage so they had plenty of room to stretch out. Many people found that disgusting, but they were clever beings, smarter than hamsters. They had inquisitive little noses and soft fur. He let them out of their cages and allowed them to run around. It was entertaining, watching them play. With all the additional room of a house, he'd realized he could have a larger pet. He'd always been a little afraid of dogs. Cats spooked him — staring at you, digging their claws in when you least expected it, drawing blood half the time. Not to mention scratching and picking at the carpet and the furniture. No, his mother had had one cat or another all his life, and he was glad to be done with them.

He couldn't recall how he'd become interested in snakes. Maybe it was something from his childhood in the swamps of Florida, seeing snakes in the yard, not growing up with the normal suburban bias to something unfamiliar and mysterious.

Antony and Cleopatra were fine company. He spent time in their room, watching them and talking to them on a daily basis. Often, he let them out of their boxes and allowed them to move around freely. He'd sometimes invited them into other parts of the house, but of course that stopped when he and Jennifer were married.

He went back to the room and returned Cleopatra to her terrarium. He lifted Antony out of his box. He stroked Antony's skin, spoke to him and told him about his frustration with the construction, apologized, hoping the noise hadn't been too disturbing.

Jennifer had never liked the pythons, and to this day it made him angry how she grimaced and shuddered whenever he so much as mentioned them. People who didn't like snakes were ruled by primitive ignorance. There was nothing slimy or inherently creepy about a snake. People who disliked them were buying into myths and sensationalism from movies and stories. It came from the idea drilled into religious people that the snake was the personification of the devil. If people used some intelligence and gave reptiles a chance, they would realize the stupidity of their beliefs. And yet, he felt the need to hide their presence. Very few people reacted well, and he couldn't get a reputation at the school as some kind of weirdo for keeping large snakes.

He put them in their feeding boxes, then went out to the garage and got the cooler where he'd placed four dead rats to thaw the night before. It was a sufficient breakfast for today, but he'd have to get to the pet store in the next few days. Sometimes he felt guilty that their diet was so tedious, but he wasn't a monster, even though Cleopatra might be. He couldn't bear the thought of feeding them sweet-faced rabbits or birds. Bats were out of the question. They had to be content with rats. Even with the rats, he couldn't watch them eat live prey. It felt cruel, yet it was the way the world was designed, so what could he do? They deserved to be well fed as much as he did. It wasn't as if he could turn a carnivore into a vegetarian just because it made him squeamish to think of the poor creatures meeting a terrifying end. Still, most of the time he gave them deceased rats. Besides, with live food there was too much risk of the animal biting back and hurting one of the snakes.

While they ate, he removed their water pans and carried them to the kitchen. He rinsed them, scrubbed them out and returned to the bedroom. He opened a gallon of filtered water and filled the bowls. Later, after the pythons had plenty of time to digest their meals, he'd return them to their terrariums.

He closed the bedroom door, went down the hallway and out the front door. He looked around the neighborhood. Despite his complaints about noise, right now he longed for the sound of human life. Sometimes he wondered if it had been a mistake to hold onto the house after Jennifer was gone. He should have moved to a smaller place. But then he wouldn't be able to have a pottery studio, and he might be more isolated from his neighbors.

A crow glided down from the redwood trees a few blocks away, screeching and cawing. Its glossy black feathers shimmered against the pale sky. It landed on Claire's roof. At least there was some sound, even if it wasn't human. He shuddered. The cawing continued, creeping up his spine like something from the grave had come to warn him of impending doom. It made him long for human voices even more. If he sold the house, he could move into a condo. He wouldn't have to put up with the construction. He could afford a very nice condo. But moving away would mean no more trips to the Farmers' Market with Claire, no more neighborhood barbecues where she was in attendance, no more taking care of Joey when she was in school. The chance that she'd eventually see him in a new light, start to develop feelings for him, would be taken away.

He loved looking after Joey. It made him feel competent. When he'd had the chance with his own child, he'd failed at the simplest task given to a man — to protect his offspring from harm. He knew intellectually that it wasn't his fault, but the feeling, a knowledge beyond words or rational thought, wouldn't go away. A baby had died on his watch. When he took care of Joey, he didn't let the boy out of his sight. At times, he was afraid to even blink.

As if thoughts of Joey had summoned him, the front door of the house across the street opened and Joey leaped onto the front porch hugging his skateboard. Brian smiled. Joey didn't go anywhere without running, leaping, or climbing. Brian's gloomy thoughts slipped away. He walked along the stepping-stones to the sidewalk. "Hey, Joe. How's it going?"

Joey skittered to the edge of his porch and put the skateboard on the front path. He stepped on, gave it a push, and flew toward the curb.

"Careful!" Brian said, now standing on his own curb.

"What for?" Joey jumped off and the skateboard flew into the street.

Brian walked out and picked it up. "You don't want to twist your ankle. Or break a bone."

"I won't."

Brian handed him the skateboard. "Where's your helmet?"

"Mom said I don't have to wear it when I'm on our street."

"Even if you can't get going as fast around here, you should still wear it. Freak accidents can happen even when you're going at a slow speed."

"I don't wear a helmet for gymnastics," Joey said. "That's more dangerous."

"You're not doing it on concrete though."

Joey put the skateboard on the ground, stepped on, and began propelling it in a ring around Brian.

"What are you doing today?" Brian said.

"Nothing. My mom's making cookies. And lasagna so we have lots of leftovers for dinners this week."

"That sounds really good," Brian said. Lasagna was one of his favorite meals. He couldn't remember the last time he'd had it homemade. It was too much to hope Claire would invite him over. She kept a very distinct wall between them, making it quite clear they were friends only. Although sometimes the rules confused him. She was perfectly willing to eat dinner at his house if he invited her and Joey to join him when she'd worked past Joey's pick-up time, but she never invited him to her house.

He waited while Joey skated to his front porch and rode the board down the slight incline to the sidewalk. When he reached the spot where Brian stood, he jumped off.

"You know, I've never eaten dinner at your house," Brian said.

Joey shrugged.

"You've eaten at my house quite a few times. And your Mom has too, six or seven times."

"Are you inviting yourself over?" Joey said.

Brian backed up to the curb. No matter how long he worked around children, he was always slightly alarmed by their truthfulness. He didn't want to discuss social protocol with a child, but he was annoyed that Claire was so casual about eating at his house while refusing to return the courtesy. As if she owed him nothing. He glanced at her house. "I was just making an observation. I would never invite myself where I wasn't wanted."

Joey shrugged again, lifting his shoulders to his ears in a dramatic mockery of a normal shrug. It didn't look as if he was going to dash into the house and ask Claire if Brian could join them for dinner. Later, he would have forgotten all about the conversation. Knowing kids, Joey would remember on Wednesday night when they were finishing the last of the leftovers. Maybe he should make his own lasagna. That might be something to keep him occupied today.

Joey stepped on the board again. He glided to the driveway

and down the apron.

"Where are you going?" Brian said.

"To look at the pit."

"There's not much to see."

"It's huge."

"But it's just a hole."

"I think it's cool," Joey said.

"I'll walk over there with you."

"If you want."

Joey pushed his foot hard on the pavement and the board shot across the street. Brian hurried to keep up. He should have let Joey go. It was clear he didn't want company. But he shouldn't be hanging around a busy street without supervision. Maybe Claire would come out looking for him.

Six

EVERY EVENING WHEN Claire picked up Joey, he begged to stop by the construction site to check out the progress on the enormous hole in the ground. She stood behind him, peering through the opening in the mesh. The pit was completely hollowed out now, a gaping hole that looked like a meteor had hit the earth. The area where the old medical center stood had never seemed that large, occupying the same amount of land as ten or twelve homes, but the hole looked much larger. There must be something about the depth, or maybe the stripped land around it, that distorted her perception.

Joey gripped the chain link as if he couldn't get close enough, as if he hoped he could transform his body into something vaporous that would slip through the steel wires and land him right in the center of the action. Of course, there was no action right now, just silence, and the rush and rumble of traffic on Billings Avenue.

A breeze wafted through the trees behind her. The air flowed over the fence and across the freshly exposed dirt below. It lifted the plastic top from a takeout coffee cup and carried it along the edge of the pit. She felt as if they were holding their breaths, waiting to see if the breeze would sweep the lid down into the hole. Behind them, there was a tapping sound. Claire turned and saw two more plastic lids skittering along the curb.

"What do they do next?" Joey said.

She turned back. "I don't know. I don't know anything about construction. We'll have to wait and see. Let's go eat dinner." It was Friday evening, the sun was sinking fast, and she was hungry, ready to relax and enjoy the weekend. Tomorrow was busy — planting bulbs before it was too late, shopping for Joey's Halloween costume, and her study group in the evening.

"I like seeing what they're working on."

"I know, but they're not working now, and you've seen it. I'm cold." She shivered. "Aren't you hungry?" She grabbed her hair and twisted it over her shoulder, as if wrapping it around her neck would keep her warm.

"I wish I could have watched them digging instead of going to school."

Claire laughed. "You saw some of it."

"But not the whole thing."

She heard footsteps behind her. Before she turned, a woman spoke. "Little boys just love big trucks, don't they."

Claire stepped away from the fence and put her hand on Joey's shoulder. She hadn't heard a car pull up, but a white *Prius* sat behind them, the nose a few feet out from the curb, the tail protruding even further into the street. The woman bent down and picked up one of the plastic lids. She took a few steps, teetering on the edge of the curb. She wore red high heels with tan slacks and a pale blue sweater. She picked up the second lid. She stared at her hands as if she'd suddenly realized the lids were filthy. She nested them into each other and held her hand out awkwardly so they didn't brush against her clothing. She smiled. "I'd shake your hand, but who knows what germs are on them now. I'm Tanya Montgomery, the Neighborhood Disturbance Coordinator for the medical center."

"Oh. Right," Claire said. "From one of the meetings."

"I was at all the meetings," Tanya said.

"I wasn't."

"Why's that? No child care?"

"Once I knew what the building was going to look like and what the schedule was, I couldn't see the point of going every week to listen to people complain. I get to hear enough of that every day."

Tanya smiled. "So you're fine with the new facility?"

Claire shrugged. "It's a nice-looking building."

"Most of your neighbors don't see it that way. They're furious."

"I know."

"But not you?"

"I work for the Bay Area Medical Foundation. I'm a receptionist in the dermatology department. It'll be great if I can get transferred here when it's finished. The perfect commute, step out the front door and I'm at work."

"What's your name?"

"Claire."

"What's your son's name?"

Claire hesitated. They weren't at a school function, bonding over children or work or clothes, although Tanya looked like she could use a straight-talking girlfriend in the clothing department. Those shoes were so wrong, so distracting, so … she didn't know what, but she couldn't stop looking at them. She glanced up. "This is Joey."

"Nice to meet you, Joey."

Joey turned his head. "Hi." He turned back, surely happy to be given a few extra minutes to stare at the hole, imagining who knew what. Simply imagining what he would do if he had access to a hole like that. Claire smiled. She loved enjoying the mysteries of life through her son; things that were commonplace to adults thrilled him. How long would that last, another year? A few months? Where did that sense of freshness and amazement go, was it still there the rest of your life, just covered up by layers of experience and memory?

"So the noise hasn't bothered you? Or the trash?" Tanya extended her hand with the cup lids out further from her body.

"Not really. The beeping when the trucks back up is annoying, but it won't last forever."

"And you don't think the building is intrusive? You're not worried about the traffic with your son playing outside?"

"We live on the cul-de-sac, he doesn't come out here to play, so it's fine. If patients use our street as a turnaround, that would be a nuisance. Of course, I'm at work all day, so I wouldn't really notice except on Saturdays."

Tanya nodded. "Has there been a huge increase in litter?" She held up the lids.

For a moment her hand trembled and her smile looked equally weak, as if she was pleading with Claire to take the burden from her.

"I haven't noticed. There are always a few things in the gutters. But most of the time the city does a pretty good job keeping it swept up."

"One of your neighbors emailed me to say there was all kinds of trash. That's why I came by." She glanced over her shoulder toward the corner, and then looked down into the gutter. She took a few steps, squatted, and retrieved a wadded up brown paper bag with the Burger King logo. "I probably should have worn plastic gloves. And brought a trash bag."

"Is that your job? To pick up trash?"

"No, but I wanted to see how bad it was. This guy said it looked like a dump."

"Oh."

Tanya nodded her head in the direction of the cul-de-sac. "I think he's more upset than most, and I suppose it's understandable since his house backs right up to the site."

"Gerard? Or Brian?"

"Brian Adams," Tanya said. "I probably shouldn't talk about him. Violating the ethics of my role and all, but ..."

"But what?"

"Do you know him very well?"

"Fairly well. We've lived across from each other for six or seven years."

"Do you talk to him much?"

"We're friends."

"Then I shouldn't say anything."

Claire studied the collection of cup lids and paper in Tanya's hands. She looked very uncomfortable, her fingers pinched with the least amount of contact possible that still allowed her to maintain her hold on the trash. If she'd come by to investigate a complaint about litter, she really should have brought a plastic bag with her.

A few strands of blonde hair blew across Tanya's face and stuck to her dark, glossy lipstick. She shook her head, trying to free herself from its grip. The hair remained. She lifted her shoulder and rubbed it along her jaw. After a moment, she spoke. "He complained to me verbally once, and since then he's sent six emails. In a week."

So what if Brian was being a pest? Wasn't that Tanya's job, to field complaints? That was her entire job, as far as Claire understood it. "He's pretty upset about the disruption," she said. "He sees it as an invasion of his space. Like you said, it's right in his back yard. And since he has the interior lot, he has a larger than average yard. He has a studio for his pottery work out there. It's a beautiful set-up, and I suppose it's lost its appeal."

Tanya nodded. "Yes, I understand. But, do you think he's …" She moved the trash to her left hand, turned her right hand palm up, and studied her fingertips, as if she'd be able to see bacteria crawling across her skin. "Do you think he's …" She moved the trash back to her right hand and studied her left fingertips.

Claire's own fingers grew twitchy. And yet Tanya was willing to stand and talk despite her obvious repulsion and eagerness to get rid of the stuff. She looked like she wanted to rush to her car and fling the trash behind her, letting someone else worry about it. Finally, Claire couldn't stand the lengthy pause any longer. "Do I think he's what?"

"Unstable?"

"Why do you say that?"

"An email complaint every day."

"That's a bit much, but like I said, his space has been invaded."

"They built that extra fence."

"That doesn't block the noise, the dirt. The fence itself is an eyesore." Claire felt disoriented, arguing for Brian's point of view. She was so used to countering his hysteria. But there wasn't any harm in a few emails. She wasn't even sure how she'd wound up talking to this woman. Joey was still studying the hole in the earth as if he expected a dinosaur to emerge. She was amazed at his ability to stare at something inert and find entertainment that must all be taking place between his own ears. "I need to get home and fix dinner. It's getting dark." She was filling space with conversation, as if she could pave an escape route with small talk, trying to end the discussion of Brian, get back onto something meaningless, then exit with a clean, sharp right turn.

Tanya took a step forward. "His emails are weird. He goes on and on and explains things in so much detail it makes him sound a little off."

"Such as?"

"He wrote about the trash, but he made it sound as if it was piling up, blowing onto your street, that the area was crawling with roaches."

"Really?"

"Have you seen a single roach around here?"

"Sure. You see them from time to time. Usually smashed on the sidewalk."

"But every day? Lots of them?"

"Maybe he was saying it could attract roaches. Not that they were already here."

"No, he said the neighborhood is crawling with them."

"Maybe he's seen some in his yard. Like I said, the digging is only a few feet from his studio."

"Then that's not related to the trash."

Claire didn't know what Tanya was trying to get at. As much as anyone, she knew Brian could be finicky. His yard was pristine. Although she hadn't spent much time in his backyard, had never seen the inside of his pottery studio, she knew the property was lined with flowering shrubs. There were several cherry trees, remnants of the orchards that used to fill the entire valley. He had a garden and a bench surrounded by wildflowers.

"I've been in this job for three years," Tanya said. "I've received thousands of emails and phone calls related to our facilities and complaints from neighbors. Not that we're bad neighbors. But you know how people are. Small things. People reporting a burned out light in the parking garage, a fallen tree branch after a storm, even if it's not in their yard, just lying across the landscaping around our buildings. You'd be amazed what people write to complain about. But I've never had the same guy send me email every day."

"Have you ever had a big construction project, or are those emails from existing buildings?"

"Both."

Claire put her hand back on Joey's shoulder. "Well it's his right to complain. Venting probably makes him feel better. He's a very nice guy."

"It's not just the frequency and the exaggeration that's making me uncomfortable," Tanya said.

Claire glanced at her feet, half expecting a roach to run

across the top of her boot. She looked at Joey's feet. In the disappearing light, she wasn't sure she'd be able to see a roach scuttling by, especially near the edge of the sidewalk or in the dirt strip. A tickling sensation ran up her legs and across the back of her neck. She pulled her hand from Joey's shoulder, twisted her hair, held it on top of her head, and rubbed her neck with her other hand. "Why are you telling me all this?"

"I want to know if I should be concerned."

"Well are you concerned?" Claire released her grip on her hair and let it fall down her back.

"I'm not sure. He's intense. I wanted to know if you thought he was someone I should be worried about. If I should escalate my concerns. I wanted to know if my instincts are correct."

"He's a nice guy. He's upset about the construction. About the traffic from a larger facility. All the neighbors are."

"Everyone but you."

"I suppose." Claire wanted the conversation to be over. "I should get going." She took a few steps back.

"So there's nothing wrong with him?"

"Of course not."

"You should tell me if there is."

"He's a normal person who's upset about something he can't control. Wouldn't you be upset if this was your backyard?" Claire waved her arm toward the chain link fence.

"That's exactly what he said."

Claire shrugged. "The people who are developing this

don't seem to realize how upsetting it is to have your property value affected and your peace destroyed and you can't do anything about it."

Tanya dropped the trash onto the dirt strip. She crossed her arms, but kept her hands extended so any potential filth on her fingers didn't touch her sleeves. "His emails sound like he's threatening me personally, or some kind of violent attack on the project."

"That's hard to believe." It was equally possible that the unstable person might be Tanya. Brian was a kind and generous person that she'd known for years. A friend, in many ways. Tanya had walked up to a total stranger and begun grilling her about the impact of the construction and Brian's psyche. "What did he say that makes you think he's threatening you?"

"He said that you couldn't assault people's way of life, steal their tranquility, and expect to get away with it. He said not everyone rolls over and lets corporations walk all over their rights. He said just because the project was underway, didn't mean it would reach completion."

It did sound a little threatening. If it was true. If Tanya wasn't misquoting, or reading in her own fears, or even making it up. Maybe she was just picking on Brian because she was angry that she had to drive over to pick up trash when she wanted to go home for the day. "Are you going to just leave that there?" Claire pointed her toe at the discarded cup lids and paper sack.

"For now. I can't put it in my car. I'll have to run to the store and get some plastic bags."

"Well, I need to get home. Brian isn't threatening anyone. He's a nice guy, a great neighbor. Everyone on the street knows him and likes him. He's a schoolteacher."

Tanya uncrossed her arms. She pulled a tissue out of her pocket and wiped her fingers. She reached into her other pocket and pulled out a set of keys. "I shouldn't have said anything."

"No. You shouldn't have." Claire glanced down. Joey was staring at her. She was gripping his shoulder. She relaxed her hand and patted his back.

"It was nice chatting with you." Tanya extended her hand. When Claire didn't immediately respond, she looked at her fingers and laughed. "I guess I better pick up some hand wipes too." She let her arm fall to her side. "I'm sure I'll see you around."

"Bye." Claire turned and walked to the corner, cutting across the cul-de-sac to her front yard. Joey ran ahead, reaching the porch before she did.

While she tore lettuce and sliced avocado for a salad to complement the last of the lasagna, she thought about Brian's emails. She wasn't sure why she didn't believe Tanya. Maybe because Tanya had exaggerated the roaches, so what else had she embellished? She felt a strange mixture of mild concern about Brian's obsessive emails and outrage at the attack on him, the implication that he was mentally unstable, that he elicited fear. Tanya was paranoid. Her job had made her read too much into minor details, overly suspicious of everyone. There was nothing scary about Brian whatsoever. He had a right to be upset.

Still, she felt unsettled, partially annoyed at Tanya for making her feel that way. Beneath her annoyance was a tiny thread of fear that Tanya could be right. Brian *was* tightly wound. Was he still grieving over his wife's desertion? What if something had snapped? If he was threatening Tanya, what did he really expect to do to follow through? Nothing. He just wanted someone to listen. He was a nice guy. He helped her out with Joey all the time. They went to the Farmers' Market together and chatted several days a week. She and Joey had eaten dinner at his house quite a few times. He'd never said or done anything to set off an alarm beyond a vague hint that he was interested in a romantic relationship. And that might be her own aversion to relationships causing her to see a threat when it didn't exist. She'd been right in what she'd said to Tanya — all the neighbors liked Brian.

She cut the chunk of lasagna in half, put each piece on a plate, and set the empty pan near the sink. When the microwave had finished heating each piece until the cheese bubbled and the noodles were soft and pliable, she called Joey.

He pulled out his chair and glanced at the counter. "There's no more lasagna?"

She laughed. "We ate it four nights this week. Aren't you

sick of it?"

"Brian wanted to come to dinner because he loves lasagna. I forgot to tell you."

Claire shivered. She got up and went into the family room to get her sweater. She returned to the kitchen. "What did he say?"

"I forget. He looked sad. But I don't like eating dinner with him, so I'm happy I forgot."

"Why don't you like eating dinner with him?"

"He chews too many times."

"What?"

"He chews a lot. Like if I chew my lasagna seven times and then swallow, he chews it twenty times, sometimes more."

"You counted?"

Joey nodded.

Claire put a forkful of lasagna in her mouth and tried not to think about how many times she chewed. Joey's insight did nothing to alleviate the anxiety Tanya had stirred up.

Seven

WHEN MICHELLE WOKE, the sky glowed with a gold tint beneath the rapidly spreading blue. Another gorgeous autumn day. She closed her eyes and smiled. An equally warm feeling expanded in her heart at the thought of spending the morning pruning roses and removing dead tissue-paper-like blossoms from the bougainvillea, followed by a light lunch, and dinner at Tao Taos with the Harcourts. Not that Saturdays were necessarily more relaxing than any other day of the week now that Gerard was retired, but lifelong patterns didn't change overnight. She only worked on her sculptures Monday through Friday, limited her housework to weekdays, and they tended to make plans with friends on Saturdays, so the weekend still felt different.

She turned and reached for Gerard's shoulder. His side of the bed was empty, the sheets cold. She opened her eyes again. For some reason, the sky now appeared brittle, the gold hue dissolving into something sharper, a hint of winter coming. She sat up. It wasn't that she didn't know where he was — right down the hall, sitting in the office, the door closed, studying the screen of his computer. She liked that he hadn't retired into a lump, one of those men who melts into an easy chair and spends his life drinking beer, eating snack food, and watching sports, once the driving force of showing up for work every day is removed from his life. She was glad he had something enticing him out of bed — checking the news, reviewing stocks, reading blogs about investing and composting and home improvement and heaven knew what else.

She wriggled to the center of their king-sized bed. She pulled the pillow lower so it supported her neck. Couldn't they occasionally cuddle in the mornings, watch the sun rise, possibly even make love outside of their routine? Although, lately, there was no routine. It was true what they said — life was busier after retirement. The days raced by. It was the freedom that came with having so many unscheduled hours. There was no efficiency to life, no planning because there was always enough time. As the years went by, they'd defaulted to making love on Saturday nights. Now, despite the somewhat slower weekend schedule, one day flowed into another. She turned onto her stomach and pressed her face into the pillow. She was deluding herself. The past three or four months, Gerard was not that interested. Exploring the Internet was officially his favorite activity, the constant flow of information, the steady, mild stimulation — one new web page after another, truly like riding the ocean surf.

Half of her body was still warm from her side of the bed, the other half cold where she'd moved into the space that was usually between them. She felt faded, her skin loose and over-used, yet inside everything was exactly the same as it had been since the beginning, wanting Gerard's hands, his clean-smelling breath, the warmth of his skin on hers.

She tossed back the blankets, got up, and grabbed her robe off the wood stand where she draped it on top of their quilt at night. She stepped into her slippers — ankle-high boots with a firm rubber sole and synthetic fur inside. After she used the toilet and brushed her teeth, she went down the hall to the office. She opened the door. Gerard preferred that she knock first because it startled him when he was concentrating and she snuck up behind him.

"What time did you get up?" she said.

He clicked the mouse, the screen changed to the CNN sports page. He turned and let her kiss his forehead. She put her hands on the sides of his face and touched her lips to his.

"I haven't brushed my teeth yet," he said.

"The bed was cold. Have you been up for a while?"

"I don't know, since about five, I guess."

"What are you doing?"

"Not much."

"French toast for breakfast?"

"Sounds good. I'll make some bacon. I'm going to shower first, though." He swept the mouse across the pad. Images from their trip to Italy the year before filled the screen, melting from one scene to another — photographs of them sitting at an umbrella-covered table on the side of a river in Milan, and all the iconic pictures of Rome, each one featuring a smiling Gerard and Michelle Reynes.

AFTER THEY ATE, while she rinsed syrup off the plates before sticking them in the dishwasher, she said, "Do you mind running to the store and picking up two bags of potting soil?"

"Are you coming with me?"

"No, I forgot to do an extra load of laundry yesterday and I want to wear my green turtleneck tonight. I think it's going to be cold."

"Can't you do that later so you can go with me?"

"Gerard, will you please just pick up some potting soil? We don't need to do every single errand together."

"I like running errands with you."

She turned and slid her arm around his waist. "I do too, but we don't both need to go for a few bags of dirt. Please."

Once he was gone, she tossed the turtleneck, two pairs of jeans, and the navy blue hand towels from the hall bathroom into the washing machine. She went into the office and woke up the computer. Gerard had closed the browser window. She re-launched it, but all that came up was the Google home page. She opened her email and pulled up the message David had sent a few days ago. *Sure*, he'd written, *there's a way to find pages you've visited in the past if you forgot to bookmark them.* She re-read the instructions and opened the history. She scanned the list. There were the usual sites he visited — CNN, Yahoo stocks, financial news, a few gardening blogs. She moved the mouse through the list, studying each url. Nothing jumped out as particularly strange. She started at the top again. *survivenow.com*. What was that? She selected it and the page loaded quickly — a photograph of smoke billowing out of both towers of the World Trade Center filled the screen. It faded and was replaced by a shot of the 2011 Tsunami in Japan. Next came an old headline proclaiming: *Dow Plummets 634 points*, followed quickly by two thick, bold words with an exclamation point: *Anthrax Threat!*

The pictures cycled relentlessly as she studied the links along the side of the page: *What you should know. Adequate food supplies. Protecting your home from biohazards. Financial preparation. Weapons. Forum — exchange ideas with your fellow soldiers.*

She stared as the images continued to cycle. It was making her dizzy, or maybe the fact that the website existed at all was making her dizzy.

The sound of Gerard's Escalade in the driveway startled her. She returned to the home page, closed the browser, moved the mouse to activate the screen saver, and pushed back the chair. She'd have to digest what it all meant later. She'd also have to find a time to come back and read through the information buried in the various categories.

The forum link made her the most curious, and slightly

anxious. Soldiers? That must be what kept him engrossed for hours at a time. There was only so much searching for information you could do online. The thing that consumed entire mornings, that made the hours evaporate, was the chat rooms and other opportunities for communicating with total strangers. She knew because she'd spent hours herself trying to understand what all the Facebook craze was about, reading the comments her sons and their wives put up, trying to keep up with her few friends that had embraced the idea of online socializing as if they'd been invited to a party at the White House. Looking at photographs, searching for people she knew, sucked away her time more rapidly than a TV drama or an afternoon at the mall.

It seemed that Gerard had some fears about the future, but no fear over discussing his thoughts with total strangers.

She walked out of the office and hurried down the hall to the bedroom. She was pulling the quilt into place when he appeared in the doorway. "Potting soil delivered and waiting on the patio." He saluted.

She stared at his awkward pose. "Thanks."

While she showered, she tried to sort through what she'd seen. Now, she considered the earthquake supplies in the spare bedroom in a different light. They'd always tried to keep extra food, batteries, and a few cases of bottled water on hand. Everyone who lived in California and followed local news was reminded once a year of the importance of being prepared for *The Big One*. Michelle thought it was reasonable to be somewhat prepared, although she didn't like the hysteria that sometimes appeared in the news, warning of massive death and a complete crumbling of the infrastructure. Most times in life, things weren't as bad as you feared. Although the construction of the medical center certainly flew in the face of that theory.

She squirted shampoo into the palm of her hand, lathered it, and worked it through her scalp as if she was working the thoughts through the various regions of her brain. It had only been four months since Gerard had retired. She'd been so enthused to see him transition without the slightest bump into spending more time doing minor repairs around the house and working in the garden. The time he spent on the computer seemed harmless. It provided intellectual stimulation and it was what everyone did nowadays.

What she didn't understand about the computer, or rather the vast online world, was the move toward replacing real life friendships and human interaction with faceless, voiceless communication via cryptic comments and humorous observations, most of which tried too hard to be clever. Not that they weren't clever, but the element of trying so hard to be pithy was exhausting. That was one of the things she didn't like about virtual exchanges, you couldn't just be yourself, you had to be a clever, entertaining, light-hearted, or carefully cynical version of yourself, never veering into too grumpy or whiney. Everything was more fraught with meaning. Mentioning your children's progress through life came across like bragging. Ditto for talking about travel or even going to a show in the city, because everyone knew how much that cost. And each poorly thought-out comment and unflattering photograph was preserved forever.

Steam filled the shower stall and drifted out into the rest of the bathroom, but she shivered. What had Gerard said in that forum? She didn't like the idea of soldiers at all, it sounded like a bunch of crackpots. Or maybe he hadn't said a word, maybe he was a silent observer. That sounded more like him. The shivering stopped although her bones were still cold. She turned the hot water knob to the left. The water burned her skin, but the chill inside remained. She rinsed her hair quickly and turned off the water. The uncontrollable shivering resumed. She grabbed two towels, wrapped her hair in one and rubbed her skin hard with the other.

She should bring it up with Gerard, ask him about it. But then he'd know she was checking up on him. He'd be hurt that she didn't trust him. Maybe he wasn't trustworthy. He clearly spent hours a day looking at the website, so he must want to hide it from her. If he'd even once mentioned stumbling across it … said anything at all about that type of people … She'd heard of that type of people. She wasn't sure where, but she had. Some groups were so radical they moved to remote places, went off the grid, stockpiled food and weapons. She supposed there could be some comfort in that, telling the government what you really thought of their attempt to control your life, letting them know that despite their efforts to care for you, there was no hope of them caring for you if something really terrible happened. An event more terrible than nine-eleven. She didn't want to think about what those things might be. She wanted to enjoy her so-called golden years. Of course, with that pit behind the fence … maybe the construction had driven Gerard to seek out groups of people who were in surreptitious rebellion.

She dressed, dried her hair, and lingered over the application of her makeup. It was something she enjoyed, even after doing it every day since she was fifteen years old and had to sneak a smear of lipstick behind her mother's back. She hung up the towels, wiped down the shower door, and went down the hall to look for Gerard. The office door was open, the room empty. She walked back to the great room and through the dining room to their new deck tucked in the corner where the two rooms joined. Construction had started over an hour ago, but she hadn't noticed the beeping of trucks, the grinding of mechanical shovels until now. She must be getting acclimated to it. She wasn't sure whether or not that was a good thing.

The deck was empty. She walked back down the hall and out to the garage. Gerard stood in front of his workbench. He held a long screw in his fingers, studying it as if he was looking for a flaw in the design. The outer garage door was open and the air flowed inside, cool but fresh. That and the smell of dry dirt, carried by the constant movement of trucks. "What are you doing?"

He lifted his head slowly. "You look nice."

"Thanks."

"I thought you were planting bulbs?"

"I'll do it Monday. I figured since we're going out tonight, there was no sense in showering twice, and I didn't think about the bulbs until I was halfway through my shower." That was a lie. She hadn't thought about the bulbs at all until he reminded her. She'd thought about subversive websites and whether or not her husband was keeping secrets from her. Was that what they'd come to after all these years? White lies and secretive encounters online?

She felt more than saw a shadow cross the driveway. She turned. Claire stood just outside the entrance to the garage. Her thin gardening gloves were bright green without a hint of soil or worn fabric. Michelle hadn't ever seen Claire working in her almost barren yard, but then, it was difficult to keep an eye on children and concentrate on what you were doing. She hadn't gardened much when her boys were small either. As much as she'd loved every phase of her sons' lives, she truly enjoyed being her own person now, no one hanging on her, demanding, wanting, needing. Although she wouldn't mind a little of that from Gerard, something besides wanting her to ride along while he ran errands.

"Hi," Claire said.

"Hi. It looks like you're working in your garden."

Claire smiled. "I am."

Gerard placed the screw back in the jar. He put the jar on

the shelf and walked to the rear of the garage. He opened the door of one of the cabinets that stretched across the back where he stored fishing equipment.

Michelle couldn't figure out why he was so listless, as if he hadn't even realized he was looking at the screw, not aware that he'd taken it out of the jar then returned it for no obvious reason. She was starting to wonder whether he was having a delayed reaction to the loss of structure his career had provided. In some ways it felt like they'd been living this new life forever, but now, for the first time, she considered whether he was in some type of mourning for a missing sense of himself, or maybe the loss of adrenaline from the daily pressure to perform, to satisfy the demands of his clients. "Are you okay?"

He nodded without turning to look at her.

That did nothing to alleviate her concern, but she couldn't pursue it with Claire standing right in front of their garage as if she was waiting for Michelle to invite her in. Michelle went out to the driveway.

"I'm planting bulbs," Claire said. "The ground is kind of hard and I don't know how deep the hole needs to be."

"You could plant them in pots."

"I don't have any."

"What kind are they?"

"Daffodils."

"They should be six to eight inches, but I've put them down five inches and they did fine. They might bloom a bit earlier than you want, and if we get late frost, you'll lose them. But that doesn't happen very often."

Claire nodded. She held out her hands and studied her gloves. "Do you know that woman who's the Disturbance Coordinator for the construction?"

Michelle crossed her arms. Although the sun glared on the concrete, forcing her to squint, making her eyes water, she felt a chill as if the sky had clouded over. She pushed her hair behind her ear. She twisted her diamond earring, rotating it slowly. It was a habit Gerard hated so she was self-conscious about it. He complained about it incessantly, said it made him queasy, watching her turn a platinum stake in her ear. He didn't believe her when she said there was no feeling in the hole, pierced through her ear years ago.

"I remember her from the meetings," Michelle said.

"You've never run into her in the neighborhood?"

"No. Why would she be in the neighborhood? Her job is to take complaints and do nothing about them. Because really, the disturbance isn't some specific event, it's the entire situation. What a mockery — Disturbance Coordinator. It's like they're laughing at us."

Claire pulled off her left glove and rubbed her fingernails with her thumb. "That's a little paranoid."

"Well what do you call it?" Michelle felt her mood sinking further, her lips pinching into a raisin, her brain spinning, as if a giant hand had reached down and was whipping up all her disgruntled thoughts with a wire whisk. "It's a permanent disturbance and they throw this useless person in there to take complaints about the hour of construction or excess trash or people parking on our street. Those are minor problems. There's a canyon in my backyard and they're pretending it's not even there."

"I guess. But you haven't talked to her?"

"No."

"I ran into her yesterday. Joey was looking at the hole and she walked up and started talking to me."

"About what?"

"She received complaints about trash."

"I haven't noticed any more trash than usual."

"That's the thing. There isn't. There were a few cup lids and a fast food bag. She was picking it up herself."

"So?"

"She drove out because of all the complaints." Claire pulled off her other glove.

Michelle waited.

"All the complaints came from Brian. He's been sending her email every day."

"I guess it bothers him. He's always struck me as an extremely tidy man."

"Does sending that many emails seem ... odd?"

"Maybe. So what?"

"Tanya was asking me if she should be worried about him."

"Tanya?"

"That's her name."

"How chummy."

"We talked for quite a while. I guess his emails are rambling. He wrote some strange things, very detailed about where the trash was located. She was nervous. She thinks he's unstable. "

"I can see that," Michelle said.

"Why?"

"Excessive attention to small details can be a sign of mental illness."

"Since when does being *detailed* make you mentally ill?" Claire said.

"*Excessive* attention." Michelle wasn't sure that was the case, but Claire seemed to accept it. Maybe she was finally realizing it was a mistake to give Brian so much time alone with her son, to use him so callously. "You seem anxious."

Claire looked up. "I'm not anxious." Her gray eyes were clear, slightly moist around the edges, giving her a look of innocence. Michelle wasn't sure whether it was an act or some kind of deep-rooted confusion. Claire trusted Brian more than she should. As far as Michelle knew, Brian wasn't being paid. There was something unbalanced about the arrangement, as if Claire was offering up her son to soothe whatever disappointment Brian was brooding over, in exchange for free child care. It wasn't anxiety, she realized. It was guilt. A low-level, subtle, barely perceptible guilt that Claire probably didn't even realize was there. She didn't recognize the unhealthy transaction she'd arranged.

"Then why are you asking?" Michelle laughed. She touched her ear and felt the weight of the diamond in her lobe. It was the heat from standing in full sun, making her feel swollen. It could bring on a migraine. She moved closer to the open garage door.

"I don't even know. Tanya seemed really worried."

"Talking to you about someone else's complaints is unethical."

"It did feel as if she was asking me to gossip about my neighbor. But do you think he's unstable?"

"Do you?"

"No." Claire's voice was firm, and her answer quick, without hesitation.

"Then why do you keep asking me? I already told you I can see that in him."

Claire shoved her hands back in her gloves. "I think she's trying to stir the pot. I wondered if you had the same sense of it. Can you come look at how I'm placing the bulbs?"

"It's not really necessary. Like I said, four to five inches is fine. Eight is better if you don't want them to come up too early. Didn't it tell you that on the package?"

"Someone at work gave me a paper bag full of bulbs. There wasn't any package."

"Why are you asking me about Brian if you think she's just trying to create problems?"

"Because I don't understand why she would do that."

"Maybe she wants to pit us against each other so there aren't any complaints."

"Have you complained about the noise or the dirt?" Claire said.

"What's the point? My complaint is the medical center." Michelle put her hand against her brow to shade her eyes from the sun. It seemed as if the sun kept moving, trying to get to her, maybe wanting to cheer her up, like it wanted to shine on her face and make her feel good about the day and her life and the world. But she couldn't. Now that her mind was back circling around how unjustly they'd been treated, she couldn't feel good about anything. Not even Claire's request for gardening help, which any other day would have given her a warm, maternal feeling, improved her mood.

Claire nodded. "That's how Brian feels."

"I know," Michelle said.

"Then why do you think he's taking time to write long emails complaining about minor issues?"

"How should I know. Maybe because he can't do anything else and he has time on his hands, so why not harass that woman."

"That would be mean. Or a little crazy."

Michelle laughed. "Writing an email about trash from construction workers to someone whose job it is to address problems resulting from construction is the least mean-spirited thing I can think of." She decided to let the crazy comment hang there, unacknowledged. No matter how much her views aligned with Brian's, she still saw something in him that wasn't quite normal.

"How do you know the trash is from construction workers?"

"My point is, complaining to her about it doesn't necessarily make him mean-spirited. I thought he was a good friend."

"I don't know if I'd call him a *good* friend."

"He watches your son, he's either your friend or you're using him."

"I don't use people."

Michelle glanced next door at Brian's house. The lawn featured curved cutouts where he'd planted agapanthus that produced tiny purple flowers, blooming their way through autumn. In the center of the lawn, partially shaded by a Japanese maple tree, stood a concrete fountain. An excessively thin female statue gazed into the bowl. It was hard to tell if the statue was looking at her reflection or trying to find something below the surface of the water.

Brian was an unusual man. There was definitely something a little bit off about him. After his wife left, he seemed distant, yet not overly distraught. Of course, she didn't know anything about his marriage, so maybe it was mutual. Although the way he'd phrased it that day made her think it wasn't mutual — *I thought you should know*, he'd said, *in case you get curious because you don't see her around, Jennifer left me.* Who spoke like that? It had been several years, and he still seemed disconnected. That was the best way to describe it. "I just think it's a bit of a betrayal to gossip about a very nice man who goes out of his way to help you look after your son. What would you do without him?"

"I didn't gossip about him."

"It sounds like you did."

"No. I listened. And she was so concerned about him being ... unstable, I couldn't stop thinking about it, and thinking that he is a little unusual."

"Then why do you let him take care of Joey?"

"I never thought he was unbalanced before."

"So you let a perfect stranger influence your feelings about a man you've known for, what? Six years? Seven years?"

"I'm just asking. She got me thinking and it's seemed a little like he's not always fully there. Since Jennifer left. Forget I said anything." Claire turned and walked to the end of the driveway.

"Do you want me to come look at the bulbs?" Michelle said.

Claire shook her head. Her hair, tied up in a flouncy, curly ponytail, bounced like it had a life of its own. "I can't dig any deeper, so five inches will have to do."

Michelle didn't push it. She didn't really care if Claire was upset with her. All she'd done was point out what a hypocrite Claire was. And given a hint that she should be more cautious about trusting a man like Brian.

Eight

CLAIRE STABBED THE trowel into dirt that was more like clay than it was soil — California adobe. She might as well be trying to carve a hole in the side of a brick using only the tip of a metal spade. Between Tanya's unsettling questions and Michelle's opaque comments, Claire felt as if both women wanted her to believe she was handing Joey over to a sociopath every Tuesday and Thursday night, selfishly feeding her own ambitions.

Was using a lot of detail abnormal? If so, who decided how much information was too much? And did an excessive focus on details prove you were mentally ill? How did you know if someone was abnormal? What was normal, anyway?

She was a good mother. She stabbed the blade into the dirt. It made a pinging sound as it struck a stone. Pain shot through the back of her hand and up her lower arm. She sat back on her heels and looked at the shallow hole, more like a small bowl scooped out of the earth. It was important to get these bulbs in the ground. Even though she hated everything about this house, hated that she walked in that front door every day, slept in the living room every night, she was going to make it nice for Joey. He needed to feel like he had a real home, even though most of the furniture was missing and the master bedroom was closed up as if it didn't exist. Until she could finish college and law school, until she could finally end her sickening dependence on Greg, she had to keep trying to make Joey's life as pleasant and normal as possible.

The memory of that woman in her bed gnawed at her stomach, especially right before dawn — a part of the night that had been permanently stolen from her — lying on the fold-out bed, feeling like a guest in her own home. It was as if this house belonged to Greg's lover. In a way, it did. She was the one who had taken over Claire's bedroom and it was her income, now blended with Greg's that allowed him to maintain two homes.

Why was the worst day of her life more vivid in her memory than most of the years that preceded it? That September afternoon, a dry, summery day, when she walked into her bedroom and saw Greg's cute little butt, his smooth back, the stunning curve of his spine, the muscles in his shoulders, and his dark hair, needing a trim, covering his strong, supple neck. Long female legs wrapped around his waist.

For a moment, she'd thought she was in the wrong house. Tears rushed to her eyes. Vomit trickled up into her mouth, but she kept her teeth clenched together and her lips closed, swallowing the putrid stuff so they wouldn't know what they'd done to her. She'd stepped out of the room, leaving it to them as if it was theirs. She hated herself for that cowardly backing away. She should have stayed. She should have screamed and kicked and bit and punched and pulled hair. She had no idea why she'd closed the door and left them alone. Her sea green 400-count cotton sheets, now soiled by their bodies. She'd torn them off the bed and stuffed them in the back of his SUV. For all she knew, they were still there, or rotting in a landfill somewhere.

Why was she thinking about sheets? Ripping them off the bed had felt like ripping the skin off her life. Yet on one level, she wasn't surprised by what he'd done. She'd known from the day she met him that Greg enjoyed looking at women. She'd known he thought he could get whatever he wanted, that even this house was a stepping-stone at the start of his path to something bigger and better and finer. Something that would provoke envy in anyone who cared about those things.

It turned out that Claire had also been a stepping-stone. As if her small, child-like figure made her a childish wife for Greg's early twenties, and then he had to move on to a more robust model, someone with larger breasts, and sleek hair. Someone wittier and more aggressive.

The spot where she was planting the bulbs was in full sun. She stood too quickly and for a few seconds, the day turned dark. She dropped the trowel. It clanged on the dry dirt. She rubbed her forearm across her eyes. She hadn't realized she'd been crying. It would be awful if Michelle or Brian, or worse, Joey, came into the yard and witnessed her runny nose and swollen eyes. She walked to the spigot and turned on the water. She cupped her hands around the end of the hose and splashed water at her face, not bothering to dry it off. She dragged the hose to the strip of dirt and let the water spread across the ground. If she let it seep in slowly, the digging would be easier.

Joey was in the house, probably watching TV. She shouldn't let him do that on a gorgeous Saturday, most likely one of the last before it got cold and the rain started. He should be outside, riding his skateboard. She should arrange a play date. She should take him to the park. She should do her homework.

It wasn't fair that Michelle was trying to prevent her from going to school. She knew that was a gross exaggeration, but that's what it felt like. Just because Michelle had been completely beholden to a man all her life didn't mean you had live like that to be a good mother. She could do both. She had to do both, and there was nothing wrong with Brian. He was a nice guy. His quirkiness came from wearing his heart on his sleeve, his obvious loneliness. Since when did that make you mentally unbalanced? And Tanya didn't even know him. She was strange herself, with those red shoes, garish and out of place with tan slacks. *Too many details in his complaint?* What was that about? It was almost funny.

She yanked the hose away from the dirt and stuck the trowel in. The ground had become soft and pliable. She left the water running onto the lawn behind her and continued hollowing out the first hole.

Brian was a schoolteacher, a good soul. He was helping her because he saw how important it was for her to continue her education. She wasn't going to listen to any more paranoia from the Neighborhood Disturbance Coordinator or from Michelle.

She smiled, feeling hopeful for the first time that day. She scooped out another shovelful of wet dirt. She hoped the water had penetrated deeply enough to allow for eight-inch holes. She wanted to plant the bulbs properly, not face the disappointment of blooms that came too early and were killed by frost.

Nine

WHEN JENNIFER HAD told him she was pregnant, Brian didn't think a man could be any happier. Although he'd desperately wanted children, he hadn't anticipated how the reality of a baby would change his very nature. The faces of the children in his classroom took on a whole new look. He studied the shape of their eyes, the curve of their lips, the height of their brows. Each was a miraculous and mysterious blending of two human beings. He noticed for the first time how truly different they all were. There might be twelve children with dark brown hair, but every single one was a dramatically unique combination of varying shades.

Knowing that he and Jennifer had created something entirely new, another member of the human race growing deep inside her body, made him feel as if his brain had exploded in a kaleidoscope of new thoughts. This was more profound than any bowl or vase he could manage to shape on his potter's wheel, more important than any child he nurtured through the third grade. It was like being God. He couldn't stop studying the photographs of babies in utero, each stage of development, first looking like fish or something that had crawled out of the primordial soup, slowly revealing more and more human-like characteristics.

Jennifer had laughed at him.

"You act as if you're the first man to ever father a child."

"People don't marvel at life as they should. It's a miracle."

"I suppose." She smiled.

She was full of life, her breasts spilling out the low neck of her t-shirt, her belly already rounded, her face soft and content. He kissed her nose. He stroked her hair, letting the blonde strands flow between his fingers. It was so soft. It seemed silkier now that she was pregnant. He hoped it stayed that way after she gave birth.

He and Jennifer had met in the pet shop where he bought rats for Antony and Cleopatra. She'd cooed over how adorable they were and said not many people wanted rats as pets, but she didn't see why, they had such cute little ears, and fuzzy bodies, their sharp, intelligent eyes. They were much more appealing than hamsters, in her view.

He'd asked her out for coffee and it wasn't until several dates later that he told her the rats were food for his pythons. Her eyes teared up when he said that. She was quiet for so long, he worried their relationship was over when it was just getting started. Somehow she'd gotten past her despair over the rats and her shock that he kept large snakes in his house.

When she met Antony and Cleopatra, she'd hated them instantly, refused to touch them, or even walk more than a few feet into their mildly humid bedroom.

"I adore you, Brian," she said. "I think you know that. But I don't want those creatures in my life, and when I come over, the door to this room had better be shut tight."

He was so relieved, he promised her she'd never have to see them again.

He and Jennifer were perfect for each other. It wasn't always easy to find a woman who was content to stay home and maintain a clean house, to fix meals and work in the garden. But Jennifer liked to keep to herself. She was happy to stay in the house all day, in fact he had to encourage her to go out from time to time. She liked to cook, bake, and garden. She enjoyed cleaning! She loved making things for their home — quilts and curtains and area rugs woven by hand. Sometimes he'd worried what she would do when every room had homemade drapes and every piece of furniture had a set of throw pillows.

Jennifer had run away from home when she was seventeen. When he met her, she was only twenty, managing to scrape by working at the pet shop, renting a room hardly large enough to hold a single bed and a small dresser, riding the bus to work. He felt like she'd emerged out of nowhere and walked into his life as if she had no past at all. She never mentioned parents or siblings, or any friends from high school, and he didn't press. Things were fine as they were. She was so beautiful, so in love with him, so good to him. Although he admired her domestic activities, he was a little nervous with her sitting in the house alone all day, nothing but the TV for company. She assured him she was perfectly fine. All she needed was him. She promised that once the baby came, she'd get out more, find other mothers to socialize with.

Occasionally she greeted the neighbors from the front yard, but she never ventured out to the center of the cul-de-sac for a real conversation and never went into the neighbors' front yards. When Brian stood on the curb and talked to Claire and her husband, before Claire threw the guy out, Jennifer hung back in her own yard, smiling, offering a casual wave good-bye when the conversation ended.

Jennifer had been horrified when Claire and Greg split up. She couldn't imagine a man bringing another woman into his bedroom. "The only other thing you love, besides me, is your clay, and those revolting creatures, right Brian?" He didn't like her calling Antony and Cleopatra revolting, or creatures for that matter, but he agreed with her that he couldn't imagine why a man wouldn't be satisfied with his own wife.

HE SET THE bag of clay on his worktable and removed the wire tie that held it closed. He peeled back the plastic, disgusted as always, by the way the film of slip clung to the inside of the bag, making the heavy plastic damp and slimy. He took the handles of the cutter and slid the wire through the block of clay. He lifted off the chunk he would work with today. Once the bag was closed and put back on the shelf, he began pounding the lump of clay, kneading out the air pockets.

There was a pile of dried out clay on one of the shelves. He kept planning to reconstitute it, but never seemed to get around to it. A hammer and chisel sat on the rack with the other pottery tools. All he needed to do was pound the hardened clay into small pieces and store them in a bucket of water covered with plastic. He vowed he wouldn't purchase any more clay until he made what he had re-usable.

A new piece would help him forget about the shelves of figures that he wasn't quite pleased with. Each time he started something new, he was certain this would be the perfect one. Despite all the mocking, faceless figures staring at him, he had no doubt that it was true this time.

The first thing he did when he sat down for a new sculpting session was to work out the kinks in his mind as well as in his fingers and wrists. He broke off a piece of clay and rolled his palms across the surface, watching the clay grow from both sides of his hands, forming a long coil. He kept it thick and after a few strokes, he had a piece of clay that resembled Antony, in form, if not in fact. He drew the mouth with a wire pick, a mockery of that beautiful jaw, hiding sharp teeth and a rapid-fire tongue. Two small bits of clay, rolled into balls and pressed into the area where Antony's skull should be, formed the eyes. He set the inadequate replica to the side and created Cleopatra. Once they were both complete, he wound their bodies together. He had no idea why he did that, it just seemed right.

Facing his workspace, the entire wall was lined with shelves, only a few inches high, but perfect to house all the snakes. They looked like children's work, but he didn't have the heart to smash them back into lifeless clay for re-use, and he certainly wouldn't throw them away, even though they'd become decidedly un-snake-like, the clay turned powdery, cracking in spots. It would never reach the pure white of fired clay, but remained a light gray, reminding him of the gunk he cleaned off the drain stoppers in his sinks every few months.

He wasn't stupid. He knew what he was seeking here in the shed. Trying, over and over, week after week, month after month, to create the form that had been his child. With his growing skill at proportion, he was able to form the figures of small boys. He had over forty attempts on the second set of shelves to his right, built with enough room to display ten to twenty-inch tall heads and full body sculptures. His talent had matured, but he couldn't create the face.

Part of the problem was he lacked the skill to sculpt a face that bore a resemblance to a specific human being. He knew, because he'd tried. He'd made several images of Claire, of Michelle, even Jennifer. He could manage decent faces that looked human and balanced, noses that had the correct relationship to the lips, ears that fit the sides of the head and looked surprisingly real. But he couldn't make the faces look like the individuals he held in his memory. Claire's face looked like Michelle's, and neither differed substantially from Jennifer's. Only the hair and the shape of the bodies varied and they still didn't look like the actual person. Their clay bodies were all the same.

Getting the face of a little boy — that was impossible. He couldn't even seem to get started. He'd create the general form, separating legs and arms, giving a rudimentary shape to the torso and the head, making sure the head was positioned correctly over the shoulders, large enough to look realistic. As a beginner, the heads had always been too small. Most people had no idea how large the human head was, unless they'd tried their hand at sculpture, or perhaps drawing or painting. It was ridiculously easy to have a head that looked like an alien. You really had to work to make the head large enough to achieve the correct proportion.

His fingers faltered when he reached the hair. It was sketchy, the hint of hair at best. He created ears and scored the clay to make them adhere properly. After they were attached, his hands stiffened. He began to form the holes that would be the eye sockets, but he couldn't pinch out a nose or the start of lips, let alone construct the entire eye. And so he'd end his session, another half-formed figure set on the shelf. And that was the part he understood so well. He was trying to replicate the face of his son, but that was impossible because he'd never seen it.

HE STILL RECALLED every minute of that day, from the

moment he unlocked the front door at five-forty. It was August twenty-sixth. School had started the week before, but it was blazing hot — disorienting in itself. When he'd entered the house the heat was oppressive. There was no smell of food cooking, no sound of the sewing machine or the TV. The temperature had been in the nineties all week, bumping up to a hundred and one the previous day. It was a dry heat, the kind that made you feel you were breathing in something sharp, the kind that even though you were sweating, your skin was on fire.

He was glad Jennifer had left the drapes closed and the windows shut to preserve what cool air she could inside the house. Once the sun moved lower, they could start opening doors and windows to take advantage of the nighttime breeze — a benefit of living in the San Francisco Bay Area. Even during a heat wave like this, refreshing breezes drifted in from the ocean at night.

"Jen?"

He closed the front door and turned the deadbolt. "Jennifer?"

He glanced into the kitchen. There was no sign that she'd started dinner preparations. He supposed their dinner might be a salad, waiting inside the fridge, but it was unusual that no plates were set on the table. Maybe she planned to eat on the back patio. His feet thudded softly on the carpet as he walked down the hallway. He called her name every few steps. Their bedroom was dark, the bed covered with her hand-stitched ivory and dusty rose quilt. The quilt was spread evenly, barely brushing the floor on three sides. The bathroom doors were open. She wouldn't have gone out to run errands, she always did that early in the day, the minute the stores opened. She preferred empty aisles and short to non-existent lines at the checkout.

One after the other, he went into the spare bedrooms — the office and Jennifer's sewing room. Both were darkened from the closed drapes, empty of life.

Finally he stood in the middle of the living room and closed his eyes. He couldn't imagine where she'd gone. She hadn't been out back and the only sign of her was her trowel lying on the patio table. The wood handle and the shiny spade that she wiped clean every time she used it, not a spot of rust on it. She hadn't left him, had she? She would never do that. She adored him. She told him frequently that he was her whole life. Did the abandoned trowel mean someone had come into the yard and taken her? That seemed impossible, yet she wasn't prone to leaving her things lying around. People didn't truly get abducted right out of their yards, especially in suburbia. Besides, there were padlocks on the side gates. Then where the hell was she?

The only place he hadn't checked was Antony and Cleopatra's room. She never went in there, would never go in there. It was the one painful spot in his otherwise idyllic existence, her hatred for the lovely beings who had given him affection and silent gratitude for a good portion of his adult life. They had an understanding. He was to keep the door closed when he spent time with them. She didn't want even a glimpse of their long, supple bodies, and she certainly didn't want to see them draped across Brian's shoulders.

He walked down the hall and opened the door to their room. The air was moist, but no cooler than the rest of the house. Jennifer lay on the floor, her back to the door, her blonde hair spread across the creamy carpet. It looked soft. "Did you think it would be cooler in here?" he said.

She didn't answer.

He stepped into the room. "You must have been really hot to be brave enough to come in here. I hope you didn't unnerve them."

She was silent. He glanced up. Even in the semi-darkness, he saw that Cleopatra's terrarium was empty. All the moisture evaporated from his eyes, his mouth, his throat. He clutched his stomach and stumbled into the room. "Cleopatra? Jennifer?!" His voice was a hoarse groan. He fell on his knees and touched Jennifer's hair. He leaned over her and looked at her face. Lurid red and purple splotches ran down her neck and across her chest. Her arms, exposed by her sleeveless top, were a solid bruise.

"Oh, God," he cried. "No! Cleopatra, where are you? Come here, baby. What have you done?"

He fell on his wife's body, wrapping his arms around her, pulling her close. Then he shuddered and let go, realizing he was pressing her to him, the last thing she'd felt, the life squeezed out of her as her bones and muscles and blood vessels and lungs were compressed until they no longer functioned. Yet he had to hold her. He moved up to her again and pulled her close.

He'd warned her that Antony and Cleopatra sensed her dislike. She'd allowed herself to be attacked and she'd killed his child in the process. His little boy. The life had been crushed out of him, as if he was nothing more than the fish-like creature Brian had seen in the photographs, swimming in its little pool, never to see the light of day.

He lay on the floor and cried until it was long past dark.

When he finally stumbled to his feet, he saw Cleopatra, coiled behind the feeding case. Then he remembered — she'd been slow to eat her dinner and he'd left her in the feeding box overnight, the cover not as secure as the cover of her regular enclosure. He couldn't punish her, she didn't know. She followed her instincts. Without any conscious plan, he went to the garage, got the shovel, went to the backyard, and began digging in the center of the flower garden.

Even though Jennifer kept the area well-watered, once he dug down six or seven inches, the earth was hard from the weeks of heat, not to mention a dryer than normal spring, with no rain since late April. He stood on the upper edge of the shovel blade, using all his weight to drive it into the ground. After fifteen minutes, his back was soaked. Sweat dripped from his hair into his eyes and trickled down behind his ears. He laid the shovel on the ground, went to the side of the house, and unwound the hose. He dragged it across the lawn to the flower garden then went back to turn on the faucet.

While he waited for the water to spread through the shallow grave, he thought about Jennifer and Cleopatra. It was a classic struggle of women battling for a man's heart. Most often it took the form of mother and daughter-in-law, occasionally a woman and her brother's wife. The same could be said for Cleopatra. She knew she'd had less freedom to roam, less frequent visits outside of her terrarium, since Jennifer had come to be the dominant female in the house.

Was it possible Cleopatra had found the will to lift the cover and escape on her own? He couldn't believe Jennifer would have let her out. Although what did it matter now? Of course, Jennifer had to be complicit, had to open the door and enter the room. It was possible Jennifer had done something to torment Cleopatra, maybe even hurt her, angered her. She'd been so adamant in her refusal to learn to appreciate the beauty of the snakes, dismissive of their perfect markings, the smooth, elegant texture of their skin, the light of sentient beings shining from deep in their eyes. If she'd shown even a hint of interest in their beauty, their right to live satisfying lives, if she'd learned how to handle them properly, perhaps she wouldn't have been vulnerable to an attack.

It wasn't that he didn't love Jennifer. He was grief-stricken, the pain was deep, sharp, all consuming as he struggled to drive the shovel into the hard Santa Clara Valley clay beneath the fertilized soil of the garden. His life would be empty without her, his heart would never feel complete peace or happiness again. But still, it was her fault this had happened. That fact was clear. She'd hurt him more than he'd realized by not only ignoring Cleopatra and Antony, but by actively disliking them. The first time she met them, the moment they shifted position she shivered uncontrollably. After that, she refused to even look at them. She shuddered and scrunched her face when he so much as mentioned their names. She wouldn't go to the store with him when he bought food. After a while, she'd insisted he wasn't allowed to put the rats and other creatures in the terrariums when she was in the house. He had to wait until she was outside, working in the garden.

Jennifer hated her, and Cleopatra knew it. She had simply bided her time.

After two hours, he finally had a hole that was long enough for Jennifer's body, and deep enough to prevent any animal's ability to detect an odor and start digging. Of course, he'd have to protect her body with plastic. He had plenty of heavy-duty bags for that.

He was surprised his grief had subsided, turned into something practical that forced him to focus on the task at hand. He only had a few hours of darkness left. He needed to be efficient.

Cleopatra had taken the child's life along with Jennifer's. Of course, Cleopatra couldn't have known she was doing that. Or had she? Did she sense another life growing inside? One that, once it arrived, would force the end of her relationship with Brian?

The loss of his child was so vast, his mind hadn't begun to grasp it. A darkness closed over him. Whatever Jennifer had done to provoke Cleopatra, she'd shown complete disregard for their baby, and now he was gone, his life snuffed out forever. Unless …

Brian dropped the shovel and ran to the sliding glass door into the living room. How long would the child survive without the mother's life? Was it possible … why had he wasted all those hours digging? Why hadn't he thought of this earlier? He ran through the dining area and skidded across the kitchen floor. He grabbed the carving knife out of the drawer and rushed to Antony and Cleopatra's room. Jennifer was still on her side, facing the twin terrariums, just as he'd left her. He rolled her gently onto her back. The hours of staring at fetuses floating in their mothers' wombs had not been wasted. He knew exactly where to insert the knife and he drew it carefully through the layers of skin and fat.

Before he even finished, the adrenaline drained out of him as quickly as it had surged through his veins. He sat back on his heels and dropped the blood-soaked knife on the carpet. Of course he couldn't save his child. It was nothing but a mass of cells, a small wiggly thing at this point. What had he been thinking? There was no way it could survive.

After he'd wrapped Jennifer's body in the quilt she'd made, secured it with plastic, and placed it in the grave, he cleaned the carpet as best he could. He covered the bloodstains with one of Jennifer's beautiful handcrafted rugs. Eventually he'd remove the carpet, put in a hardwood floor, but not yet. He needed to calm down, establish a normal life as a single man once again. Discarding soiled carpet and having workers pouring over the house would arouse suspicion if he did it too soon. Once some time had passed, he'd re-do the room and create a much nicer, more exotic environment for Antony and Cleopatra. They would have built-in terrariums with larger tree branches, pools of water, and more freedom to move about.

The sky was a pale blue when he went to bed.

HE'D TOLD CLAIRE and the Reynes about Jennifer, of course. Speaking with real tears in his voice, not something he had to manufacture, he explained that she'd left him. They weren't surprised, knowing a bit about her background, a runaway who had disappeared off the face of the earth once already. It was easy to accept that it had happened again. They absorbed his pain, soaking it in as it oozed out of his skin. That tangible, terrifying grief kept them from asking too many questions. They didn't want to know the details. They wanted him to feel better, and when he stopped talking about his loss, they were much happier. They saw him as a wounded man whose wife had betrayed him. And in reality, she had.

Ten

WHEN ALL THE bulbs were tucked neatly into their holes like tiny animals burrowing down to hibernate, Claire went into the kitchen and drank two glasses of water.

The yard was pathetic. Her forty-five minutes of work wouldn't yield any visible results until March, and even then, it wouldn't create any significant change in the drab appearance. Greg had never been interested in having a nice yard. She now realized it was because he spent all his free time trolling for hot women. He'd always said they would hire a professional landscaper to prep the house for sale when it was time to move up to something nicer. Their next house would have a spectacular yard. She supposed she could have transformed the yard herself, but without Greg by her side, she couldn't get inspired to do anything. When they first split up, she hadn't had the energy for gardening.

Even though it wasn't much, and she had to wait until Spring, she loved the idea of burying ugly, misshapen lumps in the ground that would later appear as great bursts of yellow, announcing the end of winter.

Every so often, Joey pleaded with her to plant a tree in the center of the lawn. He didn't seem to grasp that by the time a tree grew large enough for him to climb, he'd no longer be interested. It wasn't that he didn't understand how long it would take the tree to mature, it was that he couldn't comprehend no longer wanting to climb trees.

Inside, he was sprawled on the floor watching TV. He looked small and slightly lost in the semi-vacant living room with its empty walls, the sliding door a window to the equally barren backyard.

The conversation with Michelle, so soon on the heels of Tanya's probing questions, still made her feel … unsettled. She was angry with herself for listening to Tanya in the first place. A total stranger complained about a few emails and suddenly Claire found herself wondering if there was something not right about Brian. She felt disloyal. She was too easily swayed. Brian was a good guy. Yes, their relationship was occasionally a little awkward, but that was her fault for trying too hard to make sure she didn't give the wrong vibe. Nothing good came of trying to force your behavior in one direction or another. She refilled the glass again and took a small sip.

This was the wrong way to be thinking — doubting herself, doubting her choices, doubting Brian's stability. She should be focused on school, her future. Tonight she was meeting with the group from her public speaking class to prepare for their upcoming debate. The team needed to be armed with facts and arguments that disputed any evidence of global warming. All of them had grumbled that they were on the more difficult side of the debate, but hopefully the feast of Mexican food that one of the guys was picking up on his way there, and a bit of beer, would spur their contrarian creative juices. There were four people on the team, and every one of them was equally determined to win, which made it exciting.

She loved the class. It was her second-to-last general ed course. When she stood in front of the instructor and the other students to argue her views, she imagined herself in a courtroom, prosecuting people rightfully accused of all kinds of crimes. It made her feel as if she could taste the future.

She put her glass in the dishwasher and went into the living room. "I'll make turkey sandwiches for lunch, does that sound good?"

Joey nodded.

"You should get ready for gymnastics. It's already twelve-fifteen."

He wriggled across the floor to the remote, aimed it at the TV, and shut it off. He turned at an angle and rolled toward the hallway. Claire smiled.

AFTER JOEY'S GYMNASTICS class, they went to the park and then to the grocery store. She served Joey mac and cheese for dinner. She filled a mug with a few scoops for herself so her stomach wouldn't be grumbling when she arrived at study group.

The others in the group were nineteen and twenty years old. Too often, she felt like their mother, or at least their big sister. All of them were full-time students, living on schedules of their own making. Dinner wasn't the clockwork routine it was for her, geared to a child's needs and the sleep schedule required for a full time job. Eating at eight or nine at night wasn't a problem for her classmates because they probably hadn't had breakfast at all and lunch or snacks came late in the day. They lived like wild animals, eating when their stomachs echoed with growls, sleeping when, and sometimes where, their bodies collapsed.

That kind of life had slipped from her grasp like a raw egg, running between her fingers. She'd met Greg when she and her friends attended a University football game during her first year at the local Junior College, married him during her second year, and stopped thinking about school when she got pregnant. Occasionally she wondered what the big hurry had been, but most of the time she managed to keep her eyes fixed on her goal. If she'd missed her chance at that carefree life, at least she could give it to Joey.

At six, she and Joey walked across the street to Brian's. He opened the door before they pressed the bell. He grinned at Joey. "Hey! We're going to have a great time, aren't we?"

Claire tried to smile. The tone of Brian's voice sounded as if he was talking to a four year-old. She looked at him, silently willing him to meet her gaze so she could give a non-verbal hint to tone it down.

"Why are you shouting?" Joey said.

Now, Brian looked directly into her eyes. He scowled. "I wasn't shouting. I'm excited to see you."

"Okay," Joey said.

"I thought we could play monopoly and then we'll make some popcorn and watch a movie. Does that sound good?"

Joey stepped over the threshold.

"Thanks so much." Claire stepped back to the edge of the porch. "I really appreciate this."

"You don't have to say that every time," Brian said.

Joey turned and stared at her. She couldn't read his expression with any certainty. It might be that he didn't want to spend a Saturday night in Brian's house, although he still couldn't offer a tangible explanation for his objection. All he could come up with was, *it feels sad*, or *it's too dark*.

Joey continued to look over his shoulder at her. Finally it struck her. She'd implied Brian was doing a favor, that looking after Joey was a sacrifice. Of course she knew why Joey was concerned with being a burden — his distracted father. Greg only saw Joey two or three days a month, usually a Sunday and the occasional weeknight. The girlfriend always tagged along, and according to Joey, his Dad spent most of the time talking to her and *petting* her.

"What do you mean, *petting* her?" Claire had asked.

"He acts like she's a cat. He keeps smoothing his hands on

her hair and her t-shirt and …"

"What does that mean?"

"What?"

"He smoothes his hand on her t-shirt?"

"You know, like this." Joey put his hand on her waist and rubbed it up to her rib cage, moving it back and forth. "I think he forgets I'm there."

The girlfriend wasn't the only distraction. It was Greg's offhand comments, *I have a lot of errands today, Joe. I hope you're up for that.* Why couldn't he run his errands after work, or on Saturdays?

She walked back to the door and stepped into Brian's foyer. She bent down and hugged her son. She straightened and looked at Brian. "You're a lucky guy to get to spend an entire evening with Joey. He'll probably beat you at monopoly."

"We'll see," Brian said.

She wished Brian would echo her reassurance, but maybe she'd confused him with her sudden change of direction. Maybe her voice sounded as false as his had. She spoke more softly, hoping it changed her tone. "Have a great time, Joey. I'll miss you."

"No you won't. You'll be having fun with your friends."

Claire swallowed. "They're not really my friends, just classmates."

"Okay."

"And I will miss you."

"Okay."

When she walked back across the cul-de-sac there was a hollowness inside her ribs, as if she hadn't eaten in days but wasn't particularly hungry, just empty. Most of the time Joey was a happy kid, but every so often, this darker side emerged, leaving her wondering how much his father's semi-abandonment had affected him. A boy, in particular, really needed his dad. It probably wasn't fair to accuse Greg of abandoning him, even in her own mind. The reality of abandonment would be so much worse. But he had shut Joey out of a significant portion of his life, and she was certain that Joey *felt* abandoned, even if he didn't know the pain of the real thing. Dragging what's-her-face along on every outing, unable to keep his hands off her for two minutes, certainly made Joey feel like he wasn't all that interesting. Claire could only over-compensate so much.

She went inside and checked her purse to make sure she had her phone. She looked at her reflection in the glass door of the living room. Her eyes were large black spots, her features only faintly visible. She lifted her hair off her shoulders and let if fall against her back. Time to stop worrying about Joey. She couldn't fix everything that was wrong, but she could do her part to help her team win the debate, and add one more project toward an *A* in the class and a high GPA. Another inch closer to law school and a real career. She laughed at her reflection — a career, period.

Eleven

AFTER CLAIRE LEFT, Brian went into the kitchen.

Joey followed. "It's too dark in here," he said.

"I've told you before, bright lights strain my eyes."

"I forgot."

"But I'll turn on another light when we start our game. Do you want to play monopoly now? And watch the movie later?"

"Okay."

"By then you might be hungry and we can make the popcorn. I got *How to Train Your Dragon*."

"I saw that ages ago with my Dad." Joey rubbed his ear. "It's cold in here."

"You'll warm up when you start concentrating on the game."

"I don't mind watching it again, though. It was good."

Joey followed him into the dining area. Brian was continuously amazed at how children followed adults around as if connected by a second, psychic umbilical cord that hadn't yet been severed. They copied absolutely everything. The parents he encountered at the school didn't appear to fully recognize that. If they were aware of it in principle, they forgot about it in the rush of daily life. He observed the parents' nervous ticks and watched them play out in their children — crossed arms as if every encounter was a standoff, hands running through their hair when they wanted to look cool. He wondered whether Joey rubbing his ear was due to the cool air, or a mannerism picked up from Claire. Or her ex-husband. Children sometimes followed adults so closely they stepped on the heels of their shoes. It was as if they wanted to take in each gesture, memorize every word, so they could make sure to learn what they needed to do in order to turn into adults, as if they knew on some deep level that childhood was nothing but a classroom for real life.

The only illumination in the house came from the light over the kitchen sink that he'd switched on to make sure Claire knew he was expecting Joey. He turned on the chandelier over the table. The monopoly board was open, money stacked neatly on one side, and a small box containing the houses and hotels on the other. The game could be classified as an antique, handed down through two generations. It had wood buildings rather than the plastic houses and hotels that came with most of the games now.

"Do you want to play monopoly? Or do you prefer something else?"

"No, this is fine." Joey settled in the chair he used when he did his homework at Brian's.

For an hour and a half they marched their markers around the board. Brian was surprised by Joey's skill. He'd supervised Joey's homework often enough that he knew Joey was good at math, so it had been easy to guess that monopoly would be appealing, but he wasn't prepared for Joey's ability to make sure he collected whole sets of properties, to bargain for the right deal. Not that Brian would have taken advantage of Joey's age and tried to hoard all the best ones, but he'd imagined he would have to throw the game somewhat. Instead, Joey was giving him a run for his money, so to speak.

Still, the game was getting tiresome. That was the trouble with playing with two people, the game deteriorated into a passing back and forth of rent payments. Of course, no matter how many people were playing, the game tended to taper off into a dull plodding around the rectangular spaces, exchanging funds, the occasional bankruptcy, which was really just a roll of the dice. There was nothing strategic about it. Maybe it was more similar to life than he'd realized. A roll of the dice, landing in the wrong spot at the wrong time, and you were done, bankrupt — financially, emotionally, or spiritually.

Faded red hotels sat on Park Place and Boardwalk. Brian was embarrassed by his foolish love of those properties. They never delivered what they promised, because they offered only two chances to capture rent, while most of the other properties had three. Because of the game's periodic delivery of a player directly to the starting square, they regularly missed the adjacent Boardwalk and Park Place. Still he always tried to make sure he ended up with those two, regardless of the risk. He didn't understand whether it was the color, the implied exclusivity, or the vague hint of a place in the world that was reminiscent of fun and good times. Joey hadn't landed on either one in his past five trips around the board. Brian's funds were slowly getting depleted. He was sick of the game, and Joey didn't talk much, so there was nothing to distract from the clinking dice, tapping game pieces, and quiet demand, *You owe me a hundred dollars, please,* for Joey's ownership of three of the four railroads.

"My eyes hurt," Joey said. "It's still too dark in here."

"All the lights are on."

"Maybe you need brighter bulbs."

"These are energy efficient."

"Well I can't see very good."

"Very well."

Joey ignored the grammatical correction. He picked up the dice and shook his hand. "I'm gonna win."

"I think you're right. Should we end the game and agree that you won?"

"I want to win for real."

"All right." Brian felt a yawn descending from the back of his head. He tried to swallow it.

"Are you tired?"

"No. Well, maybe just tired of sitting in this chair. I'm a little hungry. I'll make some popcorn."

He went to the kitchen, pulled out a bag of popcorn, and unfolded the sides. He put it in the microwave and while the motor hummed, he got a bowl out of the cabinet.

"Your turn," Joey said.

Brian's cell phone rang, chimes pinging up and down the musical scale. He glanced at the screen — Claire. Behind him, popcorn ricocheted inside the bag, banging like something wanting to escape a cage, flinging itself hard against the sides. He moved into the hallway so he could hear better.

"Hi," he said. "Everything is going good. I'm making popcorn."

"I might be a little later than I thought."

He glanced at the microwave but of course he couldn't see the hour because it was still counting down the cook time. "That's fine."

"Maybe eleven?"

"Do you want me to have him go to sleep in the guest room?"

"No, that's fine if he stays up. Do you have enough stuff to keep him entertained?"

"Sure. I have the movie, and I have a DVD series on wild animals."

"He'll like that," Claire said. "And thanks so much."

"No problem."

After he disconnected, Brian removed the bag from the

microwave, ripped it open, and dumped the popcorn into the bowl. He carried it to the table. "Do you want something to drink? Snapple?"

"Okay."

"That was your mom. She'll be here at eleven or so." He glanced at the microwave. Eight-forty.

Joey grabbed a handful of popcorn. "I'm still cold."

"How about hot chocolate instead of Snapple?"

"Okay."

"I'll turn on the heat for a few minutes. Just to take off the chill." Brian went to the thermostat and turned the dial. It would smell stale because this was the first time since summer that the furnace had been fired up. He should check the humidifier in Antony and Cleopatra's room. The warm air was so drying, he adjusted the setting whenever he turned on the central heating. But it would only be on for ten or fifteen minutes, so they'd be fine. He returned to the kitchen.

After the hot chocolate was made, they finished the game. Joey decided he'd rather watch the jungle segment of Brian's nature collection. Joey was a funny kid. Often, he seemed older than his years, racing around the cul-de-sac, doing stunts on his skateboard that bigger kids couldn't pull off, and now this. He supposed Joey had considered it and decided seeing the dragon movie a second time wasn't so great after all. New was always better. He hoped it hadn't been a mistake to offer the option of the nature DVDs. Joey would love the animals, but there were a few scenes that might be too violent. He should have checked with Claire.

He inserted the first disk. As Joey watched in silence, his eyes round, pupils dilated, Brian longed for a classroom full of kids like Joey, interested in the world, not jaded at the age of seven or eight, too impatient for board games or television shows that didn't shoot images at their retinas at the rate of sixty frames a second.

After a while, he paused the DVD. "Hang on." He went into the kitchen and got the bucket of red vines. He started back to the living room and realized his usual habit of eating out of the bucket might not work with Joey. He pulled out two handfuls, put them in a beer mug, and carried it to the living room. He set it on the coffee table. Joey looked at him as if asking permission. Brian nodded and Joey grabbed one of the candies.

Joey chewed on the red vine. After a moment, his lips turned the color of blood. "I wish I could have a monkey."

"That would be cool. What's your favorite animal?"

"I think lions. And monkeys. I wish I could have a pet. Mom said when I'm ten."

"That makes sense. What kind are you thinking about?"

"I want a turtle."

"Not a dog or cat?"

"Everyone has dogs and cats. That would be good too, but I want a turtle."

Brian didn't think there were any turtles in this segment, but it certainly had its fair share of exotic birds and insects. It also had snakes. What would Joey think of Antony and Cleopatra? Most boys liked snakes, didn't they? He re-started the DVD.

It might be interesting to introduce Joey to Antony and Cleopatra. None of his neighbors knew about the snakes. The negative reactions from the few people he'd told over the years had been too upsetting. Even if boys liked snakes, adult men were less impressed, looking at you with surprise. They didn't freak out like women, but they certainly read something unflattering into it. There was a *you're not normal* look to the set of their eyelids and the sudden slowing of the conversation, if not an abrupt end. The reaction confused him. What was wrong with having snakes? They were fascinating creatures. He knew Joey would love the pythons, but was fairly certain Claire would not. There was a ten percent chance she'd be okay with it, she was easy-going, but the other ninety percent said she'd go ballistic at the thought of her son being around such large and potentially deadly creatures.

While he nibbled another red vine and watched a giant macaw sidle along a branch, he mulled over the question. He wasn't sure why he'd never shown the snakes to Joey. Joey had spent countless hours at his house, yet the thought had never occurred to him until this minute. Maybe because he was used to keeping them hidden. Maybe because the topic of pets had never come up before, and Joey was usually occupied with homework. More likely it was a feeling of exposure, knowing their potential, and being irrationally afraid that someone might figure it out, that they'd remove his beloved companions from his home.

Joey stared at the TV, the half-chewed red vine lay on the table, soggy and squashed together on the end he'd been nibbling. On the screen, children were trapping spiders the size of their hands and cooking them on large tropical leaves over a small fire they'd built themselves. Spiders that, if they weren't cooked correctly, would release deadly poison. The scene must surely make a modern child realize that he lived in an insulated world, prevented from exploring or taking risks on his own, effectively kept under lock and key. Seeing the pythons might make Joey feel more in touch with life. Could he convince Joey to keep a secret? Or did it not matter? Surely Claire wouldn't prevent Joey from entering his house. After all, what other options did she have?

He didn't understand why he was so hesitant. It was no big deal. Even if Claire hated them, if she didn't want Joey around them, all he'd have to do was promise to keep their room secured — easy enough.

"Are you going to finish that red vine?" Brian said.

Joey glanced at the table then back at the TV.

"Do you like watching all these creatures you've never seen before?"

"I've seen most of them on other shows."

Brian smiled. He'd wait. Only twenty minutes or so remained on the disk.

When it was over, Joey grabbed his half-eaten candy and curled it so the whole thing fit inside his mouth at once. "Can we watch another one?"

It was ten, Claire wouldn't be there for at least another hour. Brian yawned. Getting up and visiting Antony and Cleopatra's room would get his blood flowing so he didn't nod off during another hour of soothing, even-toned voice-over. "I want to show you something first."

Joey looked at him.

Brian stood. "Come with me. I'll introduce you to my pets."

"I didn't know you had pets."

"Let's go see."

He led the way down the hall and paused in front of the room. "You have to be confident and calm because if they sense you're scared or tense, they'll get upset."

Joey nodded.

Brian opened the door and turned on the lights.

"What's in there?" Joey said.

Brian walked to Antony's case. Antony lifted his head and turned it slightly. He slithered closer to the glass wall. Brian opened the top and reached inside. He wrapped one hand around Antony's mid-section the other just below his head. He lifted him out of the case.

Joey stepped closer. "That's awesome." His voice was a whisper, so soft that Antony didn't seem to notice the unfamiliar sound.

"His name is Antony. That's Cleopatra." Brian nodded toward the other case. "Do you know who Antony and Cleopatra were?"

"I heard of them."

"Cleopatra was a ruler of ancient Egypt. She fell in love with Mark Antony, a Roman general."

"Why did you name them that?"

"Their love transcended the ages — he died in her arms."

"Can I touch it?"

"Not *it*, him."

"A boy snake?"

"Male." Brian lowered Antony so his head was level with Joey's.

"Will he bite me?"

"They don't bite unless they already have their prey. Or if they're provoked."

"I thought snakes bite people, and kill them."

"Not all snakes are poisonous. And this kind of snake, a python, squeezes its prey to death."

Joey didn't flinch. He reached out one finger and ran it from one of Antony's spots to another, as if he was connecting the dots.

"Isn't he beautiful?" Brian wasn't sure why he suddenly felt vulnerable. He needed Joey to love the snakes, to see them as he did, to recognize they were the most regal creatures on earth. He wanted Joey to ask to hold part of Antony's body around his own shoulders. He wanted Joey to think this was the greatest moment of his life so far. Perhaps he wanted Joey to demand his own pet python.

Joey continued petting the snake. After a moment, he walked to the other case. He fiddled with the clasps on the cover.

"Don't open that." Brian lowered Antony back into his case, slightly depressed that although Joey was quite taken with the snake, he kept himself at arm's length.

"I thought you said it wouldn't bite."

"She. Cleopatra is the female."

"Are you going to take her out?"

For a moment, it was on his lips to ask Joey if he wanted to hold part of her body. But that wasn't right. He wanted the desire to come from Joey, not a forced response to his offer. It was possible the kid recognized they were too heavy for him to hold on his own, so he didn't bother asking. But Brian could support the bulk of the weight.

He walked to Cleopatra's terrarium, opened the cover, and lifted her out, gripping her more firmly than he had Antony. She was much stronger and more easily startled. Not to mention her history of jealousy.

Joey stood close to him and stroked Cleopatra for several minutes. After a while, they returned to the TV. For the rest of the evening, Brian struggled fruitlessly to keep himself from sinking into melancholy.

Twelve

SUNDAY WAS A day that felt out of order — nearly eighty degrees even though the calendar was closing in on Halloween. Claire sat on the patio staring at her back fence, a naked expanse of grayed wood. The backyard was as barren as the front, except for an apricot tree, and she hated apricots. One thing at a time. She'd buried the daffodil bulbs, maybe next spring she'd buy a few flowering shrubs to plant along the fence, something that grew quickly and could withstand the full sun it would receive for most of the day. She constantly vacillated between wanting to make things nice for Joey and not wanting to bother investing any energy, or money, in a place she couldn't wait to escape.

Landscaping was the last thing she should be thinking about right now. She should be focused on what Joey had casually mentioned over turkey sandwiches and cheddar cheese crackers — pythons. Right now, Joey was asleep on the living room floor. He'd been cranky from staying up so late. After lunch, she'd let him watch a movie, hoping he'd doze off.

She was afraid to close her eyes. Even basking in the sun, a chill crept down her spine as she thought of Brian's *pets* and their love of baking in hot, breeze-less air. Or was that only rattlesnakes? Did tropical snakes, like she supposed his were, prefer moist, steamy environments? That seemed more likely. She could almost feel their thick, heavy bodies slithering across her skin. Her stomach and chest convulsed. She squeezed her hands around her upper arms.

She prided herself on not being the type of mother who gave schoolteachers or her parents, or even Joey's father, explicit instructions on the care of her son. She figured most aspects of good childcare came from instinct, from commonly accepted caution, and treating a child with respect. Anything that didn't fall under those categories wasn't a matter of life or death, so it wasn't a big deal. It had never occurred to her, would never cross her mind, to tell Brian, *by the way, please don't introduce Joey to enormous, deadly snakes*. She couldn't imagine what he'd been thinking. Knowing she'd lived across the street from those things for all these years made her afraid to think about sliding under the blankets and turning out the light at night. She shivered, once again feeling them move across her body — dense muscles, creeping slowly, silently. Snakes looked as if they belonged on an alien planet, their faces cruel and demonic.

Joey must have known how she would react, because he

was cautious when he told her, at first underplaying how large they were. Twelve feet! Between the involuntary shivers repeatedly racing down her spine, there was a slow burning rage that Brian had compromised Joey's safety. How could she have known the man all this time and never heard a word about his snakes? If one of them got out, if it attacked Joey, did Brian have the strength, or the know-how, to protect him? Would he kill his pet if Joey's life were in danger? Surely he would, wouldn't he?

She went into the house. Joey was curled up on the floor. He looked so exposed, sleeping without a blanket. She took the quilt her grandmother had made off the back of the rocking chair and laid it over his hips and legs. She turned the volume down on the TV, went into the kitchen, and grabbed an apple out of the bowl on the counter. Biting and chewing her way around the circumference, she walked into the entryway and stared out at the cul-de-sac, studying the statue and fountain in the center of Brian's lawn, trying to determine whether there was anything in his overwrought yard that indicated he was hiding deadly animals inside the house. Had the snakes lived there when he was married to Jennifer?

She returned to the kitchen and shoved the apple core into the garbage disposal. She went out the front door, closing only the screen so she'd hear Joey if he woke and called for her.

Elaine, who lived in the house at the center of the cul-de-sac, next door to Brian, stood in her front yard holding her infant daughter. Claire waved and walked to the sidewalk. Elaine crossed the curve of the street to meet her.

"I haven't seen you in a while," Claire said.

"Because all I do is try to rock Molly and sleep. Since the construction started, she cries all day. It's awful."

Claire pulled her hair over her shoulder and combed her fingers through the curls. "Everyone complains about it."

"They do," Elaine said. "But I'm not everyone. We're not going to just sit around and whine about it, doing nothing."

"What can you do?"

"We're going to stay with my parents."

"Good for you."

"And we're starting a major remodel. We're gutting the house. Mark's been talking to contractors. We'll sink the back yard so the fence seems higher and you won't be able to see the medical center. We're building an enclosed patio and adding a second story that only has windows looking toward the park. The second floor will be a master suite and the wall without windows will have a mural."

"That sounds like major work."

Elaine shifted the baby's head so it was nestled between her breasts. Molly closed her eyes and smiled briefly. In the space of a single breath, the movement carried Claire back, remembering Joey's face, hiding dreams and thoughts that no one would ever be privy to.

Elaine continued talking, oblivious to what had just

happened a few inches from her lips. "We're selling the house. We didn't buy here to live in an industrial complex."

"The medical center was already there."

"I know, but it was small, almost invisible. Now it's taking over the neighborhood."

"Are you worried you won't get what you paid for it?"

"Oh, no. We'll get more. The remodel is really slick. Granite, imported tile, recessed lighting, high tech — we're putting in a wireless network. The lights and maybe the heat and AC will all be controlled by a cell phone app."

Claire let go of her hair and slid her hands into the pockets of her jeans. "A realtor told the Reynes they couldn't ask what they wanted for their house now that the medical center is quadrupled in size. Even after their remodel."

Elaine turned to face Michelle and Gerard's house. Her hair, short, dark, and silky swung across her face. She shook her head to toss it out of the way. It looked as if she was gazing up at the sky, searching for further proof that they could get what they deserved out of a house that was sitting in the shadow of a yearlong construction project. "They didn't do enough. Two new rooms and a deck, a little paint and some landscaping provides a nicer facade, but there's no unique selling value. Our house will stand out from everything else in the neighborhood."

"But won't people that can afford something so nice prefer to look in an area that's purely residential?" She had no idea why she was arguing about this. Elaine acted as if she had it all figured out, there was a tone that said all the others in the cul-de-sac were suckers, or stupid.

"No. It's targeting a certain kind of buyer. We know what we're doing."

"I'm sure you do."

"The timing is perfect. We'll stay with my parents, and they'll be able to enjoy their granddaughter in the first year of her life. I can go back to work without worrying about daycare and nannies and all of that. Our house can get a complete makeover and by the time it's done, the medical center will be complete, so it won't be a noise and dirt issue, and we can put it on the market."

Claire shoved her hands further into her pockets but they'd already reached the bottoms, so all she succeeded in doing was yanking the waistband against her hipbones. "It sounds like you have it all worked out. That's fantastic." She still had no idea why she was so annoyed. Attitude was everything, or something like that. And Elaine's attitude was self-important. She and her husband had the money to create a dream home out of a tract house. Not everyone did. She smiled, hoping she looked kind. Actually, this conversation with Elaine had been a good thing. She was in a better frame of mind for talking to Brian. Instead of discounting everything she knew about him, focusing on nothing but his deadly pets, she was reminded of their long-standing friendship. She wondered what Elaine would think, knowing there were predators right next door. Those snakes could escape and her baby's life would be in danger. Of course, within a few days, Elaine and the baby would be gone, so maybe she wouldn't care. "I need to go talk to Brian. I better get going."

"Sure. I should put my sweetheart to bed. The one day a week when she can get uninterrupted sleep." Elaine kissed Molly's nose.

"When are you moving out?"

"This week."

"Be sure to come over and say good-bye before you go."

"I will. But we'll be stopping by on a regular basis to check the progress."

"Good to know."

Elaine walked back across the street and up her front path. When she disappeared inside the house, Claire couldn't escape the feeling that Elaine had disappeared from her life. It was likely that Elaine would come by in the daytime to check the progress of the work, and entirely possible that Claire would never see her again. It amazed her how easily people slipped in and out of your life without you even noticing, until you looked back a few years later and wondered what had happened. Until you sat in front of a fire on a winter evening and thought about the people who had been swallowed up by time. But that wasn't something for an October afternoon. She pulled her hands out of her pockets and walked across the street to Brian's. She rang the bell.

The house was silent. His Honda was in the driveway. Goosebumps speckled her bare arms. Standing in the shade of the porch, it was clear the heat was the autumn kind, only present in full sun. She shouldn't have worn a tank top. Or maybe she was shivering because she imagined Brian in the window-less room with one of the snakes draped around his shoulders, the other slithering across the floor. Her shiver turned into a full-body shudder that made her nauseous. He was taking too long. She rang the bell again. Maybe it seemed longer because her imagination was going wild. Maybe from his perspective, she was standing there relentlessly poking the bell.

The door opened. "Hi," Brian said. "What's up?"

"Can I come in for a second?" The minute she spoke, she regretted it. Where were the snakes? How was she to know whether they were safely in their room? How was she to ever know that again? Yet, she'd been in the house numerous times and never felt any uneasiness.

Brian moved back and she stepped inside. Her feet sounded unnaturally heavy, even on the thickly carpeted floor. He led the way to the living room. The drawn chocolate-colored drapes and matching carpet made the room quite dark.

"It's beautiful out, you should open the drapes."

"Not right now. Have a seat."

"I wasn't planning to stay, I don't even know why I invited myself in."

"You can sit for three minutes. Or less, if that's all it takes."

"You know why I'm here?"

"I have a suspicion."

"Your pets."

He nodded.

"I didn't know about them."

"Why would you?"

"I'm surprised you never mentioned them. After all these years."

"Most people don't react well. I tend not to bring it up. Antony and Cleopatra are used to keeping to themselves, they know how humans usually respond."

Claire swallowed. Joey had told her the snakes' names, but she hadn't been prepared for Brian to refer to them as if they were self-aware, with opinions and feelings of their own. She shivered again. She could feel his eyes on her. He knew she was repulsed. His thin lips looked pouty, as if he wanted to be kissed, or patted on the head. His hair was damp around the roots, making the rest of it look even finer in contrast. At first she thought he looked insulted, then she realized he was hurt.

"I wish you would have checked with me before you let Joey see them."

"Would you have said yes?"

"I would have wanted to be there."

"Really?"

Okay, he had her there. She didn't know what she wanted. She did not want to see them, and she didn't like Joey's fascination with them, and she didn't like knowing there were deadly animals living across the street while she and Joey slept in blissful ignorance. Even worse was that they lurked behind a flimsy door while her son sat at the table doing his homework. "I don't like them."

"Snakes? Or mine in particular?"

"They have the potential to kill you."

"I know what they're capable of. Their terrariums are secure."

"What if Joey got in there, or they got out?"

"They can't get out. They don't have opposable thumbs, you know."

Was he mocking her? He still looked more hurt than anything else. Did he really expect that she'd be excited about them? That she'd be okay with what he'd done? "It's dangerous."

"Lots of things are dangerous. People have foolish mythological biases. Cars are more likely to kill you. In fact, so is a skateboard."

She didn't know how to argue with that.

"To be honest, I'm disappointed," he said.

"Why?"

"You've always struck me as a very open person."

"This has nothing to do with being open."

"You're closing yourself off to a part of the world. You're preventing your son from discovering new things."

"I am not. Discovering new things and being in the house with deadly snakes is not at all the same. I expose Joey to lots of experiences." She leaned against the corner of the wall.

Brian tilted his head as if he was trying to interpret her change in position. "Please don't be upset, Claire. Take a step back and look at it logically. Do you want to meet Antony and Cleopatra? So you can see how secure their terrariums are?"

"See, that's weird. That you call them by their names."

"Why wouldn't I?"

She stared at him. Somehow it made them seem more human, as if they had distinct identities. And they didn't. They were snakes. Cold blooded, with its well-deserved connotation of not caring, of lacking feelings, referring to creatures that changed to suit the environment.

Brian took a step toward her. His eyes were teary. She hadn't meant to upset him, but he'd upset her terribly. She didn't understand why he couldn't see that.

"Does this mean you don't want me to look after Joey anymore?"

She knew that's what it sounded like. It was a natural conclusion. She couldn't go to school without Brian's help. Was she really considering risking her son's life for supplemental childcare? But that was ridiculous. She wasn't *risking his life*. Yes, the creatures were dangerous, potentially deadly. But Joey said they were in cases with lids. She imagined them pushing at the covers, hoisting themselves up and over the sides. She shuddered. Even if they could do that, which she didn't want to spend another moment picturing, they couldn't get underneath the door, could they?

"Can I see the room?" she said. "I don't want to go inside, I just want to reassure myself that the door is secure."

Brian walked past her. She followed. He stopped in front of the bedroom door adjacent to the master bedroom. She realized she'd never ventured into this part of his house, never gone further than the hall bathroom. The door was like any bedroom door in a tract house. For a moment, she flashed on Elaine's exotic remodeling plans. She wondered if Elaine would have thicker doors — solid oak — in her effort to make a veritable fortress out of her house, as if adding insulation and a second story and a networked interior could shut out the parts of the world she didn't like. Not that Elaine would be there to notice.

"I thought snakes could flatten themselves," she said. "Can they get under the door? If they got out of their boxes?"

"They can't get out of their terrariums," he said.

"If they did. In the one in a million chance they figured out a way … if there was an earthquake and the boxes fell over."

He looked at her. Did she imagine a smirk flitting across his face? She wasn't being over-protective. They were enormous, she'd looked it up. They were close to one hundred-pounds, for God's sake. He had to see her point of view.

"Will you let Joey come over if I put something along the bottom edge of the door?"

"So they can flatten themselves?"

"I'm trying to make you feel comfortable. Joey likes the

snakes. Even if he happened to wind up alone with them for some reason, they wouldn't hurt him unless they sensed a threat. Not that he'd be around them. Ever."

She wondered how a snake felt anything, much less threatened. Her resolve was weakening. Not weakening exactly, Joey's safety was the most important thing in the world, but she knew there was some kind of visceral hatred that was driving her thoughts about the snakes.

Brian smiled. "Are you sure you don't want to meet them? It might calm you down. They say facing your fear is healing. You'll see they're lovely creatures."

"Maybe another day." Claire wondered if she'd ever get a peaceful night's sleep again. Despite her monumental effort to not let fright overtake her mind, there was a steady chill trickling across her neck.

Thirteen

IT HAD TAKEN a significant effort, but Michelle had managed to get Gerard out of the house so she could do more investigation on the computer. She'd nudged him all day Sunday, gently reminding him that winter was coming, he might not have many more chances to play golf. It was yet another symptom of something not quite right. Before he retired, Gerard nearly salivated at the opportunity for a round of golf. Now, it seemed there was always time — later. She'd urged him repeatedly to call his partners, to see if he could get a last minute tee time. Finally he'd acknowledged how long it had been since he'd last played, and made the calls. At seven-thirty that morning, he loaded his clubs into the back of the Escalade and drove out of the cul-de-sac.

The office was cooler than the rest of the house, the wood shutters closed most of the time to prevent a glare on the computer screen. There was something about the fact that computers were easier to read in the dark that gave them a sinister quality. Yes, she enjoyed the ease of email. She could more or less see the appeal of the online socializing, sharing photographs and activities, but in the end, a computer screen looked like a great blank eyeball, staring at you, demanding all your attention, and functioning best in a dimly lit room, shutting you off from the real world.

She wasn't sure why, but she closed the office door. The room had been David's bedroom when he was a child. There was an easy chair, an old-fashioned roll top desk where she crafted her tiny, colorful sculptures, and a second utilitarian desk that held the computer. The walls were bright blue, a remnant from David's childhood, and covered with more relics — photographs of fishing trips with his Dad and brothers, ribbons from science fair wins, and a poster of *The Matrix*, his favorite film. David's love of that film was something that baffled her every time she looked at the poster. She'd found the movie tedious with a few mild gaps in logic, but David thought it was brilliant.

It wasn't difficult to navigate to the website she'd looked at before. The name had burned itself into her brain. She'd found herself mindlessly chattering to herself — s-u-r-v-i-v-e-n-o-w. She woke thinking about the phrase in the middle of the night, and wondered whether she'd been dreaming about it.

As she entered the first few letters, the computer remembered the url and filled out the remaining characters. Yet another unsettling aspect of computers — their growing ability to give the impression they knew what you were thinking. It was unnerving the way a shopping website remembered her address and phone number. She didn't like ads appearing everywhere that echoed the topics she mentioned in her email or searched for on the Internet. She didn't want her whims and curiosity tracked by a machine that remembered everything forever.

The *survivenow* website provided reams of information, including downloadable files. There were lists of food items and recommended quantities that should be kept on hand. Detailed instructions explained how to secure cash and other valuables since any crisis would wipe out all access to credit cards and debit machines. Cash would be hard to come by. Survivors were advised to stock valuable items that could be traded. And what was valuable now, would not be valuable then — *WTSHTF*. Yes, they even had an acronym, everything did now — *When The Shit Hits The Fan*. She thought the choice of that term indicated the organization was over-populated with juvenile-minded young men. How had Gerard gotten involved in this?

All week she'd wracked her brain, thinking back over recent conversations, trying to recall a definite shift in his behavior that hinted he'd taken a turn from normal thinking into a state of acute fear. She supposed some of his fears were fed by the novels he preferred — stories of terrorist attacks, apocalyptic government breakdowns, conspiracies, and massive social disruption. Not that she knew the details of the books he read, those were the bits she picked up reading the back covers. The past two years, he'd used an e-reader so she really had no idea what kinds of books he was devouring lately.

Since he'd retired, she hadn't noticed any significant changes besides his desire to tag along with her everywhere. But that was mostly cute, sometimes irritating, and not hugely abnormal, based on what she'd heard from other women at her stage in life. At the same time, he hardly touched her, even casually. His distance left a hollow space from her throat to her belly, and the tagging along made her feel as if her constant companion was a child rather than a lover.

Did that mean this had all started before he retired, perhaps years ago? It was funny how many things it was possible to forget in four months. She couldn't really recall how much time he spent on the computer before he retired. Probably because she never really thought about what he was doing. He'd filed their taxes and used it for business and web surfing for years. It was the gradual awareness of the hours spent in this room, now that he was home all day, which piqued her concern.

The question was, had he stumbled upon this forum and gotten sucked in, or had something slipped in his brain and he'd sought it out?

There were so many topics, she didn't know where to start, discussions of politics and religion, all with their own sub-categories. There was a thread that posed the question —

when did you become a survivalist? It contained a hundred and fifty-three pages of responses. Some of the answers were almost incoherent. Some talked about the past when people had to pay a great deal of attention to acquiring food and supplies. In modern times, human beings had grown disconnected from taking care of themselves, relying upon more and more external help, from insurance companies and all kinds of services delivered by the government. The phrase, *the government*, was fraught with tension in many of the posts. People seemed to believe it was its own entity, a cancer growing out of control that was set to destroy the United States, and that America would drag other countries in its wake. One essay filled an entire page. The story gave a detailed account of a man's experience working for a supermarket, his observation of gradually escalating food prices and declining profits, which led him to believe that eventually the supermarkets would collapse. The result would be food shortages, as it became impossible to remain in any type of business either growing or distributing it. This was followed by a description of his fear for his particular situation — out of work, gas prices rising to six dollars a gallon and more, followed by a complete inability to support his family. His pain was palpable.

Her breath grew heavier, as if she'd been standing in a tiny closet, the door locked, rather than sitting in a comfy chair with a mesh back and padded arms for the past ... she glanced at the clock at the top of the screen ... hour and forty minutes. No wonder Gerard spent so much time in here. She'd been completely transported to another world and the time had disappeared as if it never existed. She stood and stretched her arms overhead. She sat down again, so gripped by the drama on the screen that even stretching out her tight muscles had lost its usual appeal.

At the top of the page was a box for logging in. She put the cursor inside the box and typed a *G*, hoping he'd used his first initial and the computer would fill out the rest of his user-ID. Nothing. She looked at some of the names on the page — *batboy23, toughgirl_kate, extremewarrior, defense_expert, BeTheMan113.* There was no way she could figure out what strange persona Gerard might have adopted. Was it one of bravado? Intellect? She sighed and scrolled down to make the entire side navigation bar visible. There were quite a few links about food. Growing it, storing it, and even preparing it. One entire section was devoted to weapons. Handguns, semi-automatic rifles, shotguns, advice on buying your first weapon, storing ammunition, and even information about archaic devices like crossbows.

She browsed for another hour, and although she learned a lot about the fear and the rage lurking on the Internet, she learned nothing about Gerard. The website had fourteen hundred members, which wasn't a lot when you thought about the three hundred million-plus people in the United States, and assuming fear was global, the reported seven billion on the planet. Still, there were over a thousand people, many of them posting comments in forums and engaging in live chats for hours a day, according to what she could gather from the time stamps on their messages. Most of the states were represented, as well as the UK and Germany. Did some regions have a higher concentration of so-called survivalists, people terrified of losing their jobs, or already out of work, people who worried they would lose access to food and water, that their families would be threatened? The members of the site were afraid of earthquakes, terrorist attacks, the bankruptcy of the government, and complete societal breakdown.

She'd never been a worrier, but when she finally closed the browser window, her hand shook on the rounded back of the computer mouse.

As if they'd been silent until that moment, or she'd been sucked into the web pages with all her senses and hadn't heard them earlier, she was suddenly aware of the rumble of trucks behind the back fence. She hadn't thought about the construction or the invasion of her life the entire time she was reading. Now, her rage over the noise and dirt and resulting three-story building rising up behind her home seemed pathetic. What was a medical complex in light of national or global collapse? She had shelter, food, income from their investments, and social security and healthcare coverage. There was a thin trickle of fear that she was foolish to believe all of that would last, that there was any security at all beyond your own bags of rice and beans and produce from a highly recommended indoor garden.

Part of her wanted the rage to return. It was the only thing that would cut out the subtle thrumming inside her head, telling her she'd deluded herself, that even with their better-than-average collection of emergency supplies, she was clinging to a cardboard support system that couldn't keep her safe in the event of a true disaster. Of course, she'd always believed you couldn't actually prepare for a disaster. Look at the victims of tsunamis. When walls of water washed over your home, it didn't matter how many packages of dried soup you had.

She ran her hands through her hair, letting the strands caress her fingers. She bent over and touched the tips of her toes, exposed in her sandals. It was a beautiful day and she was shut up in this room, the collective fear of strangers nibbling at her brain. Is that what had happened to Gerard? Had he stumbled upon this by accident, and a ghoulish curiosity brought him back over and over again, once he was caught up in the individual stories? It wasn't that he'd started out seriously considering apocalyptic disaster, but the constant association with these people, cowering in their dark rooms, stirring up and enflaming one another's fears, had infected him.

She went back to the computer, and selected the menu to shut it down. She needed to get outside in the real world, yet she couldn't enjoy her own backyard.

She walked down the hall to the kitchen and took the

teakettle out of the cupboard. She filled it with water and turned on the gas. She got out a white mug with an image of a starfish on the side and dropped a peppermint tea bag inside. Part of her wanted to eat lunch now, something to make herself feel grounded in physical reality. The light was too bright, her pupils still dilated from the dim office, watery from reading too much text on a sage green background.

While she drank her tea, she tried to think about how to approach Gerard. She wasn't sure why she needed to think it through. She should just ask him, but it felt as if she'd been spying on him. She didn't want him to think she didn't trust him. And if he hadn't told her, if he'd truly spent hours reading and talking to these strangers, why was it that he hadn't even *tried* to bring her into this new world? Was he afraid she'd laugh at him? That she'd insist he stop? She didn't understand why he'd shut her out. They'd always shared their thoughts easily, even when they weren't in complete agreement, like the time she first voted for a Democrat for president — Bill Clinton. Maybe that's when things changed. Perhaps it had been years that Gerard was leading a secret life. He hadn't liked it that she was on the fence politically. She still was, although in his view, she was veering too far over to the left side, in danger of falling.

Maybe that had sent him looking for like-minded people, because most of the comments she'd read leaned toward a mistrust of the government, a belief that it was destroying human nature, and those views tended to be from the right side of the political spectrum. If he'd gone looking for others to share his views, perhaps they'd lured him further and further from that center line. Perhaps she didn't know him at all any more. And if she didn't know him, what else was he hiding from her?

Fourteen

BRIAN SIGHED WITH pleasure when he thought of Joey's damp, partially open lips and gentle stroking of the snakes' tough, smooth skin. After all these years, it was so affirming to have someone interested in Antony and Cleopatra, someone who recognized and revered their unique beauty, who touched them without shrinking away. People didn't realize how cruel it was to pull away from someone with revulsion. It was the most painful feeling on earth. He saw it in children at school as they huddled in groups, deliberately putting space between themselves and those who were different — boys that were too frail, children that were overweight, the odd child who picked his nose or surreptitiously sucked her thumb. Worse, he remembered it in his own life. His brother closing and locking the bedroom door, his brother's friends howling with laughter at the dark stain on the fly of Brian's shorts. He'd meant to use the bathroom. Instead, he'd been consumed with attracting their admiration for his skill at hide-n-seek. He'd waited too long under his mother's car, parked in the driveway.

He squirted cleanser into the bathtub and scrubbed a gray spot near the drain that he could never get rid of.

What was it about human beings that they needed so badly to be physically desirable? And why were they often compelled to reject those who weren't? Some reptilian programming, a longing that couldn't be defined. That's why shunning had been such an effective punishment throughout history. Now, shunning was subtle, unspoken, but it was still used. He had to believe Antony and Cleopatra, and all living beings, had similar needs, if not actual feelings.

Claire didn't realize how her rejection of his pets hurt him. Of course, he'd always known it would be that way. Women, especially, had some kind of groupthink hatred of snakes. Their screams were almost staged, as if they thought it was expected. It was really irritating. Not all women had it, he'd encountered women online who kept snakes, who adored their pythons as much as he did. But it wasn't as if those women lived nearby, and a love of snakes didn't seem like a very firm basis for a relationship. Although it would certainly avert the kind of ending he'd experienced with his marriage to Jennifer.

The moment Claire had looked at him with that horrified expression, no, that look of pure revulsion, he'd known there would never be anything more than casual friendship between them. Although she'd always been clear that she didn't view him as a potential mate, he'd held onto a strand of hope. You never knew what the future held. It wasn't that he sat around desperately wanting her attention and a shift in her feelings toward him. The desire was just there, a comfortable presence below the surface of conscious thought. They had an easy companionship. And she was beautiful. That long dark hair, skin so smooth she didn't need makeup, yet her features were distinct, giving the impression she'd added color and shadow to her dark, dramatic eyebrows and her large eyes with their thick lashes.

He straightened and rubbed his hand on his lower back where it was tight from bending over. He had to do something to keep himself busy. It wasn't as if Joey would have stayed this late, but since he hadn't been there at all, Brian had eaten dinner early and then found an empty evening stretching endlessly ahead of him.

Claire had shown up early at Joey's after school care. She smiled but looked past him, as if she was greeting someone behind him. When he turned, no one was there.

"I'm skipping class tonight," she'd said.

"Why?"

She gave him a vacant look and said nothing. Surely she wasn't dropping out of school. She'd change her mind in a few days, she'd realize how much she needed him.

He could have occupied his evening grading his students' journals, but he'd felt the need for something physical, something that required every muscle in his body, and kneeling over the side of the tub, reaching all the corners with the brush and sponge, qualified. Now the tub sparkled. Of course, he rarely used it, so it wasn't really that dirty. It was six forty-five.

He could write another email to that woman. The noise had been awful when he came home from work. The pile driver slammed into the earth, making him feel as if some kind suburban monster was ramming a spike into the top of his head. The sound rattled his brain until it felt as if it had detached from his skull, knocking against the bone, his teeth tapping each other. He gritted them until his jaw ached. But he'd already sent several complaints about the pile driver. It had been operating throughout the previous week, late in the afternoon every day, almost as if they waited until people were in their homes before starting.

Besides, despite the jarring sound, he wasn't really in the mood for composing email. He was more upset by Claire's reaction than he'd realized. At first, he'd been insulted. The hurt had taken some time to accumulate. Alongside the pain, was a nagging thought — why had he hidden the snakes from her all these years? He knew the answer before the thought completed itself. It wasn't just a casual lack of opportunity to tell her about them, to invite her to meet them. He'd hidden them because he knew she'd hate them. He pretended it might not play out that way, but the odds hadn't been in his favor. The delusion of thinking she might care for them had kept him going. Now he knew there could never be anything between them.

The sense of loss made him realize how deeply the fantasy had penetrated his life. He imagined carrying Joey into the house, perched high on his shoulders, ducking as they went through the doorway, laughing as Brian deposited his new stepson on the living room couch like he was shedding a jacket. Then he would lead Joey down the hall to show him the spare bedroom transformed into a boy heaven. The room would have a brand new computer, a collection of things boys liked — dinosaur bones or arrowheads or something like that. As Joey explored the sports equipment in the closet and bounced on his new bed, Brian would return to the front porch where Claire waited, her dark hair spilling over her arms. He would lift her and carry her over the threshold. He'd take her to his room — their room now — and place her gently in the center of the bed. Of course, they couldn't make love until after Joey was asleep, but he was patient.

None of that would ever happen. If she did come over again, Claire's fear and disgust would turn into something solid that filled the air, seeped under the door into Antony and Cleopatra's room. Cleopatra would sense Claire's feelings, and bide her time.

He put away the cleaning supplies and went into the snakes' room. Immediately, they knew he was there, turning their heads to study his movements, waiting for him to approach, to stroke their flawless skin, to talk in a gentle voice, praising their beautiful markings, the strength of their bodies as they moved, coiling themselves in intricate patterns, always moving, searching, wanting something.

He lifted Cleopatra out of her terrarium and placed her body around the back of his neck. She felt warm and affectionate. The weight of her was reassuring, although he didn't know why he needed assurance. Maybe all he needed was love. Everyone did.

Fifteen

CLAIRE LEANED AGAINST one of the trees that lined the street alongside the construction site. Joey stood near the fence, peering through the hole in the canvas backing. His fingers curled around the chain link like spiders clinging to a web.

For three solid days, she'd tried to come up with an alternative childcare solution. There were no other possibilities. It was either Brian, or drop out of school. Brian, or remain beholden to Greg and his girlfriend for another five years. Brian, or a lifetime of dependence on her ex-husband's income. She couldn't live like that. Quitting school now would be more than a temporary deferral, she'd lose momentum that she might not get back.

The expression on Brian's face when she'd met him at the school and told him she was skipping her class this evening had been a mixture of hurt and disappointment. Or were those the same thing? The twist of his lips and way he widened his eyes made him look younger than his thirty-seven years, young and vulnerable.

Eventually she had to make a decision about whether she was simply going to trust that nothing would go wrong. The snakes had been there all along and never escaped, but now that she knew of their existence, she couldn't put them out of her mind. It didn't matter that Joey had been safe when she was ignorant. At the same time, she didn't want to raise a nervous, anxious child. There was no fear of that, yet. Joey charged into everything with his arms flung open, as if he was welcoming the world inside of him.

Still, she felt betrayed. Brian had deliberately avoided mentioning he owned two enormous snakes. For years. Why hadn't he said anything? Why didn't he want anyone to know?

Just as she opened her mouth to tell Joey it was time for dinner, there was a voice behind her. "Hi, Claire."

She turned. Tanya stood a few feet away, her blonde hair almost glowing against the dark purple sweater. She wore black skinny jeans and purple shoes with four-inch heels.

"Hi." Claire put her hand on the tree trunk. A loose piece of bark, like peeling skin rubbed against her index finger. She picked at it. The piece broke off in her hand.

"I got a bunch more emails from Brian," Tanya said.

"Really? What about?"

Joey let go of the fence and walked toward the corner of the cul-de-sac, trailing his fingers across the chain link. He stopped at the next opening in the canvas mesh and looked through. She couldn't imagine what was different about the view from fifteen feet further along, but he liked to check each angle.

"Three of them explained in agonizing detail, with attached photographs, the location of a dirty tissue, a cup half-full of milkshake, and a crumpled cigarette box."

Claire still felt the urge to defend Brian, but it had weakened considerably. A room harboring deadly snakes had dampened her loyalty. "What were the others about?"

"I don't know if I should tell you."

"You brought it up."

"They were disturbing."

"You make it sound like he's psychotic." She was startled at the word she'd chosen, upset that it had appeared out of nowhere. She didn't think that at all, she never had. Tanya was fixating on a bit of mildly obsessive behavior and creating something dangerous out of it, trying to provoke fear, or something.

"I'm worried about him. I wonder how you've lived near him for all this time and never noticed anything strange."

Claire hugged her arms. She glanced at Joey. She was cold and hungry and she didn't want to talk about Brian. The reason she'd never noticed anything strange about him was because he kept his oddities closed in a spare bedroom and hadn't bothered to tell her about them. "So why were the other emails disturbing?"

"He said he had very special *beings* living with him and the noise was making them restless."

Claire laughed. So, he wanted to hide his snakes even from a complete stranger.

"It's not funny," Tanya said. "He said the *beings* were upset and weren't eating and he was worried it was harming their health. He sounded insane. Why would he say he had *beings* living with him?"

"Why did you come over here? Aren't you supposed to respond with email or a phone call to the person who complains? If you're worried, shouldn't you report it to your manager?"

"I have to observe the situation before I do that. It's frustrating to have to come by every time there's a stray piece of trash. Sometimes it's gone when I arrive, if it was even there to begin with. The emails were mostly the same, going on for five or six paragraphs with all these unnecessary details, describing the consistency of the milkshake and the smell of sour milk. But it's these *beings* that freaked me out. Does he think he's channeling someone? Or has angels living with him? What does that mean?"

Claire giggled. Would Tanya be more upset over giant snakes or imaginary beings?

"Why do you keep laughing? Do you know what he's talking about? Does everyone on this street already know he's mad? If he is, why didn't you tell me that last time? I would have handled this differently."

"How would you have handled it?"

"I'd report my concern to the police, which I still might."

"That's a bit extreme."

"I don't understand why you think this is so funny. He could be dangerous."

"He's not dangerous. Although his *beings* are."

"Does he think he has vampires in his house or something?"

"He has snakes."

"Oh. How would the construction disturb them? I didn't know snakes could hear."

"I don't know if they can hear or not. I don't think they have ears."

"Then I wonder why he thinks the construction is affecting their appetite. He does go on and on — you can't imagine how specific he is."

"I guess he wasn't that specific, since he left out the part about two giant pythons."

Tanya stepped closer. She twisted her hair into a coil, then flipped it behind her shoulder. "He has pythons?"

Claire nodded.

"What do they look like?"

"I've never seen them."

"Why not?"

Claire pulled the sides of her jacket together, keeping the lapels crunched between her fingers. "I didn't even know he had them until a few days ago."

"How can that be?"

"He never mentioned them."

"How did you find out?"

"He showed them to my son when I was with my study group."

"Why didn't you ask to see them?"

"I don't want to."

"Are you afraid of snakes?"

"Yes."

Tanya smiled. If she'd started the day with lipstick, it was gone now, and her lips looked almost white. Even in the fading light, Claire could see tiny flakes of dried skin around the corners of her mouth. She knew she was imagining things, overly upset about the snakes and Brian's deceit, but she felt Tanya's lips had a slightly reptilian look.

"They can't hurt you," Tanya said.

"Are you kidding? Joey told me they're ten or twelve feet long. They could crush you to death."

"Well they wouldn't. Not unless they're threatened."

"How do you know so much about pythons?"

"Everyone knows that."

Claire glanced at Joey. He was gripping the fence again, staring through the opening, transfixed by the pit and the concrete pillars with strands of rebar spilling out the tops. "Let's go, Joey."

Slowly, he uncurled his fingers from the fence.

"Do you think he'd let me see them?" Tanya said.

"That's not very professional. I thought you were supposed to be addressing his grievances."

"I should see the snakes, to see if they're being harmed."

There was something unnerving about Tanya's sudden change of focus, her eager interest in the snakes. Two minutes ago she implied Brian was mentally disturbed, now she was trying to get Claire to act as a go-between so she could get inside his house and see his snakes?

"Will you ask him for me? I could respond to his email and tell him I'm interested, but then he'd wonder how I knew. And if I said you told me, he might get annoyed with you. It seemed like he didn't want me to know he has them. Why do you think that is?"

"I have no idea." Claire turned. Joey had managed to climb a foot or so off the ground by wedging the toes of his shoes into the chain link. "Joey! Get down, let's go."

He dropped to the ground and sauntered over to where she stood. She put her arm around his shoulders. "You can't climb the fence."

"That's right," Tanya said. "It's dangerous. Don't you see the signs?"

Claire felt a prick of annoyance. She never liked other people telling her son what to do. It was none of their business, unless it was his teacher. She didn't need this worried, snake-obsessed woman interfering.

"The signs say don't *trespass*, but they don't say not to climb up," Joey said.

"You're supposed to figure that out," Tanya said. Without pausing for a breath, she added, "So will you? Ask him if I can meet the snakes?"

"How would you be able to know whether they're okay? Are you a snake expert?"

"Brian could explain it to me."

Claire smirked. Tanya probably didn't notice, it was nearly dark now. And cold. "We should go. Joey needs to do his homework. Nice talking to you." She turned. Joey darted ahead, around the corner, and looped the cul-de-sac, reaching their front porch before Claire got to the corner.

"Are you going to ask him?" Tanya called after her. Her high heels clacked on the sidewalk as she followed Claire. "Will you? Please?"

Claire walked up the front path and inserted her key in the lock. What a freak. First she acted like Brian was a threat to her safety and now she couldn't wait to get inside his house and drool over his snakes. She shivered.

"What's wrong?" Joey said.

"I keep thinking about the snakes."

"Why was that lady asking about them?"

"Who knows."

"I don't mind going to his house so much, now that I've seen his cool pets."

"I don't want you in that room. And I told Brian that."

"It's the only interesting thing in his house."

"Last year you liked going over there."

"I don't any more. His house is too dark and it's boring. But now that I can look at his snakes, it's not as boring."

"No snakes," Claire said.

"Whatever." Joey turned to go his bedroom.

"I'm serious."

"Okay."

Claire wasn't sure if he was stomping his feet or if his footsteps had a heavier thud because she was already feeling edgy.

Sixteen

ON WEDNESDAY GERARD had an appointment for a physical. He asked Michelle to go with him.

"That isn't necessary. It's not like you're having surgery or a procedure."

"You could sit in the waiting room and read or knit. We could have lunch."

"We can have lunch out another day."

"Why not? You'll be doing the same thing at home, how is it any different?"

"It just is. You're asking too much."

He left, looking defeated and slightly apprehensive. Or had she imagined the fear in his eyes? Was he worried something was wrong? Maybe he was hiding a lump in his stomach or blood in his urine, along with everything else. More likely, he didn't want her alone in the house because something on the computer alerted him that she'd been prowling around. He was worried she'd find out about his new, or not so new, hobby.

Now, more than ever, she wanted time alone in the house. This thing was so huge, she had to know how serious he was. And she needed to see whether he was hiding anything else. Perhaps most people weren't quite as well stocked with emergency supplies — not as many weeks of food and water, no tent or propane stove like the Reynes kept in the office closet. But after sitting like an eavesdropper on that website, she wondered if there was even more food, wondered if he had a detailed escape plan like some of them. She needed to know if he was hiding cash. If he had money she didn't know about, they could have sold the house and not worried about losing some of the value. They could have escaped that nightmare on the other side of the back fence. But more than anything, she wondered if he had weapons, which so many of the visitors on the SurviveNow site seemed to be preoccupied with. And if that was the case, he might be nurturing a whisper of madness, like the others who expressed their views in long, rambling, grammatically incorrect sentences, riddled with misspelled words.

She had no idea where to start looking. There was the tool shed in the backyard, but she went in there at least once a week, and unless there was a false floor, it contained nothing but garden tools, discarded flower pots, and various fertilizers. The house didn't have a basement. There was the attic, more of a crawl space. Gerard never went up there that she was aware of, and even if she could manage to remove the cover from the opening, she certainly couldn't hoist herself from the top of a step ladder up through a small square and land in the attic without hurting herself, or slipping off one of the beams and falling through the plaster. No, if he was hiding things, it would have to be somewhere with easier access.

She wandered slowly down the hall from the great room, past the three bedrooms that had once been occupied by their sons — the office that housed the computer with so many secrets hidden in its electronic guts, and the other two made up as guest rooms for when their boys came to visit. The house was simple, a typical California ranch, featuring the decks as living space as much as it did the interior. There weren't many hiding places.

She entered the master bedroom. It was quiet, full of light from the sliding glass doors that opened onto a second, smaller deck facing the garden and a gazebo. She sat on the edge of the bed and looked around the room. Every part of the house was like this room — clean, spacious, decorated sparely, influenced by a Zen style. The dresser was pine with small, simple knobs on the drawers and a large mirror hanging above it. The headboard and footboard of their bed matched the dresser, smooth pieces of wood, unadorned with carving or any other fussy details. In the corner opposite their shared dresser was an armchair with pale green cushions. Next to it was a round table with long legs, the top large enough to hold nothing more than a cup of tea.

There wasn't a single place in the house that offered hidden crevices, unused closets, locked cupboards, or dark corners that might be concealing the physical evidence of what Gerard had kept buried inside the computer all this time.

She stood and went to the armchair. She sat down and looked at the room, trying to get a different perspective. Usually when she sat in this chair she either worked on her knitting or read a book. She wasn't accustomed to gazing at the room, and now it looked unfamiliar. She closed her eyes. She wanted her mind to stop racing in circles, trying to figure out something that could be solved so quickly if she simply asked Gerard. And it was possible that what she was looking for didn't exist. Maybe he only went into that forum as a voyeur, like she had. Maybe there was no user ID and password, maybe he hadn't made a single frightened, paranoid, or angry comment. Maybe he hadn't made friends there. It could be his own form of reality TV, watching moderately deranged people, which had the effect of making you feel quite sane.

While she'd been exploring the forum, she'd forgotten all about the construction project. The racket slipped to the background like a painting you didn't really care for, but were so used to looking at, you stopped really seeing it. It might be Gerard's own form of escapism. Maybe that's why his rage over the new medical center had dissipated. She wanted to believe that. More than anything she wanted to believe that, but her mind continued twisting around itself, straining to think of secret storage places in their home.

She got up and went to the dresser. She pulled open the narrow top drawer on Gerard's side. A rush of guilt flowed through her chest, ran down her arms, and dripped into her fingertips. She never went through his things. She was like a suspicious hag, searching for evidence of another woman. The drawer contained nothing of interest — a few receipts, a money clip he'd received as a gift but never used, a box of coins, a shoehorn, also never used, and a handful of screws, nuts, and a ring of keys. The keys were small, made for padlocks, not doors. She slid the drawer closed.

She walked back past the bedrooms that still echoed softly with boys' voices, first child-like, then transforming, seemingly overnight, into the baritones of men. She went into the great room that encompassed an eating bar and the kitchen, and featured floor to ceiling windows. Off the great room was the dining room they'd added in ignorance, unaware of the coming invasion. Nestled at the point where the two rooms joined was the main deck where they often ate lunch, and sometimes breakfast on summer mornings.

The dining room looked unused, and it was. They mostly ate at the bar in the great room unless they had friends for dinner, or the boys came home. It was strange that they'd added a dining room after the boys were gone. They used it less than once a month, but when they did, it was nice to have plenty of room to insert extra sections in the table, bringing in a second table when they really had a crowd.

Her clogs sounded like mallets on the hardwood floor as she walked to the doors that opened out onto the deck. The builder — a man Gerard knew through his real estate connections — had done a great job. The addition looked like it had always belonged to the house, inside and out. It almost seemed as if the house had only been partially complete when it was first built, waiting for Michelle and Gerard to add the finishing touches. She opened the door and stepped out onto the redwood planks. Now her clogs produced a hollow sound. She walked past the round wood table and pulled out one of the chairs. She sat down and looked back into the dining room. Instead of seeing inside, she saw the ghost of her reflection on the glass.

There was nothing here. Whatever Gerard was up to, she was going to have to ask him. She wasn't sure why she hadn't done that from the start. What did it say about her marriage that her first instinct was to snoop around on her own rather than simply asking him why he spent so much time on the computer, why he visited that site?

But she knew the reason she hadn't asked. Because, although she couldn't admit it, although she denied it to herself, she'd been scared he was doing something sordid, and then when she found out what he was up to, it scared her even more. She didn't want him to become one of those half-crazed old men, railing at the government. Or maybe he'd always been that man. Look how he'd come unglued over the construction project, at first. She'd been upset at the coming intrusion into their tranquility, the visual eyesore, the traffic, all the things that would lower their quality of life. Gerard's rage had been different.

He focused on the government conspiracy. He'd never used that word, but now that she thought back over his behavior when they were first notified of the plans to expand the medical center, she realized that's how he viewed it. One evening in particular stood out.

It was the previous summer, the air like the warm, sweet breath of a baby. They'd held hands as they walked to the community center for one of the many public meetings. She'd worn a black sleeveless dress. She was proud of herself, thanks to endless hours of yoga practice, that she could still show off her firm arms and shoulders. She wore black gladiator sandals and while they walked, she admired her red toenails, a splash of color to match the thin red crystal hanging from a chain around her neck.

When they arrived at the community center, the parking lot was nearly full. Inside, only ten or fifteen empty chairs remained in a room that accommodated a hundred people.

The meeting opened with a viewing of the artist's rendition of the building, the bi-weekly attempt to sell them on its beauty, and an updated overview of the construction timeline. Next, the Disturbance Coordinator, Tanya Montgomery, stood and read complaints and questions that had been submitted by email. She read each one, supplied the official response, and then allowed brief questions or comments from the audience. Essentially, all of her responses circled back to a reassurance of temporary disruption.

When she indicated there were no more complaints and she believed she had addressed them all to everyone's satisfaction, Gerard rose from his seat. They all knew her flat statement, insisting everyone was satisfied, was a lie. People were simply beaten senseless from the repetitious answers. Everyone but Gerard.

He walked down the center aisle, his shoulders straight, not turning to look to either side. His pale blue shirt, and possibly the fluorescent lights, made his hair look even grayer. He approached the microphone at the front of the aisle. He raised the stand. The room was quiet. He turned away from the mic and cleared his throat. The mic still picked up the sound — a deep, angry scratching. A woman seated close to the loudspeakers winced.

He turned back and put his hand on the base of the microphone. "You haven't addressed the primary concern."

"I answered all the comments that were submitted by email," Tanya said.

"You didn't answer mine."

"Well in the case of duplicates, I only used one that was representative."

"Nothing you've said was representative of my complaint."

"What was that, sir?"

"The city council is behaving like the federal government."

"How is that?"

"You think you can just take over our lives. You do not have the right to lower our home values, destroy our peace of mind, and build whatever you please because you're more interested in growing tax revenue than in the citizens who live here."

"Oh, I remember that one," Tanya said. "I represent the medical foundation, so I can't address city government issues. I forwarded that on to the planning commission."

Gerard cleared his throat again. This time, he didn't bother to turn away from the mic. The bark that echoed through the room was loud and rough. The five members of the planning commission, seated on a platform behind Tanya, pulled back at the burst of unpleasant noise.

"The government has become corrupt, they have too much money and they think that gives them free reign to do as they please. They steal from the people they were elected to serve and they're bankrupting the country. This is a residential area and we've tolerated the existing facility because it was a single story, and only had a few offices. This new thing is like a metropolitan hospital and I guarantee you that someone is getting either contracts or outright cash from this deal. They're ignoring the will of the people, making decisions behind closed doors, and destroying this neighborhood. I want someone to own up to that and tell us why this was decided without consulting the people it impacts."

Michelle's neck and chest burned despite the thin tank top and the air-conditioned room. She looked at her feet, swollen and red, her ankles puffy, as if they were in a roasting pan, in need of basting. She hadn't consumed enough water today. She wondered why she was thinking about bloating when her husband was raving in public, making himself look like a mad man.

Tanya turned to the members of the council, arranged behind her like a string of guardian angels watching over the proceedings. Her blonde hair swung across her shoulders. The lone woman on the council put her hand around the table mic in front of her. "Excuse me, sir."

Gerard raised his voice. "This is an outrage. Government run amok. We bought our homes in good faith and the city is destroying our property value."

"Sir. What's your name, sir?"

"Gerard Reynes. I'm not finished."

"Mr. Reynes, the project has been approved, and ..."

"It was approved behind our backs. We have a right to vote."

"There was no change in zoning. This is a simple property improvement, like any property owner is allowed, with approval of the planning commission. Please sit down."

"You invited us to express our complaints."

"About any issues with the construction."

"I have an issue with the construction!"

Sweat sprang up under Michelle's arms, across the back of her neck, and beneath her breasts. She wanted to lift her hair off her neck, but didn't want to raise her arm and expose the odor of her armpits to the woman on her right. She uncrossed her legs. She wished she'd worn flip-flops so she could slip them off and rest her feet on the cool linoleum.

Finally, thankfully, Gerard ran out of steam. He turned and glared at the planning commission members. When he looked back at the crowd, his face was tight, his lips pulled down. He trudged back to his seat.

On the way home, they did not hold hands. For two days, she hadn't spoken to him, then slowly they'd worked it out. Or maybe it simply dissolved on its own like so many disagreements did over the course of so many years. After that, she stayed out of the politics and tried to focus on thinking positive thoughts that the city would come to see what misery they were inflicting on the surrounding residents. They hadn't, and now she realized Gerard had deflated after that brief outburst.

She stood and walked to the steps that led from the deck to the ground where stepping stones wound through a small rock garden, ending where the lawn began. The pile driver had stopped. It was noon and there were no other sounds coming from the site. They broke for lunch as regularly as those following a religious call to prayer. If she was quick about it, she could make a glass of instant iced tea and enjoy her gazebo for a few minutes before activity resumed. As she turned and hurried back across the deck, her clogs made the hollow sound she'd noticed briefly when she first came outside, but as she approached the middle of the deck, the sound grew thick and dull. She stopped.

The thought pierced her skin as if she'd been stung by one of the wasps that sometimes tried to build a nest under the eaves — Gerard had been out here every day, hovering around the contractors after they completed the dining room and started work on the deck. In fact, he'd been such a pest, one of the workers had made several comments to Michelle. "Your husband is a wannabe builder."

She'd grimaced and said nothing, annoyed that the construction worker was mocking the man who was paying his salary.

She turned and walked back across the deck. There was definitely a dull sound near the center when she passed close to the table. She pulled away the chairs and dragged the table a few feet to the left. She tapped her foot and listened to the thud that was mostly under the table area. There was no doubt that something solid had been built beneath the boards in this section. She kicked off her clogs and went to the edge of the deck. The lip was only about a six inches wide and there was plenty of space for a man, or woman, to crawl under the deck. She picked up her clogs and went back into the house. In the bedroom, she slipped out of her Capri pants and top and pulled on the jeans and a t-shirt she wore for heavy-duty yard work.

Back outside, she looked under the deck. Enough light filtered between the boards to reveal a box that had been constructed near the center. She wondered whether the construction workers built it, or if Gerard had done it while they took their lunch breaks, after they were finished laying the boards so they wouldn't notice the addition. Of course, the guy running the project was his friend. Maybe he constructed the box and the jeering comment from the worker had been related to Gerard's interference in the design.

There were bugs under here, spiders and ants, possibly earwigs. She forced herself to focus on the destination and willed the creepy things to run from her in fear.

The easiest way to get under the deck was to lie on her stomach and use her elbows to propel herself toward the center. It wasn't difficult to drag herself across the hard-packed dirt.

The box was wood with metal strips along the seams. On the narrower side that faced the dining room wall was a hinged door, secured with two padlocks. Damn. Why hadn't she thought of that? Now she had to crawl out, brush herself off so she didn't track grit into the house, comb through Gerard's drawer, and then come back out and crawl under here again. She rapped her knuckles on the side of the box. The sound was heavy and solid. It was nearly seven feet long and three feet wide — about the size of a coffin. She laughed at herself. Being under the deck, knowing the bugs were watching her, getting ready to explore her body, trying to see them in the dim light, was filling her head with morbid thoughts. When she returned with the keys, she'd bring a flashlight. That would chase the bugs back into the shadows. She crept to the edge, eased herself out from beneath the overhang, and went into the house.

By the time she reached the box again, she was perspiring. Her feet were grubby and her fingernails caked with dirt. Hopefully she'd be able to take a shower before Gerard returned. She'd lost track of the time and hadn't thought to look when she was in the house. Oh well, too late now. If he came home and found her under the deck, maybe that wouldn't be so bad. She wouldn't have to spend any more time trying to figure out how to approach him about whatever was going on. And she was moments from finding out exactly what that was.

Part of her was afraid to unlock the container. Her earlier thought of a coffin made her irrationally anxious that there would be something disgusting inside. If that fear was realized, how quickly could she crawl out of the tight space?

She'd put the keys in a tin so she wouldn't be required to fish them out of her pockets. She laid the flashlight on the ground and popped the lid off the tin. There were eight keys. The third one she tried worked in the top padlock. She pulled the lock out of the hook and then went to work on the second. When she had that opened, she moved the locks and the tin of keys to the side. She scooted back, picked up the flashlight, and pulled open the door.

"Michelle?" Gerard's voice was distinct, indicating he was on the threshold of the dining room. "Michelle? Are you out here?"

She closed her eyes. If she didn't answer, he'd search the house and eventually start to worry. He might go to Claire's, maybe even Brian's, then he'd be frantic. If she answered, she wasn't sure whether he'd immediately crawl under the deck and drag her out before she had time to investigate the interior of the box. She whispered, "Five. Six. Seven." The seconds were passing.

Then she knew. If he went to Claire's and later they asked where she was, everyone would find out. "I'm down here," she said.

His foot thudded on the deck as he took a single step out the door. "Where are you?"

"I'm under the deck."

"Oh God."

She waited for him to say more. To announce he was joining her, or demand that she come out immediately. She could imagine him counting the beats as she had a moment earlier. For some inexplicable reason, she thought of her current knitting project. She could almost feel the soft, peach-colored yarn, and she realized she was longing for a life that didn't involve spying on her husband and reading terrified diatribes online. More than anything in the world, she wanted to be sitting in her armchair, or in the front room, her needles clicking and her mind at rest, filled with nothing but the intricate pleasure of transforming a strand of fiber into a blanket or a scarf.

Gerard was still silent. She shone the flashlight into the wood container. In the front was a large metal lock box. She supposed one of the other keys fit that lock and she assumed the box was filled with cash. It was about two feet long, room for a rather large amount, depending on the denominations. She tugged and it fell forward, hitting the dirt. She pulled it the rest of the way out and set it near the keys and open padlocks. She'd look at it later. Now, she'd be opening it while Gerard watched. Or maybe he'd pry it out of her fingers and refuse to let her see inside.

The rest of the wooden container was filled with guns. Hand guns, rifles, and two strangely designed things that looked like something out of a film about the Mafia. A second, larger metal box closed with a simple clasp. It contained ammunition.

As far a she knew, Gerard had no idea how to shoot anything more complicated than a nail gun.

"What are you doing?" His voice was directly above her.

She rolled onto her back, not caring if dirt got into her hair. A tear slid out from the corner of each eye. She was suddenly too tired to push the cash box to the edge of the deck, too tired to close and lock the door, too tired even to drag her body out from under the deck.

As if to torment her further, the pile driver started up again.

Seventeen

BRIAN LOOKED OUT across his front yard. Michelle knelt on the sidewalk plucking weeds out of the ground beneath her rose bushes. It had to be painful, but she didn't appear to be uncomfortable. She wore designer sunglasses, not a normal part of her weed-pulling attire. That, and the yard had six tiny weeds, at best. He struggled to see anything but the occasional tendril with a delicate cluster of leaves at the top.

He adjusted the wand on the mini blinds. If she glanced up, she wouldn't notice he was watching her. He wasn't really watching, just intrigued that she would weed the yard wearing faded jeans, a bright white sweatshirt, and bare feet — but complete her outfit with those sunglasses. From the neck up, she looked as if she should be strolling around Union Square in San Francisco, but from the neck down, tending to her weed-free garden.

The subtle change in the angle of the blinds made it more difficult to see her, and it probably didn't matter whether he took care to hide himself, because she stared at the ground with the intensity of a woman searching for a lost diamond ring. He was amazed that she managed to methodically find and extract weeds that weren't visible from where he stood.

He should go out and speak to her. It was rare that he came directly home from school instead of working in the classroom, and it had been a while since he'd talked to her or Gerard. In fact, he couldn't recall whether they'd spoken more than two words since the construction started, and not many more since that night near the end of the railroading job by the city planning commission when Gerard growled into the microphone about conspiracies and scared everyone in the room. Possibly that public display of anger and incoherent thinking had directed Brian's subconscious to put some distance between him and the Reynes and he hadn't been aware of the shift until this moment.

He would go out and talk to her. Standing at the window, fiddling with the blinds, trying to hide himself was not healthy behavior. He twisted the wand again and set the blinds back to their original position, parallel to the windowsill. He grabbed his jacket off the living room couch and went outside. He closed the door firmly behind him, so he wouldn't startle Michelle by creeping up on her. She was a fragile woman, thin bones in her wrists and ankles, a thin face, thin hair, and a seemingly thin barrier between health and pain. When her husband had spoken out at that meeting, she'd looked like she was trying to fold her body inside of herself.

"Hello, Michelle. You certainly are vigilant about the weeds."

She glanced up at him, not looking at all surprised that he stood a few feet to her left. She hadn't turned to see him approach, yet she seemed fully aware that he'd been walking toward her. "It's better to get them when they're small." She pushed the pile of weeds farther away from the dirt as if they were in danger of creeping back in and re-planting themselves, like young children that needed to be corrected again and again before they finally learned their boundaries.

"I try to do the same. You're just better at it than I am."

She sat back on her heels and pressed the limp weeds into a smaller pile.

"Don't your knees hurt?" he said.

"I'm used to pain."

"Your migraines?"

She nodded once.

Is that why you're wearing the sunglasses?" It wasn't that bright out. The sky was mostly white with clouds, and a few splits where blue showed through as if it was covered by a torn piece of fabric.

"No. Not today."

He waited for her to explain.

Michelle stood and picked up the clump of weeds.

"Done weeding?"

"I think so. How's your sculpture coming along?"

"Not very well."

"When are you going to invite me over to see some of your work?"

"It's not ready." It irritated him that she repeatedly asked to see his sculpture. Every three months, as if she noted it on her calendar.

"You always say that. You have to more be confident in your work. I didn't think I'd ever sell my sculptures, and now I've made a nice amount of money that pays for a few dinners out and gives us extra cash for vacations. It's very satisfying to earn an income from your art."

He coughed. He wanted to laugh, and not in a kind, convivial way. She called her brightly colored clay figurines *sculpture* — tiny cats and dogs with silly faces, cows and horses, turtles and mice. Putting them on the same level with his serious efforts was insulting in a way he couldn't begin to explain, not that she asked or would even understand. He wanted to smack her on the back of the head and tell her how stupid she was. He worked with his clay in privacy, not throwing it out in the world before it was ready. Not that hers would ever be ready. Her creations were child's play, crafts. She didn't realize that every time she made that comparison, he intensified his vow to never, *never* show her his studio. It had been a mistake to come out here, to engage her in conversation when he should have known she would take the first available opening to steer the subject to their supposedly common ground of art. He stepped back. He felt his upper lip start to tremble. He forced his muscles to remain in a neutral position.

"You shouldn't be so shy, so critical of yourself. I'm sure you're very good."

"And you shouldn't assume you know anything about another person's work when you're quite obviously clueless." He smiled. This time he let his lip curl in a dramatic lift that he could feel creasing his face and pushing his nose to the side. Michelle looked hurt, even from behind her dark glasses, so large they touched her cheekbones. Two red spots appeared near the corners of her mouth. Her lips quivered like bees hovering near a blossom on her rosebush. He wondered whether her glasses hid teary eyes. Too bad. She had no right to call him shy, or assume he lacked self-confidence. Shyness was for weak children who were afraid of the world, not a man as accomplished as he was.

"I didn't mean to hurt your feelings, Brian."

"You didn't."

She stood and brushed off her kneecaps, although Brian couldn't see any dirt or bits of weed on her jeans, which implied it was more a gesture of submission.

"I don't know why you don't want me to see your work. We could be supportive of each other. I might be able to give you some suggestions about how to make it polished, if that's your concern."

Before he could figure out how to respond to that gushing display of ignorance, Brian glanced at Michelle's front porch.

Gerard stood in the shadows. "Are you coming inside?"

It was unusual that he hadn't greeted Brian. There must be something going on here that had nothing to do with him.

Michelle touched one of the many red blossoms, still soft, brilliant with color, even in autumn. She had a variety of colors, planted in no particular pattern — yellow, red, white, and pink. She stroked the petals as if she was encouraging the rose to open further. She didn't glance at the front porch or give any hint that she'd heard Gerard call out to her.

Gerard stood with his hands tucked under his armpits. Brian expected him to walk out to the sidewalk, to start a conversation, most likely about the pit yawning behind their houses, but Gerard didn't move. Brian felt caught in the center of an elaborate drama he couldn't interpret.

There was a constant pull between wanting to be friendly and connected to his neighbors, until he was faced with the reality of their personalities, and then he wanted to close all his blinds and drapes and ignore them, coming and going only in the dark.

Eighteen

AT SIX O'CLOCK that evening, Brian waited for Joey outside the after school care center at the back corner of Hickam Elementary School. Claire had been forced to relent, calling and asking him to pick up Joey because she had to stay late for a last-minute staff meeting.

She no longer fully trusted him to look after Joey. Even when she used that meek, guilty tone of voice, he could tell that she was only asking because she was desperate. She had no backup plan. She had limited resources when it came to raising her child. The father was unreliable at best. Not because he was a drifter, but because he had other priorities. A child had to be the first priority, and Brian felt sorry for Joey, who surely knew his father gave more attention to everything else in his life, including his dogs. The dogs rode in the SUV, sitting directly behind the girlfriend, whenever Greg came to pick up Joey. They got to see Greg seven days a week, while Joey was relegated to one Sunday a month and a few, randomly scheduled weekdays.

The doors to the after school care center were closed. A few parents stood nearby, heads bent over their smart phones. They tapped at the screens. All were silent, except for two women who managed to simultaneously text and talk to each other. Brian shoved his hands in his pockets. He supposed he could yank out his phone and peck away like the others, but he'd checked his email at home before driving back to meet Joey, so he knew there wasn't anything to look at there. Browsing the web on a three-inch screen was not his idea of a satisfying experience.

He strolled down the corridor. Outside the covered area it was even colder. He hunched his shoulders and walked back.

After a few minutes the door opened and the other adults rushed inside to claim their children. Brian waited.

When Joey emerged, his facial expression was the same as always. He might not even know why his mother had skipped class. He might not have made the connection between the revelation of the pythons and the change in their schedule.

"Did you have a jacket?" Brian said.

"It's in my backpack."

"You're not cold?"

"Nope."

"Okay, then. Let's go."

They walked across the campus to the teachers' parking lot. Brian unlocked the doors with his remote and Joey climbed inside.

When they drove past the construction site, he saw a piece of rebar lying in the gutter. Something else for the Disturbance Coordinator. He was still waiting for a response to his last email. Her replies were intermittent, at best. It was as if there was a policy that dictated answering every third complaint. In the end, they really didn't care. The DC was only there to make the residents feel as if someone was listening, so they didn't take aggressive action. Although what they would do, he had no idea. The question was, why did they bother? He wondered again if she was aware of her uselessness or if she actually thought she had a bona fide function.

At home, he got Joey settled at the kitchen table with a math worksheet. "Do you have any questions about your homework?"

"No. It's easy," Joey said.

Brian used the bathroom and then took a few steps further down the hall. He jiggled the doorknob to Antony and Cleopatra's room. Of course it was secured, why had he checked? Because Claire made him feel badly, made him anxious for no logical reason. The snakes could not get out of the room, even if they managed to escape their enclosures, which was impossible, as long as he didn't leave them in their feeding boxes. Besides, Cleopatra had attacked Jennifer because she was attacked first. She probably sensed animosity through the door, but would not act on it unless someone entered her space. And Joey seemed to like the snakes. At the very least, he was fascinated with them. Even if he didn't overtly love them, he didn't have a negative attitude toward them.

He thought about going inside and saying hello to Antony and Cleopatra, but it was better to let them alone for now. There was plenty of time for interaction after Joey went home. Claire had made it clear Joey wasn't to enter the room again. Although there was something about that directive that stirred up a desire to do the opposite of what she'd asked.

He went down the hall to the kitchen. Joey's head was bent over his paper.

"Do you want some cocoa?"

Joey nodded.

While he waited for the water to boil, he started to feel a little guilty. Antony and Cleopatra had been alone all day. Today was a feeding day and they were probably getting restless. It wasn't fair that Claire was dictating their schedule. She kept Joey away from him, then suddenly needed help, and Antony and Cleopatra had to pay the price for that?

By the time he'd dissolved the cocoa, he'd made up his mind.

He set Joey's mug on the table. "I need to feed Antony and Cleopatra. Are you okay with your homework?" He knew he was blowing it out of proportion. There was no reason they couldn't wait for an hour until Claire arrived. Even if he fed them now, there'd been no reason to announce it. Still, he liked the eager look on Joey's face.

"What do they eat?" Joey laid down his pencil and pushed the cocoa away.

Brian knew he should cut off the conversation, but it was like writing the emails to the Disturbance Coordinator, once he got an idea in his head, he couldn't remove it until he acted it out. It had been the same when he buried Jennifer's body. The thought came and he knew he had to follow through, no second-guessing. It was important to be decisive and follow your instinct immediately without dithering, analyzing your behavior forever. "Mostly rats."

"Alive?" Joey looked disgusted and excited at the same time, his eyes glassy. He licked his lips.

"No."

"Can I watch?"

"No. Your mom doesn't want you in the room with them any more."

"I won't tell her."

Brian pushed Joey's cocoa back across the table. He wasn't sure what to say. Joey's unhesitating willingness to deceive his mother startled him. Brian had hardly finished speaking before Joey had blurted out the suggestion. "No. That wouldn't be right."

"She's just scared. But I'm not."

"It's not a good idea. Later, you'll feel bad for disobeying her. Maybe you can convince her to change her rules."

Joey scrunched down in his chair. Brian hadn't noticed until this moment how much taller Joey had grown the past few months. His legs were long and skinny. It was possible Brian was witnessing the very first seed of teenaged rebellion. Of course Joey wasn't even close to being a pre-teen, but he certainly looked ready to take his life into his own hands in whatever small way he could find.

"She won't know."

"You can't be hiding things from her."

"It's boring here. I want to do something exciting. Like feed the snakes." He straightened, almost bouncing in his chair, as if his energy would infect Brian and force a change in direction.

Brian walked to the kitchen door. "Ask her again. But not this time." He left the room and went out to the garage to get the two rats he'd removed from the freezer that morning. Half of him hoped, almost knew, that Joey would follow. But the kitchen was silent. Had he really gone back to work on his math without any further complaint? It was so difficult to predict kids' behavior. When you expected them to do one thing, they did something else. He went into Antony and Cleopatra's room and closed the door.

Both snakes lifted their heads as he approached Antony's cage. Brian set the box containing the rats on the floor. He opened the cover, lifted Antony out of his terrarium, and placed him in one of the feeding boxes. He picked up the aluminum pole with pinchers on the end, stuck them into the box, and grabbed one of the rats around the middle. He held it over the cage. Based on Antony's languorous movements, coiling around, flicking his tongue into the air, he wasn't yet aware of the rat. Brian dropped the rat in the cage. Antony moved quickly. His head shot up and he coiled the upper section of his body around the rat.

He shouldn't leave Joey alone for too long. The math had been going well when he'd left the kitchen, but it was possible Joey could run into a roadblock. He lifted Cleopatra out of her box and draped her around his neck. He stroked his hand along her smooth, satiny skin. She lifted her head and extended herself out from his body. He supported her a few inches below her head and she turned, looking back at him with equal intensity. It would be the highlight of his life if he could know her thoughts, or whatever they called brain activity in something non-human — the desire to fulfill her needs, whether hunger or a simple observation of the world around her.

As he lowered her into the feeding case, he worried, not for the first time, that the snakes didn't have enough stimulation, shut in this room, secured in their terrariums most of the time. He'd never followed through with his plan for re-doing their room. He should at least study the possibilities. He dropped the second rat near her head and she sprang at it.

His cell phone vibrated in his pocket. "Hello?"

"It's Claire. Some of us from the office are going out for a glass of wine. Do you mind giving Joey a sandwich to tide him over? I should be there by seven-thirty at the latest."

Brian swallowed. Three days ago, she was terrified to let

her son in the same house as the snakes and now she wanted an extra favor without any advance warning. It was becoming clear that she was a bit of a user. Or maybe he was someone easily used, he wasn't sure. "Okay."

"Thanks so much. I really appreciate it."

He waited. After a moment of silence, he decided she wasn't going to recognize her own inconsistency. "Have a good time."

"I will. Thanks."

He ended the call, shoved the phone back into its case, and approached Cleopatra. The house was silent. Obviously Joey was doing fine without him, so he had a few more minutes to watch Cleopatra finish her dinner. After she was finished, he left them alone to digest their meals. He stepped into the hallway and closed the door. The house was awfully quiet. He didn't hear the scratch of Joey's pencil, or the sound of the hot chocolate mug thumping on the table. He hurried to the kitchen.

Joey's chair was empty. "Joey? Joe?"

He went into the living room, then back to the hall, and glanced at the bathroom. The door was open and the room dark. He walked to the doorway and looked inside. "Joey?" He returned to the living room and opened the sliding glass door. The backyard was silent and dark. He stepped out, calling Joey's name again. He went to the pottery studio but the padlock on the door was in place, then he realized the sliding glass door had been locked. Joey wasn't outside. He stood in the center of the yard. This was not good.

There had to be a logical explanation. Joey had his own house key, it was possible he'd gotten bored, or gotten it into his head that he needed something from home. He hurried back inside and went down the hall and out the front door. Claire's house was dark.

He jogged across the cul-de-sac and tried the front door. Locked. He rang the bell. Where could he have gone? He was sitting there focused on homework and hot chocolate. Brian hadn't been in the room with Antony and Cleopatra for more than twenty minutes. Maybe thirty.

He walked into the center of the cul-de-sac and looked around. Would Joey have gone to the Reynes? Their lights were on, but if he checked, he risked alarming them before it was necessary and they might tell Claire.

It felt as if the tool he used to pick up the rat carcasses was fastened around his intestines. It wasn't possible for the kid to simply evaporate into thin air. And it wasn't as if someone could have entered the house and snatched him. All the doors were locked. Unless Joey had opened the door to a stranger, but the odds were against that. Besides, he would have heard the doorbell. He jogged to the corner and glanced along the fence surrounding the construction site. Nothing. He walked back to his front path.

His door stood open, he'd run out so quickly, convinced Joey had gone home. He walked up the front path and went inside. Was it possible Joey had hidden, waiting for Brian to leave the house looking for him, and then entered the snakes' room? Of course. He wanted to see them, had begged to watch them eat dinner. He probably didn't understand why his mother had forbidden him to have any contact.

Brian hurried down the hall. Against all reason, driven by panic, he opened the door to Antony and Cleopatra's lair, knowing he'd see how foolish he'd been. The room was dim and silent, except for the rustling of his pets. He backed out and closed the door.

He stood in the hallway. A sob pressed against the inside of his chest, swelling until he thought his lungs would rupture. He tried to calm himself. Nothing terrible could have happened. Joey was just hiding, sulking. "Joey?" He wondered if he should call out the all clear like was done in a game of hide and seek. No, that would be silly. If Joey were playing a game, he wouldn't give up that easily.

He went into the living room and sat on the couch. He closed his eyes and tried not to cry. He couldn't have Claire arrive to find him sobbing like a toddler. Worse, he couldn't have Claire arrive to find he'd lost her son. He glanced at the clock — seven-ten. Maybe she'd linger over her glass of wine longer than she'd planned. He got up and began a methodical search under furniture and through closets, gasping for breath, trying to convince himself that Joey had to be inside the house.

Nineteen

CLAIRE PULLED INTO the cul-de-sac. She parked in her driveway and walked across the street. More lights than usual glowed behind Brian's covered windows. Most of the time when she picked up Joey, only the porch light was on. Brian would be in the living room with Joey, the kitchen dark, the blinds closed tight. She supposed she wasted electricity, making sure Joey always had a pathway lit from his bedroom to anywhere else he might want to go in the house. After he went to sleep, she still kept a nightlight in the hallway so he could easily make his way to her hide-a-bed in the living room.

She walked up Brian's front path and rang the bell. Behind her, the fountain in the center of his lawn splashed and burbled. It soothed her, mingling with the effects of the wine. She and her friends had shared a plate of gyoza and California rolls. She felt mellow and only mildly anxious about the snakes.

Why was Brian taking so long to answer? Any other time, it wouldn't have bothered her, but now that she knew about the snakes, the feeling of contentment snapped in two. She knocked on the door and punched the bell again.

She was about ready to pound the side of her fist on the door when it opened. Brian stood a few feet back from the threshold. For a moment, she couldn't figure out why the door seemed to open so quickly. It was the deadbolt — she hadn't heard him turn the lock. "What's the matter?" She stepped into the entryway and Brian moved away until his back was pressed against the kitchen doorframe.

"I don't know how to say it."

"What happened? Where's Joey?!" A spasm gripped her throat and the words barely made their way past her lips.

"I don't know. He was doing his homework and then he..."

She rushed past him, turned, and stumbled down the hallway.

"He's not in there. I've looked everywhere." Brian was right behind her.

Claire swallowed, trying to catch her breath, hating herself. She hadn't wanted to go into that room, and for half a breath, the relief that she wouldn't have to was stronger than her panic. "What happened? Where is he?" She shoved Brian and he tripped backwards into the hall bathroom, grabbing the edge of the counter to keep himself from falling.

"He has to be here, or nearby. I've searched the whole

house twice, and was ready to start again. He might be playing a game."

She could tell by the shaking in his voice that Brian didn't believe that any more than she did. "How could you lose him?" Her throat was still tight and dry, her voice strangled. "Are the police on their way?"

"I haven't called them."

"Why not?" She reached into the side pocket of her purse and grasped her phone. How did it work if you dialed 9-1-1 from a cell phone? Did she have to give her location? She wasn't sure what Brian's house number was. After seeing it every day for years, she should know, but she didn't.

"Don't call them yet. He must be here."

"You said you searched the whole house."

"I did, but ..."

"Did you check the construction site?" Her heart beat faster, blood pulsed with such ferocity she could feel it in her neck.

"Yes. We should check with the Reynes."

"Why would he go there? How did he even get out of your sight?"

"I only left the room for five minutes or so."

"Or *so*? And he just disappeared?" She ran down the hall and shoved open Brian's bedroom door. She flicked on the light. "Joey?" She yanked open the closet door and pushed his clothes aside. There were three pairs of shoes on the floor and only half the rack was filled with clothing. She left the door open and got down on her hands and knees. She pulled up the comforter and looked under the bed. Brian stood in the doorway. His breathing was loud, heavy. It sounded damp, as if he needed to cough out phlegm.

She stood. "I'm calling 9-1-1."

"Do you think he could be in your house?"

"Did you check?"

"The door was locked. I meant could he be in there with the lights off, hiding?"

"Why would he do that?"

"He might have been angry with me."

"For what?" She pushed past him and walked down the hall and into the living room. "Did you check your garage? And the yard? Why was he angry with you?" She was panting, as if she'd been hiking a steep incline. She pressed 9-1-1 on the keypad of her phone. The high-pitched tone deep in her head was louder than the ringing phone. She felt hollow and hyper-aware of her hands, the shape of the phone, so small and so critical. She'd never called 9-1-1. It was a series of numbers you thought about all your life, but how many people ever tapped them into a phone?

It was taking forever to connect. She pulled it away from her ear and looked. The phone was searching. "Where's your phone? Why are you just standing there?"

Brian turned and went into the kitchen. She heard the phone lift out of the base. She felt a small prick of relief that he had a land line. She didn't. Most of her friends didn't. The whole world was nuts, thinking they could rely on such unstable devices. When you really needed them, they failed.

IT SEEMED LIKE twenty minutes, maybe more, before a lone police officer rang Brian's doorbell. Claire knew it hadn't been that long, but she couldn't say how long it *had* been. She wasn't even sure what time she'd arrived, wasn't sure how much time she'd wasted talking to him, looking in his closet and under his bed. She couldn't believe he hadn't called the moment he finished searching the house. How much time had been squandered, walking across the street, conducting a second search, talking to her… ?

The officer, a woman with longish brown hair and too much mascara with a tint of blue almost the same color as her uniform, remained on the porch while Brian explained Joey had been missing for about fifty minutes.

"Where was he when you last saw him?"

"At the kitchen table doing his homework."

"And where were you?"

Brian glanced at Claire. He looked back at the officer, lifting his chin so he was staring past the top of her head. "In the other room."

"For how long?"

"I think…" He coughed. "I think about fifteen minutes. Maybe twenty."

"What were you doing?" Claire said.

"I was feeding Antony and Cleopatra."

"Who are they?" said the officer.

"His snakes," Claire said. "He has two huge pythons. Is that legal?"

The officer stared at her. "Where were you?"

"Out with some friends."

"Did your husband call to let you know your son was missing?"

"He's not my husband," Claire said. "I live across the street. He picks Joey up from after school care. He watches him in the evening sometimes." Why did she feel so guilty? She wasn't a bad mother for letting her neighbor, her friend, take care of her son. Until Joey started complaining that he didn't like going to Brian's, until she found out about the snakes, she'd trusted Brian completely. Until now … She still trusted him, it was just that it had grown flimsy, as if her trust had been as fragile as a tissue all along, and now it had gotten wet and was coming apart in her hands.

"Have you checked your house? Does he have a key? "

"He has a key. But I haven't checked. I wanted to call you right away. It's been an hour." Her voice was shrill, on the edge of breaking.

"Shall we?" The officer turned and stepped off the porch.

Claire followed the police officer down the front path. She heard Brian, breathing too loudly, right behind her. Again, his breath sounded damp. Was it always like that? She'd never noticed, and she didn't like it that she was noticing now. Every thought should be of Joey. She knew he wasn't at home, the house was dark, and he would have turned on at least one light that would be visible from the street. Still, she hoped. Her stomach twisted and flopped as if she'd swallowed a cup of worms.

She unlocked the front door and reached inside to turn on the light. She went into the house. "Joey?" The silence was endless. She walked into the living room and flicked on the light. "He's not here."

"Let me check."

Claire wanted to cry as she watched the officer walk slowly into the kitchen, open the garage door, then come back through the entryway and walk toward the bedrooms.

When the officer returned to the living room, she said, "Where's his father?"

"We're divorced."

"How far away does he live?"

"Three or four miles. Joey wouldn't go there."

"Have you called him? Does he have any friends who live nearby?"

Claire shook her head. "The closest is about eight blocks away."

"You should contact all his friends. After you call his father." The officer looked at Brian. "What was the last thing he said before you left the room?"

"He wanted to watch me feed Antony and Cleopatra, but I reminded him his mom didn't want him near them."

Another surge of guilt flooded Claire's lungs. Why was

everything making her feel this way? Tears swam into her eyes. Maybe he was hiding in the room with those horrid creatures. She coughed, barely able to speak. "Are you sure he didn't follow you in there, that he's not hiding?" she said.

"Yes. There's no place to hide."

She turned to the police officer. "What are you going to do?" Tears poured down her face, then dried and started again.

"First I'll talk to your neighbors. Is there anywhere else he might have gone? Has he done anything like this before?"

"Never."

The officer asked Claire for a photograph, then pulled out a business card. "If you find out he walked to a friend's house, call me."

"Can't I go with you? To talk to the neighbors?"

"It's better if you don't."

"What am I supposed to do? Sit here alone when my son is…" A sob gripped her throat and chest so hard, she couldn't release any sound. She gasped for air, her whole body shook.

The officer put her hand on Claire's wrist. "Have a glass of water. Make those phone calls. I'll stop back by after I talk to your neighbors."

"I'll stay with you," Brian said. His voice was soft and uncertain.

"No." She felt Brian looking at her, but she kept her attention on the empty living room. At some deep level she knew it wasn't entirely Brian's fault. Joey had gotten up from the table and gone somewhere on his own volition, whether someone had come to the door or he'd simply wandered outside, it could have happened just as easily in her own house. She knew that. Yet right now, she hated Brian. He cared more about those beasts lurking in his spare bedroom than he did about her son. He knew how Claire despised them, knew that he was tempting Joey's curiosity by feeding them when Joey was around. He could have waited an hour. It's not like the things had to have their dinner right at six o'clock. She shuddered thinking about them, their slithering moves, their ugly faces. The whole world felt ugly right now.

Brian followed the officer outside. Claire stood in the entryway, unable to close the door without Joey in the house. Cold air rushed in, wrapping around her until she felt like she was embedded in a block of ice, but she didn't care.

As she watched the officer walk up the front path to the Reynes, she thought about all the moments when she'd lost track of Joey, that heart-stopping panic in the grocery store when she turned and found he hadn't followed her around the end of the aisle, distracted by the junky little toys hanging near the gift cards and office supplies. She'd run back down the aisle and there he was, fingering a tiny replica of a tow truck.

Once when they'd gone to the park, her attention had been arrested by a couple arguing near the picnic tables. She hadn't realized how much their drama had absorbed her until she turned back to face the slide with a small wood fort built around the top landing. Joey had disappeared. She'd jumped up, twisting her ankle, and stumbled to the edge of the play area. She stepped into the sand-filled area around the play equipment, not breathing, tripping forward, her flip-flops tossing sand at the backs of her legs. She'd glanced up and Joey poked his head out of the fort, waving at her.

This was entirely different.

Across the street, Gerard opened the front door. She wondered exactly what the officer was saying. Gerard glanced across the street. He didn't wave, which she was glad of. The officer glanced over her shoulder, then quickly turned back to Gerard. While they talked she dialed Greg. He knew nothing. She wasn't surprised.

Finally, Gerard closed the door. Claire hadn't expected him to provide any useful information, he hardly ever said more than two or three words to Joey. Still her chest ached when his front door closed. Mrs. Bennett, next door to Claire, would know even less. Gerard hadn't bothered to call Michelle to the door, but what did that matter? None of them knew where he was. They'd been inside, eating dinner, watching television, whatever it was people did in the evenings when their children were grown.

The entryway behind her was getting colder, but she still couldn't bring herself to close the door. She leaned on it as if a man stood next to her and she needed to collapse into his solid, unyielding strength.

A moment later, the Reynes' door opened. Gerard and Michelle stepped out onto the porch. Gerard held a flashlight in his left hand. He flicked it on and they proceeded down the front path. Michelle continued into the street and across to Claire's yard. She paused just past the sidewalk edge. "We'll find him."

Claire's damp fingers squeaked on the edge of the door as she slid down to her knees. Tears poured out of her eyes and she sobbed with a deep coughing sound. A moment later she felt Michelle's hand on her shoulder. "Gerard told the officer, it's not like someone would come to the front door and snatch a child. Joey must have wandered out of the house. He has to be around here."

Claire looked up. The police officer was cutting across the yard from Mrs. Bennett's to Elaine's house, lifting her feet, shod in heavy, thick-soled boots, to step over a tarp-covered pile of brick stacked in the front yard. It was all a waste of time. Despite the minutes she'd spent on Mrs. Bennett's front porch, the officer had surely come away empty handed. Mrs. Bennett probably wasn't even sure who Joey was. Elaine and Mark weren't there. She should have mentioned that to the officer. The house looked uninhabited, but that didn't stop the officer from ringing the bell.

"He's a smart kid," Michelle said. "It's not like he's going to get lured away with candy or a puppy or some such thing."

Claire wasn't so sure. Especially the puppy. She couldn't stop crying, couldn't do more than mumble things that even she couldn't decipher.

"I think it's better if you stay here," Michelle said. "Shut the door and go lie down on the couch. You'll feel better, get some blood into your brain."

Claire nodded. She pulled herself up on the edge of the door and let Michelle pry her fingers off the knob. The officer was headed back in her direction.

The officer explained that she'd call another car — they'd check the surrounding streets, the elementary school, and nearby parks.

Brian had disappeared into his house, probably seeking comfort from his snakes.

The beam of Gerard's flashlight bobbed and jerked as he walked to the end of the cul-de-sac. Michelle cut across to join him and they continued to the corner. As the light disappeared with them, Claire stepped outside, slammed the door, and ran to catch up. Joey must be looking at the construction site. That's what he wanted to do every day. Brian hadn't looked hard enough. She'd been too fixated on the snakes to think clearly.

She walked the three sides of the construction site with the Reynes, but Joey wasn't standing in any of his usual spots, peering into the pit. They called his name, one after the other, then in unison. Their voices sounded weak and thin on the night air. When she started shivering so hard her teeth chattered, Michelle told her to go home.

The Reynes returned half an hour later. Their tight lips and slightly unfocused eyes hinted at anger more than fear for Joey. Claire had the feeling that looking for Joey had been of secondary interest. Michelle was turned slightly away from Gerard as they stood on her porch, refusing to even glance at him. At the same moment, both of them reached out and patted Claire's forearms, Gerard's hand on her right arm and Michelle's on her left.

She watched them cross the street back to their house, wondering if they noticed the space between them grew wider as they walked.

The streetlights looked inadequate, and when the Reynes entered their house and turned off the porch light, everything was too dark. She started to cry again. She never should have agreed to a glass of wine, never should have trusted Brian once she found out about those snakes. They said something about him, that his priorities were misplaced, or simply indicated that he wasn't normal. No one could be trusted. Everyone eventually betrayed you.

She stood on the porch. The officer had told her to wait, but she couldn't stand here and do nothing. She went inside and got her coat, a flashlight, and grabbed her purse. She would call the parents of his friends while she walked. If she had to spend the whole night walking around the entire city, it was better than sitting on the couch.

Twenty

AT SEVEN ON Friday morning, Brian went out onto the front porch. He carried his coffee mug in one hand and his cell phone in the other. The mug was full, the coffee still too hot to drink. He hadn't slept much and desperately wanted to gulp down the entire mug. He wondered whether Claire had slept at all. He also wondered whether she'd ever speak to him again.

Inside the house, Joey's math papers were on the kitchen table where he'd left them. The chair was pushed out in the exact position Brian would have expected if Joey had decided he was definitely bored with adding up three-digit numerals. When he'd seen the papers, he'd turned away quickly, made the coffee, and looked out the window while he waited for it to brew. The papers would have to remain until Joey was found. Of course, for all he knew, Joey had been returned last evening and Claire was so upset, she hadn't bothered to pass on the information, wanting to punish him by making him suffer all night. Did other people do that? Try to inflict emotional suffering on someone who had hurt them? He knew he was tempted in that direction more often than he'd ever admit. Was that normal?

The frost on Claire's roof was losing the white sheen in the center. It was only a light coating, a precursor of winter. He blew on the coffee and took a quick sip. It hadn't cooled as much as he'd expected.

His heart felt like a wedge of clay that hadn't been properly stored. Slick and wet and sloppy on the inside, covered by a dry, hardened exterior. He would give anything to make that feeling go away, anything to go back in time and change his decision from the night before. He knew he'd been tormenting Joey, trying to get back at Claire, prodding Joey to complain to his mother, possibly to look at her with disdain, to stop following her rules. And wasn't that exactly what had happened? Joey had decided to do as he pleased.

He took another sip of coffee. It burned his tongue and he knew he'd be touching the sore spot all day.

He wasn't sure how long he stood on the front porch, blowing and sipping, but after a while, a police car pulled into the cul-de-sac. A different officer from the one the night before got out and went to Claire's door. So Joey hadn't been found. Brian turned and went inside the house. Looking at the accusing math papers and Joey's backpack on the chair near the window was preferable to watching Claire open her door, glance across the street, and refuse to acknowledge his existence.

The thought of forcing himself to shave, take a shower, eat a bowl of cereal, and proceed to get ready for the school day felt like a betrayal of Claire. Surely she wasn't thinking about such trivial things. It was seven-twenty. In sixty minutes, thirty-three children would be waiting for him outside his classroom. He couldn't mope around the house waiting for a miracle. He put the half-empty mug on the counter and went into the bathroom to begin his routine.

At ten minutes to eight, he was ready. He would walk to school instead of driving. The sky was cloudless. Walking quickly would give his mind something to do rather than circling around his mistakes and his less-than-pure motives. His guilt. No matter how much he recognized that Joey had misbehaved, he knew the razor blade of guilt in his throat was deserved. He had earned every intermittent stab.

He stuffed his papers into his bag, shoved in a water bottle and two power bars, and went outside. He locked the deadbolt and hurried to the corner, forcing himself not to look at the police cruiser, empty and accusing in front of Claire's driveway.

As he started across the opening of the cul-de-sac, he looked back over his shoulder. The black and white car drew his eyes, wouldn't let him go after all. He walked faster, his head still turned.

"Look out!"

He turned too late and plowed into the Disturbance

Coordinator. "Sorry." He took several steps back.

"Why were you looking behind you?" she said. She looked past him. "Oh. Is the police car there because of the little boy that's missing?"

"How did you know about that?"

"My supervisor told me."

"How did your supervisor know?"

Tanya took a sip from her silver coffee container. She had a large mouth with full lips. Her fingers were thin and long. A drop off coffee glistened on the nail of her index finger.

"Is that why you're here?"

"No. I stop by most mornings now, just to check things out. Making sure there's nothing else for you to complain about."

"Well aren't you diligent."

"I hope you'll stop bombarding me with email. It won't change anything."

"I know that."

"Then why do you do it?"

"Because it's important to express one's opinion."

"Even if it's pointless?"

"Especially when it's pointless."

"Okay."

He stepped around her. "I need to get going or I'll be late for school." He continued across the street in the opposite direction of the construction. The sound of trucks firing up, gates being dragged open, told him it was eight. He walked faster.

"Hey!" Tanya shouted.

He lifted his hand to wave good-bye.

"Wait," she called.

Her high heels clickety-clacked across the street.

"I'm late." He nearly shouted, not wanting to waste time turning his head.

The sound of her heels grew more rapid until she was right behind him.

"I heard you have snakes," she said. "Pythons?"

He stopped. "How did you know that?"

"The boy's mother, Claire? That's her name, right?"

He nodded.

"She told me. That's really cool. Especially pythons."

"You like snakes?"

"Yes. They're so elegant. They're always sizing you up, not like mammals who look at you as if they want something from you."

"Huh," Brian said.

"They're beautiful."

"Do you have snakes?" he said.

"No. And I don't know why. I've always admired them, but I guess it's a lot of responsibility."

"That's true."

"Can I see them sometime?"

"We'll see." He started walking, but she kept pace with him. "Is that what you get used to saying, being a schoolteacher?"

He laughed. "Yes."

She reached into her suit pocket and pulled out a business card.

"I have your email address," he said.

"Here's my phone number. Please let me know. I could bring a bottle of wine or something."

Was she asking for a date? Because of the snakes? He smirked and took the card.

Twenty-one

SEEING THE POLICE car pull up to the curb had spun up a thin web of hope in Claire's throat that felt worse when it was torn away. The officer hadn't supplied any useful information. In fact, by the time she closed the front door after him, she'd wondered why he'd stopped by. Was it a PR move to make sure she knew they were doing their jobs? *Hard at work? Searching high and low?* She couldn't remember if he'd actually said those words — *searching high and low* — but that was the impression she'd been left with. She also didn't know what that entailed. She supposed they'd issued an Amber Alert. Or did a child have to be gone longer, have a confirmed sighting of an unsavory adult talking to him, or an ex-spouse … They'd spent a fair amount of time on that topic. Someone had talked to Greg, and his girlfriend, and seemed more or less satisfied that Greg had nothing to do with it. Of course he didn't, she had to beg him to take Joey for an entire weekend, Greg wouldn't kidnap him.

After walking around the neighborhood last night, shouting Joey's name until her throat burned and no more sound would come out, she'd felt like all of her insides had withered into a pile of dead leaves. Each organ was so brittle, it seemed as if it would flake into a thousand tiny bits if she touched it.

By the time she'd walked all the streets within fifteen blocks, pausing every few steps to check her cell phone, believing each time that it had rung and she hadn't felt the vibration, she was ready to collapse. Still, she hadn't slept. She'd sat on the couch, not bothering to open it into a bed, staring at the glass doors, darkness leaning against them. She couldn't bring herself to go through the motions of making tea, or opening a bottle of sparkling water. She'd had nothing to drink but infrequent sips of tap water. About three a.m., she ate two wheat crackers.

She wondered whether she should call her parents. They were on a two-week cruise. Making the effort to reach them would be an admission that Joey was … but he wasn't. He was just lost. Or hiding. He wasn't … gone. There was no need to call her parents.

She stood in the center of the kitchen. A beam of sunlight came through the mini blinds. She'd never closed them during the night. The light ran across the tops of her feet. Her skin appeared transparent. Her feet were cold, but she couldn't put on her socks, now stiff with perspiration. Getting a clean pair would require walking down the hall to the spare room, passing Joey's room. That wasn't possible.

The light across her feet had dimmed. She wasn't sure if clouds had appeared in the sky or if the sun had moved enough that it no longer shone directly through the blinds. It was upsetting to be tormented with these tedious, wandering thoughts, but there didn't seem to be any way around them. She would think about Joey for a few minutes and then her mind froze before wandering off to some other bit of trivia. It had been that way all night.

She opened the refrigerator. A box of juice for Joey's lunch sat on the top shelf. A sob shoved up out of her belly. She slammed the door and walked to the entryway. For what seemed like the thousandth time, she pulled her phone out of her pocket. The screen was blank. The last text had been an hour ago — a line of *xxxxxxx's* from her friend at work. One for each year of his life. That also made her sob with a rough, gasping sound she didn't recognize.

After sucking in a deep breath, she hurried down the hall, refusing to look toward Joey's room. She stopped outside the master bedroom door. The knob felt warm when she would have expected it to be cool. She turned it but didn't push the door open. She had no idea why she wanted to look inside. Now. After all this time. Was she trying to gouge a hole in her heart so that the pain of not knowing where Joey was, what had happened, would be lessened by piling on agony from the past?

She pushed open the door.

A hint of mildew from a bathroom that hadn't been

cleaned in two years hit her nostrils. Of course the bathroom hadn't been used either, so there should be no cause for mildew. Maybe it grew on its own from the memory of wet tiles. The bed looked like something in a showroom, not a piece of furniture that had anything to do with her. She walked closer and placed her hand on the mattress. She pressed down. It was hard, as solid and cold as a block of ice.

A whole lifetime had taken place on that bed. Making love to her new husband, conceiving their child, sleeping with Joey in her womb, waking up and feeling her water break, nursing her new infant, comforting a toddler after scary dreams. Then, finding that while she wasn't looking, something had inserted itself into the middle of her life and split it in half, like an ax slicing through dried wood. She sat on the bed but she didn't cry. All the tears for Greg were finally gone. Her tears for Joey had solidified so that her stomach and intestines and throat felt as if they were filled with cement, on the verge of hardening.

She lay on her back. Her lower legs dangled over the side. She stared at the ceiling and closed her eyes. Maybe she'd never wake up.

THE DOORBELL RANG. Claire's eyes didn't immediately open. She knew she was in her bedroom but in her dream she'd been standing just inside the door. Greg and his girlfriend were sprawled in sweaty abandon across her sea green sheets. They'd wanted her to leave, but instead, she'd taken two more steps into the room.

The girl yanked the sheet up to her neck and was fumbling to cover Greg. "Can you leave us alone for a minute?"

"You're in my bed. With my husband."

"We need some privacy."

"Then you shouldn't have chosen my bed." Claire smiled at her wit and strength. She smiled even more at their growing discomfort. It wasn't shame for what they'd done to her. It was the reaching under blankets, scurrying across the floor to collect discarded clothes, tugging a thong over sweaty legs, watching it curl into an impossible knot. It was a bra strap twisted the wrong way because she put it on while keeping an eye on Claire, rushing to leave behind the weakness of being naked. Greg was immobilized, asking in a dull voice, "How come you're here?"

They'd slunk out of the room and she'd whipped out a cigarette lighter, the first indication she was dreaming, and held it to the sheets, breathing in the sharp odor as the flame crept through the fabric then sprang to life when it reached the feathers inside the comforter.

Not wanting to leave this improved version of her life, she squeezed her eyes tighter. How long had she been asleep?

The doorbell rang again and she opened her eyes. The light hitting the curtains suggested it was mid-morning. It might be Michelle. If it were Brian, she wouldn't open the door. If it was a police officer, she didn't want to hear any change in status, any news, or answer any more questions. She pulled herself up to her elbow and looked at her feet, reluctant to touch them to the floor.

The doorbell rang a third time. She stood and shuffled across the bedroom floor. She went out and closed the door firmly behind her. In the entryway, she looked through the peephole. It was hard to see who was on the other side. It was blurred and almost looked like an eye peering back at her.

She opened the door.

Joey was perched on a man's shoulders, leaning forward to press his brow against the peephole. "Oh my god!" She lunged at him, pulling his head toward her face, burrowing her nose in his hair. It was cold. "Where were you?" she sobbed.

The man bent down and let Joey dismount as if he was getting off the back of a horse.

Claire grabbed Joey, squeezing his upper arms close to his body. She lifted him off the ground and his feet dangled against her shins. "I was so scared."

"I'm sorry, Mom. I didn't mean to."

"What happened?" She glanced up. The man was just a few inches taller than her, with wide shoulders and longish blonde hair. "Who are you?"

"Doug. Doug Branson. I'm on the construction crew." He glanced toward the opposite side of the street. "I was the first one there this morning, and I found this guy sleeping under a tarp."

Claire released her grip on Joey and lowered him until he

stood on his own. She put her arms around his shoulders and pulled him against her hip. He didn't object.

"Sleeping?" She looked down. "How did you get inside there? You're not supposed to … it's locked. Isn't it?" She looked up at the man.

"I climbed the tree," Joey said. "It hangs over the fence. That one tree on the end."

"And you jumped down?"

"I hurt my ankle."

She pictured the surface of the ground on the other side of the fence — a narrow strip before the ground sloped abruptly.

"Anyway," Doug said. "I'm sure you had a horrible night. But here he is."

Claire started to cry. "Thank you. Thank you so much." She blinked away the tears. He was staring directly into her eyes. She should look away, she wanted to look away, but she couldn't.

Doug stepped off the porch. "I didn't do anything."

"You did."

"Alright, then. Take it easy." His gaze locked onto Joey's eyes in the same way. It was really remarkable. Most people glanced all around your head, their focus dancing from your nose to your forehead to some spot beyond your ear. "Bye kiddo." He turned and walked down the path.

"Thank you so much for taking such good care of him." She knew she was gushing but didn't care. She hugged Joey, squeezing him so hard her arms ached.

Doug turned onto the sidewalk. He waved and cut across the street and disappeared around the corner.

"Can you walk?" she said.

"Sort of."

"I should call the police. I need to let them know you're okay."

"The police were looking for me?"

"Oh, God, Joey. I was terrified. I thought you were … why didn't you call me?"

"I lost my phone."

"Why did you leave Brian's? Why did you climb the tree? You know you're not supposed to go inside there. That's why they have the fence."

"Well they're not trying very hard to keep me out, with that big branch hanging over. It was easy."

She pushed the door open wider. She put her hand under his armpit and helped him limp up the step into the house.

"I'm gonna be late for school," Joey said. "My backpack's at Mr. Abram's."

"I think you'll stay home from school today."

"But my math homework is due."

"You're staying home. We need to go to the doctor. Have them check your ankle, and make sure everything else is okay."

"What else would be wrong?"

"It's just a good idea." She picked him up and settled him

on her hip like she had when he was two or three. He was heavy, and her back ached, but she could still carry him. She took him into the living room and settled him on the couch. "What do you want to eat?"

"Captain Crunch."

He was only allowed that kind of stuff on special occasions. It was clear he was feeling fine and going to make the most of the situation. "I'll get you some juice first. And call the police."

"Did they put their sirens on?"

She laughed. "No. But they were looking for you all night."

"Sorry, Mom."

"I walked past there four or five times last night, I was shouting your name."

"My foot hurt really, really, really bad. I could hardly walk. I laid down under the tarp because it smelled good. Like rain. And there was a sweatshirt on the ground. I guess I went to sleep."

"I guess you did."

She wanted to know why he'd left Brian's house, why he felt it was okay to climb the tree, in the dark. She wanted to chastise him. Mostly she wanted to sit on the couch and hold him.

Twenty-two

MICHELLE AND GERARD had been at a standoff since she'd found the weapons and cash. When Joey Simpson went missing, they'd been distracted enough to stop arguing. But now that Joey was home, she was determined to get inside Gerard's brain and find out exactly what sort of plans he'd been making without her.

It had suddenly become too cold to eat breakfast on the back patio. If she waited to serve it as brunch when there was a chance the temperature might be pleasant, their meal would be destroyed by banging and shouting and gear grinding. Her forehead pinched just thinking about it. The back patio was preferable for breakfast or lunch because Gerard was more prone to linger over the meal when they ate outside. At the bar facing from the kitchen into the great room, he was all business. First, he cut up every piece of food on his plate, as if he was preparing to assemble a mechanical device and needed to lay out all the parts. Then he worked quickly. He didn't exactly shovel food into his mouth, but close enough. When he was finished he pushed his plate to the side, drank a few sips of water, or finished his coffee or wine, depending on the meal, stood and carried his plate to the sink, rinsed it and placed it in the dishwasher.

The only other time he was prone to linger was when they ate in the dining room. She considered serving breakfast in there, but it would be such a departure from their routine, he'd misread it as an ominous sign, viewing it as obvious preparation for an important conversation. She was preparing for just that, but she wanted to work into it slowly, not start off as combatants. There was a more than definite chance that's where they'd end up. She'd just have to make sure to start right away, before he could polish off his meal and disappear.

She cracked three eggs into the non-stick pan, dribbled in a few tablespoons of low-fat milk, and scrambled them quickly with a plastic whisk. She splashed in Tabasco sauce, then finished scrambling them. In the perfect timing born of thirty-eight years of cooking the same breakfast for the same man, the English muffins popped out of the toaster, alerting her it was time to turn off the burner under the eggs. As if he also was on a timer, Gerard appeared in the doorway. He pulled out one of the long-legged chairs and seated himself at the bar.

When she was settled next to him, she took a bite of eggs, then put down her fork. "We need to talk."

"A dreaded phrase in a man's ears."

"This isn't a game."

He ate a forkful of eggs and took a bite of his muffin.

"How long have you been into all this stuff?"

"Which part?"

"Let's start with the guns, although that's not even the most alarming piece of this."

"What's alarming?"

"The people in those chat rooms."

"I suppose a few of them are a little militant."

"*All* of them."

"Don't over-generalize."

Michelle ate several bites of egg. The Tabasco burned at her throat. She might have overdone it. She was so busy thinking about this conversation, she'd added more than usual.

"There are one or two crackpots in every crowd," he said.

"Every single person that commented on that site is paranoid."

"I'm sure you didn't read every comment."

She was off track already. The subject was too vast for breakfast, too complex to tackle all at once. She'd wanted to start with the guns. She needed to know how long this had been going on, what he thought he needed them all for, but the people he was associating with were more frightening than an entire garage full of weapons. "I didn't read any rational comments."

"It depends on what you call rational. Is it rational to have a sixteen trillion dollar national debt? Is it rational that our entire economy is smoke and mirrors?"

"People who are a lot smarter than you are working on the economy." She glanced at him. He looked hurt. The face she'd known when he was a twenty year-old boy flickered to the surface for a moment. She suddenly felt they were on a date and he was trying to impress her and she'd slashed at his ego with a fillet knife. "I'm sorry. That didn't sound the way I wanted it to."

"How did you want it to sound? Like me and the others who are concerned about the direction our country is headed are stupid?"

"No. It's that nothing is ever solved by pulling away from the tribe."

"Maybe the *tribe* is deranged."

"People need to work together, not separate themselves and rely on hoarding and weapons to bolster their sense of security."

"This isn't about a sense of security. This is about protecting the people we love."

"It's crazy. If the stock market crashes, you're going to hole up in the house and shoot anyone who comes by looking for food?"

"The stock market crashing doesn't begin to touch on how things could fall apart."

She pushed her plate away. She couldn't eat any more eggs;

they felt like clumps of hot wax sliding down her throat. She could already feel the heartburn eating across her stomach. She hated to think she was getting too old, her stomach lining too sensitive, to enjoy Tabasco sauce. She picked up her muffin.

"You're naive if you think everyone would remain civil in the face of a national, or global disaster."

After a moment, when he didn't say any more, she laughed. Apparently he wasn't as concerned about bruising her ego as she was about his. "We can't live our lives in fear."

"I'm not. Preparation eliminates fear."

"What does that mean?"

"Fear comes from believing you're helpless, or not capable of surviving. I know we have food and supplies and cash. If the worst happens, we have the means to defend ourselves."

"You really think we're going to have warfare on the streets of suburbia?"

"You never know. But I don't have to be afraid, and neither do you."

"I'm not."

"How can you look at that fence, and listen to that incessant racket," he waved his arm toward the sliding glass doors and the backyard beyond, "and not understand that the government doesn't give a rat's ass about you and would stop at nothing to get its way?"

Now they were way off track. But when she tried to think what track they should be on, what she'd expected from this conversation, she couldn't remember. Everything he said made sense, but when she read the comments in the forum, they sounded like they'd all gone mad. Of course the world was fragile, full of risk, death always hanging over the human race. But that was life. One way or another, they would all die. And was it really healthy to fixate on the worst-case scenarios? "Why were you doing all this behind my back?"

"I knew you'd react this way."

"So you lied to me?"

"When did I lie?"

"You don't think building a secret compartment under the deck and filling it with guns and cash you siphoned off from our *joint* account is lying?"

"No." He pushed his plate to the side. He left his half-full mug on the placemat and stood. He carried his plate to the counter.

She closed her eyes. She couldn't watch him rinse it and put it in the dishwasher as if he was filing away the entire conversation.

"I'm going to ride the stationery bike for a while," he said.

"You should digest your food first."

"I'll ride slowly."

"Aren't we going to talk about this?"

"I don't see what there is to talk about." He left the dishwasher door hanging open and returned to the counter. "Are you finished?"

She nodded.

He picked up her plate, carried it to the sink, scraped off her eggs, and stuffed the rest of her muffin into the disposal.

"I need to understand," she said.

"You're not trying very hard."

"I don't know what I'm more upset about — that you're paranoid and hanging out with a bunch of crazy strangers, letting them poison your mind, or that you hid something so huge from me."

"I was waiting to see when you would be open to it. I have to do what I think is right to protect our family."

"How does any of this protect the boys? Are we going to have them all move back in here while we hide out and wait for Armageddon?"

He walked back to the counter and leaned on it. His eyes were wide, slightly blurred behind his glasses. "I love you. I'm doing this for you."

"It doesn't feel like I have anything to do with it." Her eyes filled with tears.

He pressed his ribs against the counter as he leaned across and put his hands on her upper arms. He rubbed her left arm gently, rhythmically.

The tears spilled over her lower lids and liquid dribbled out of her nose. She lifted her head. She looked at him but didn't connect with his gaze. He could provide all kinds of explanations about not living in fear and protecting themselves and being naive. She might be naive about what could go wrong in the world, but she was not naive about mental illness, and Gerard was demonstrating some abnormal behavior. The insistence that those on the fringe were in the mainstream, and the unquestioning acceptance of their views. The obsessive need to go everywhere together, to never be alone, except when he chose to close himself up in front of the glow of the computer screen.

She knew what happened when someone ran obsessively, single-mindedly, after a single thread, letting the rest of life fall by the wayside until they were unable to function around normal people. She would not allow him to slip over the edge as her brother had.

With only sixteen months between their birthdays, she and Paul had done everything together, rode their bikes, built forts in the backyard, and played Risk and Canasta. On month-long summer trips across the country to visit relatives, they had only each other and they enjoyed enough of the same things — books and hiking and swimming — that they'd remained close through high school and into college.

It all went sideways during Paul's junior year. When he'd returned home for the summer he'd lost interest in leaving the house, even for a movie. He hardly slept. He sat at the far corner of the backyard, smoking one cigarette after another. After a few nights of this, Michelle had gone out to join him. As she gagged on cigarette smoke, she peppered him with questions to which he gave near-monosyllabic answers.

"Why won't you tell me why you're behaving this way?"

"Not important."

"Everything's important."

"Wrong."

"What's happening to you?" She slipped off her chair and knelt on the grass. Even though it was past midnight, the grass was warm and dry. For a moment, she worried night bugs might crawl out from the roots and up her legs. She shivered and lifted her knees off the ground so she was half-squatting.

"Nothing."

"I feel like you're disappearing."

"I'm here."

"Your body, but where are *you*?"

"Here."

"You don't laugh, you don't talk. I wonder if you even think. It seems like your mind is a screen and the movie has stopped playing."

He was silent.

"Why won't you tell me what's going on?"

"Caroline."

One painful, disconnected word at a time, she extracted the story. He'd fallen in love, his first girlfriend. Probably not his first crush, but the first one he did anything about. After only three months, they'd even talked about marriage. At least he had. He bought her a ring with a chip of a diamond on it. She wore it, for a while. Then she started hanging out with hippie types. Her hair got longer, which he liked. She stopped shaving her legs and under her arms, which he didn't like. It repelled him, made him feel as if she was becoming an animal, not a clean, silky-skinned young girl. It scared him. They tried pot. He hated it, she loved it.

Then she stopped wearing the ring and started talking about how monogamy was a construct of civilization, meant to control people, meant to tie women down, a concept that was developed when sex always resulted in babies. Now, women could enjoy sex like men did, without ending up bearing six or seven children. He and Caroline had gone to a party. She disappeared into a tiny bedroom, a shed really, built on to the back of a house. When he went looking for her, thinking she was simply smoking more pot, he found her naked on a mattress, her limbs wrapped around three nude guys sprouting beards, long hair, and bead necklaces.

Paul never recovered. He couldn't seem to pull himself out of wherever he'd gone. He didn't go back to college in the fall. He stayed with their parents, who didn't know how to handle him, so they looked the other way and kept feeding him, hoping he'd get better. He didn't. When he was twenty-two, the voices started. He'd go on for hours over dinner about the need for better control of the human race, how people didn't know what was good for them, and they should have more regulation, less ability to destroy their own lives. The government should control who had children, and when, and how many. There was too much freedom. The human race was hurtling toward annihilation.

For the rest of his life, Paul had been on medication that

swallowed him in a sleeve of plastic. He didn't seem to really hear anyone who spoke to him. At least when he'd sat in the backyard smoking, his eyes had life. With the medication, his eyes went flat. Her best friend disappeared.

Of course, her brother had been an entirely different story from Gerard. Still, she knew how easy it was to get lost inside your own head. The human mind was nothing but a block of clay. The older she got, the more she believed that. It was so easy to mold it into something obscene.

She stood and walked around the counter. She put her arm around Gerard's waist and leaned her head against his shoulder. "Can we talk about it some more?"

He stiffened.

She squeezed him more tightly. "I want to understand. I promise I'll listen."

"It's not complicated."

"Over dinner. I'll make spaghetti tonight. We can have a bottle of wine and eat in the dining room and you can tell me all about it."

"Sure."

She hated herself for caving. She wanted to grab his shoulders and shake him until his teeth clattered like dice, but she could see he wasn't going to relent. It was better to take a softer approach. Or a subversive one.

Twenty-three

BRIAN WAS HURT that Claire hadn't told him immediately when Joey was found. She didn't seem to appreciate how much he cared for Joey. He wouldn't feel any more protective if Joey was his own son, but that fact was lost on her. She was really quite a selfish person in some ways. She trusted him with the most precious part of her life, she expected him to keep a close watch, yet she expected him to give that same care without feeling any anguish over what had happened. He was there picking Joey up from childcare with as much dedication as his mother demonstrated. Of course, Claire worked miles away, bound by clogged roadways while he was right there on the school grounds. But she wouldn't be working toward her degree if it weren't for him. And he wasn't helping with Joey just to get her attention, just because he'd wondered whether something might grow between them. He did it because he cared about Joey. Almost as much as he loved Antony and Cleopatra.

Aside from Joey, he wasn't overly fond of children. It wasn't that he didn't like kids at all, the students in his classroom were okay. Some of them were quite intelligent and entertaining. But he didn't feel anything for them. A number of his colleagues acted as if their students were a part of their families. He wasn't deluded enough to believe he would stand out in these kids' lives ten years, even five years, from now. He did his part in the educational process and that was it. He wasn't any more special or important than a robot on an assembly line, and the teachers who thought they were didn't have a very firm grasp of reality.

He walked through the house and out to the backyard. There were papers to grade, but those could be put off until tomorrow afternoon, even Sunday. Right now, he wanted to work on a sculpture. He'd given up too easily the last time, and slacking off was not how one became an adept, accomplished artist. Developing talent required long hours of hard work. No wonder he wasn't pleased with his efforts. You got what you gave.

The yard was dark, but he didn't need to waste electricity by turning on the patio light, he knew his way to the shed blindfolded. He inserted the key, unhooked the padlock, pushed open the door, and reached inside to turn on the light. Of course, everything was as he'd left it. That was one good thing about not having a child on a permanent basis. Everywhere that Joey went in the house, things changed, bathroom towels hung crooked on the racks, sofa pillows were moved or tossed on a chair where they didn't belong.

Claire was so worried about Joey getting into the room with the snakes. That told Brian she didn't know him very well. He would never let Joey near the snakes unattended. Who knew what idea would enter his head? Look at the random impulse to walk out of the house, climb a tree, and drop over the fence into the construction site. Joey was lucky he hadn't broken a leg. Or that someone hadn't snatched him when he was wandering along the street in the dark.

Brian's current sculpture sat on the table, covered with a damp cloth, a sheet of plastic wrapped over that. He lifted the plastic off the object and placed it at the end of the table. He pulled out the wood chair and sat down. The faceless children seemed to be looking down from the shelves. Despite their missing eyes, he felt as if they stared at him while he worked. Some had heads too small, ears too high, hands disproportionate to each other, legs that looked more like snakes than muscled human legs with kneecaps and ankle bones. But if he started at the top shelf and moved his attention slowly down, he could see some signs of improvement over time.

He lifted the damp cloth off the clay and ran his hands over it. It was the perfect consistency — moist and pliable, not mushy from over-use of water. He picked up the metal blade and scraped it along the neck to remove a slight lump. He put the blade back on the table and pressed his fingertips against the bridge of the nose — a non-descript nose that failed to remind him of any particular person. He wasn't even sure it looked like a child's nose. It was just a nose. How did a child differ from an adult anyway? They were smaller — that was the only differentiating feature he could come up with. But in a sculpture, smaller was irrelevant. He supposed their features were softer. There were no lines in the skin, but he didn't have discernible lines in his face yet, either, so that wasn't it. He lifted his hand and touched the sides of his nostrils. He ran his finger down the cartilage, hard as bone, that formed the shape of his nose. It was bigger, thicker, the cartilage more pronounced. It was... Maybe he should work on the eyes. He pressed his thumbs on either side of the nose to create depressions where he could begin carving out eye sockets. How would a child's eyes be different?

He couldn't believe he stared into the faces of thirty-three children every single day, spent time with Joey multiple times a week, and he couldn't come up with one single thing that made a child's face differ from an adult's. Nothing he could capture in clay. Or maybe he lacked the talent to recreate life. He put his hands in his lap and stared at the half-formed child, the blank face. He was no longer sure why he was doing this. His baby was dead, he would never see its face, never have a child, and now Joey had been ripped out of his life through no fault of his.

The figure stared back at him, questioning, waiting.

Brian grabbed the hammer off the hook on the wall behind him. He slammed it into the figure's shoulders. He raised it again and hit the head. The clay was dense and it took a few strokes for the skull to collapse. He dropped the hammer on the table, wrapped his hands around the head, and pressed them together. He tore at the side of the head, gouging it so that it looked like it was the victim of a gunshot. He ripped the arms off the shoulders. It was surprising how much force it took to make it unrecognizable, as if it didn't want to give up its form, its life.

He sprayed water on the cloth, laid it over the mutilated pile of clay, then covered it with plastic. He sprayed water on his hands and wiped them with a clean towel. He went out of the shed, closed the door, and secured the padlock.

Inside the house, he pried clay out of his fingernails, washed his hands more thoroughly, and sat down at the computer to check his email. There were three new messages. One from his cell phone provider with a gleeful reminder that his bill was available to check online, *now!* The second was a message from one of the teachers at school, and the third was from the Disturbance Coordinator — Tanya.

He clicked on her message and studied the three lines of text.

Hi, Brian. I hope you're doing well. I hope this isn't intrusive of me, but I do love snakes, and I'd love to meet yours and talk to you about them.

This has nothing to do with the construction project, just a personal request. Give me a call.

She signed it simply — Tanya. Her cell phone number was

typed on the line below her name.

She hadn't acknowledged his last three concerns. All she cared about were his snakes. He pushed his chair away from the computer desk, startled by the thought. He closed his eyes and tried to think what his most recent complaints had been. He couldn't remember. He'd write back to her separately, later, and demand a response. But right now, he would call her about the snakes.

This was the best thing that had happened to him in a while. Maybe forever. His own words spread slowly through his brain — *all she cared about were his snakes*. It was almost unbelievable. Ever since Antony and Cleopatra came into his life, he'd been waiting for someone who recognized and appreciated their regal beauty. And here she was — a virtual stranger inviting herself to his house because she wanted to meet his snakes. It was too good to be true. He should be delighted. And he was.

HE STOOD BEHIND the front door, waiting for Tanya to ring the bell. He'd seen her car pull up to the curb, seen her sit inside for a few seconds longer than he would have thought was normal, and then check her make-up in the rearview mirror. Through the small, semi-circular window near the top of his door, he glanced at Claire's house. What would she think if she noticed Tanya coming inside? He wasn't sure if what he was doing was strange, or if it was none of Claire's business — no one's business. Still, he felt exposed. He wished she'd parked near the construction site and walked, but then, if someone saw her, it would appear even more unusual that she was walking around the cul-de-sac. At least this way she only had ten or twelve steps to his porch and then he'd sweep open the door and she'd step inside before anyone registered who it was.

And why did it matter? Why was he second-guessing himself like this? Who cared what any of these people thought? They had their own lives and problems. They had no say in what he did or whom he chose to be friendly with.

The bell rang. He took three slow breaths before he turned the deadbolt and opened the door. He moved back so she wouldn't feel crowded. She stepped into the house and smiled. Her lips looked uncertain, as if she wasn't sure whether she was supposed to be smiling.

She wore pale gray slacks and a snug-fitting sweater that was greenish but had the hint of another color he couldn't identify. Her blonde hair was loose, hanging down the center of her back.

"Thanks for inviting me over."

He wasn't sure he had, but there was no need to argue. "Do you want anything to drink? Tea? Dr. Pepper?"

She laughed. "Dr. Pepper? Is that the only soda you have?"

"Yes, why?"

"It's a rather strange choice."

"Why?"

She looked at him and giggled. "I've only known one

person in my whole life who drank Dr. Pepper. Everyone drinks Coke or Pepsi."

"Now you know two people. Do you want some?" He could see her considering the options as she glanced past him at the living room. If all she did was march down the hall and look at his snakes, it seemed rather voyeuristic. But she probably didn't want to stay long enough for him to make tea. He waited.

"I'll have some tea, if you have any regular flavors."

"I have green tea, black tea, cinnamon, and I think some herbal thing that claims to calm your nerves."

"Green tea is good."

He gestured toward the living room. "Do you want to have a seat, or come into the kitchen while I make it?"

"I'll watch you make it."

He frowned. It was an odd way of putting it. Did she think he was going to poison her? He went into the kitchen and picked up the kettle. He filled it with water, set it on the stove, and turned on the gas. Without an invitation, she walked to the table in the dining area and sat down in the chair Joey usually sat in. He got out mugs and tea bags, green for Tanya, black for himself.

After the tea was ready, he handed her a mug. "Should we go sit in the living room? I don't want to bring tea into Antony and Cleopatra's room. In case you get startled."

"Oh, I won't get startled. I love snakes, they don't scare me. But let's sit and drink this first so I can hold them. If that's okay?"

She waited a long time for her tea to cool before drinking any. His mug was half empty by the time she took her first sip. They talked about the elementary school, but studiously avoided the topic of her job or the construction project. It occurred to him that this would be a good time to get answers to the emails she'd ignored, but he didn't want to put a sour tone on things.

When their mugs were nearly empty, he took hers and put them both in the kitchen. He led her down the hall to Antony and Cleopatra's room.

"How long have you had them?"

Brian put his hand on the doorknob. He paused. Jennifer had died a little over a year ago; he'd lived in this house alone ... ten, almost eleven years. "Twelve years," he said, surprised at how time had passed so quickly. He'd been with Antony and Cleopatra longer than almost anyone else in his life.

"Where did you get them?"

"I ordered them from a reptile supplier."

"What made you decide you wanted snakes?"

He opened the door, but stood blocking the way. He didn't want to be explaining things when she first saw them. He wanted her to drink in their beauty in silence, or near silence. "I grew up in Florida. There were lots of snakes in the area, they came into our yard all the time, and I saw them at reptile parks. I always liked them."

"That's all?"

"That's all." He stepped into the room.

"Why pythons? Surely you didn't have them crawling around your backyard when you were a kid."

"Do you want to see them or ask questions?"

"Well I'm as interested in you as I am in the snakes."

"I'm not that interesting," he said.

She put her hand on his forearm. He stared at her fingers, long and thin. The joints were almost nonexistent, so her fingers appeared limp and weak, like pale earthworms. He decided to ignore the touch, her fingers would slide off as he moved into the room. "When I started getting your emails, I thought you were a mental case."

He blinked. "Why?"

"Your messages had the same traits as emails from other weirdos, people who ended up threatening me. We get a lot of them, you know. Every neighborhood has one person who's a little off. And you write a lot of detail that's not necessary."

"I'm trying to be explicit so you understand the situation."

"It's not necessary, and it's a very recognizable pattern across the emails and hand-written letters we get from people who are … Well, they're unstable."

"Oh." He stepped away. He couldn't decide if he was angry or hurt or embarrassed.

"I don't think that any more. Okay? So don't look like that." She laughed. "Why did you name them Antony and Cleopatra?"

He waited for her to step inside, and out of habit, closed the door behind her. "The names are regal, don't you think? And they have a regal appearance."

She walked to the center of the room and looked at their cases, first Cleopatra's, then Antony's. "They're beautiful." She moved closer to Cleopatra's box. She unclasped the lid and reached inside. She ran her finger down Cleopatra's back. The snake moved forward, rearranging her body in response. Tanya continued to stroke the snake's skin with her index finger, keeping her hand well away from the head. After several strokes, she placed her palm over the body, cupping her fingers slightly. Brian was struck again by the boneless quality of her hands. "Can I hold her? How heavy is she?"

"She weighs about ninety pounds."

Tanya nodded. She pulled her hair back and twisted it into a coil. She wound it up and tucked the end into the top so it formed a loose knot. It immediately sagged down onto her shoulders. Blonde strands slipped out and touched her cheeks.

"You should probably tie your hair more securely."

"I need to go get my purse."

He opened the door and waited while her high heels thumped down the hall to the living room, stopped, and then thumped back. When she returned, her hair was tied into a twisted loop at the back of her head. The red band was stark against her pale hair.

"Antony is a little friendlier, and he doesn't weigh quite as much — about seventy pounds." He approached the terrarium.

"Can't I hold both?"

"Cleopatra sometimes gets jealous of other females." He didn't look at her, and wasn't sure if he imagined it or if he heard her breath catch in her throat and stop for a moment. "I'll hold the upper half of his body and then we can place the rest of him around your shoulders."

He lifted Antony, keeping a firm grip on his upper body, talking to him softly. The snake moved his head, turning as if he intended to look Brian in the eye. "This is Tanya," Brian said in a low voice. He moved closer to Tanya, suddenly aware of her scent, which was like lemons, but not exactly. "You're sure you aren't going to freak out? He gets upset if people panic. They can sense that, even if you don't scream."

She shook her head and the coil of hair flopped across the back of her neck.

He placed the snake's mid-section across her shoulders. She smiled and stroked his skin. "He's so beautiful, so strong."

"He is. They both are."

"Can I hold him alone?"

"Do you think you can manage?"

"Yes."

He lifted Antony's upper body closer and Tanya placed her hands around the section below his head. "He is heavy," she said.

"He's a big guy. You should feel Cleopatra. I can't hold her for long, it gets tiring."

"Why do you think she's jealous? I don't think animals, especially reptiles, really have those emotions, do you?"

He knew without a doubt Cleopatra was jealous, and vindictive. Look at what happened to Jennifer. But he'd never talked about it and he didn't know how to explain it without mentioning his wife's death. He glanced at Cleopatra's box. She stared through the sides, flicking her tongue, watching her partner.

"How do you know?" Tanya said.

"Maybe I'm imagining it." He laughed. "It's just a feeling I get."

"Have any women ever held her?"

"Not since I've had her."

"Maybe I can the next time."

He would let that pass. He wasn't getting into that kind of conversation now. He needed time to think this through.

After a few minutes, Tanya indicated she was tired. He removed Antony from her shoulders and placed him back in his box.

As they walked down the hall to the entryway, he said, "Don't tell anyone about the snakes."

"Why not? Who would I tell?"

"Just in case. Don't tell my neighbors. Most people don't react well. They're not like you."

"I guess I can understand that."

"Claire's the only one who knows. She hates them and she's

never even met them."

"She said she's afraid of snakes."

"Like I said, most people hate them." He realized that wasn't exactly what he'd said, but she got the point, there was no need to correct himself.

Twenty-four

MICHELLE LOOKED OUT the picture window in the front room. Gerard stood on the curb in front of Brian's house. He was talking to the Disturbance Coordinator. What was she doing on their street? Usually she lingered in the area where the fence ran along Fairview. As far as Michelle knew, she'd never ventured into the cul-de-sac.

Gerard's hair, streaked with black, despite being mostly gray now, looked as soft and luxuriant as Tanya's long blonde hair, which she had tied up into a messy knot with a red hair band. She wore slacks and high heels and a sweater that was a size too small.

The sun was far to the west, below the tree line. It would be dark soon, and it must be getting chilly out there, yet Gerard didn't look cold, wearing only a t-shirt and jeans. He had on the steel-toed work boots he'd ostensibly bought for doing heavy-duty yard work, but lately he wore them most of the time. Most likely preparing for his imaginary battle with sinister forces. She laughed softly, but the sour humor caught her throat and she had to swallow to fight back tears.

She went into the kitchen and took plates out of the cabinet and set them on the bar. Despite her earlier suggestion that they'd eat in the dining room, that she was willing to listen to radical ideas, his seemingly rapid descent into a world she wanted nothing to do with, she was planning dinner at the counter, something simple. She was too tired. It was Saturday night, a night for socializing or watching a movie, not thinking about anything serious. She wasn't in the mood for a confrontation. She placed flatware near the plates, folded two blue cloth napkins and put them under the forks, and carried a vase with a clipping of wisteria to the counter. It would be nice to cuddle on the couch in front of a movie, forget about guns and hidden cash and the end of civilization and all the crazy people huddled over their computers across the country, madly typing out whatever needling fears had gripped their minds that day.

She returned to the front room to close the drapes. Gerard was still on the curb, dropping his heels below the level of the curb, then rising on his toes as if he was doing calf-strengthening exercises. At the same time, he was gesturing broadly. She watched, fascinated, afraid he would fall, amazed at his ability to keep his balance, all the while talking at what looked like a furious pace.

Tanya stared at him. Even in the fading light, Michelle could see her lips were parted, her eyes wide. Every few seconds, she nodded, and the mass of hair bounced and then slipped lower as if it was preparing an escape from the hair tie.

Suddenly Michelle realized what was going on. He wasn't complaining about the construction. If he were, Tanya would be talking, spouting off her canned phrases. He wouldn't dare tell her about his weapons cache, his food supplies, his conviction that the government and society overall had irreparable cracks and was on the brink of collapse, would he?

She yanked the cord. The drapes swung wildly toward the center. She grabbed her jacket off the back of the chair and went out the front door, leaving it open behind her, as if the light and warmth of the house would suck Gerard back inside the minute he glanced in that direction. She cut across the lawn to the sidewalk in front of Brian's house. At first she heard only his voice, then the words became clear. "You should do some research."

"Seriously?" Tanya said.

"I think it's much closer than even most of us who are prepared realize."

"It all makes sense. The debt ... it's such a huge number, we'll never pay it off."

"That's right. The debt per person is over fifty thousand dollars. And you know lots of people don't even pay taxes, so it's really more than that."

Tanya laughed, her voice shrill.

"Scary, isn't it."

Michelle walked to Gerard's side and looped her arm through his, pulling it close to her waist. "What's going on?"

"Your husband's explaining how close we are to a major financial crisis and the violence that could happen."

"How did that come up?"

Gerard pulled his arm out of her grip. "Tanya commented on my work boots."

Tanya laughed. "They seem a bit much for pulling weeds."

"So we started talking about survival."

Michelle didn't see how the subject would have moved that quickly from a pair of boots to Gerard's survivalist activities, but she supposed he looked for every sliver of opportunity to mention it. Now that Michelle knew what he was up to, maybe he wasn't going to be cautious any more. Or, had he been hiding it only from her? The sudden realization hurt. How many people knew about this? Had he talked to Tanya about it before? She tried to think back to when he might have seen Tanya alone, or first met her. Maybe they'd chatted privately at one of the community meetings last spring or summer. It could be everyone knew about Gerard's inclinations but her. That he'd been talking about it for years, to his co-workers, to people he met at the hardware store, to his golf partners. She couldn't believe his golf partners would buy into this kind of extremist thinking, but what did she know? They might be eating it up. Tanya obviously was.

"It'll be a miracle if I survive the construction," Michelle said. "My migraines have doubled. That's the kind of survival you're supposed to be working on." She tried to smile at Tanya because she thought her tone sounded harsh. It was harsh. She didn't like it that Tanya was feeding Gerard's paranoia, lapping it up like some young, dumb kid that didn't know how to think for herself.

"It's fascinating, when you think about it," Tanya said.

"What is?" Michelle said.

"We really are on the brink. Not just the US, but the whole planet. Everything's going wrong — global warming, the debt, the wars, that tsunami in Japan awhile back."

"That's how the world's been since life began," Michelle said.

"I don't think so. Gerard is right. There's no real money any more. And there is a certain kind of lawlessness. In the old west you had a few bad guys, but now, no one obeys the laws."

"Oh come on," Michelle said.

"You know it's true," Gerard said. "Think."

"I do think." Michelle didn't like snapping at him, didn't like arguing in front of this girl, but even more, she didn't like this girl encouraging him and agreeing with every word when she didn't know what she was talking about. What did she know about the national debt?

"It's like he was saying, it wouldn't take much for everyone to freak out. An extended power outage where all the traffic lights were out, and no one could watch TV or use their computers. And if it lasted even two or three days, all the cell phones would die. People would go nuts."

Gerard nodded.

Michelle wanted to smack him. Or her. Or both of them. She shouldn't have come out here and now she couldn't see how to quickly end the conversation with a little grace and dignity.

"Gerard said when he was younger, people obeyed the small laws, like stopping for red lights and pedestrians, or following the speed limit in residential areas."

"So? What does that have to do with a widespread power failure?"

"I'm not explaining it very well." Tanya brushed a piece of hair off her face.

Michelle wasn't sure any hair had been there. It must be an insect. Or a habit. She didn't have to look at Gerard to know how he loved hearing about his skill in explaining complex subjects. The conversation was making her nauseous. Whether it was inside their pants or inside their skulls, men's egos were so easily aroused. She could almost feel him glowing, feeling important — a well-read, well-studied man who understood difficult concepts. She sighed. The nausea was real. It might be a migraine coming on, and then how was she supposed to fix dinner? She glanced at the house. The light looked dimmer, as if the house was straining to stay alive. As if it was hinting that this was what they would face, darkness everywhere, receding light ending in total blackness.

She shivered.

"The connection is that people used to be more restrained, less animalistic," Gerard said.

"People haven't changed. We've always had an animal nature."

Tanya leaned forward slightly. "Let him finish. You said you didn't understand the connection, and he's explaining it to you."

Gerard didn't seem to notice the tension between her and Tanya, he kept on as if he was giving a lecture. "If people can't even slow down when a traffic light turns yellow, because they could care less about everyone else on the road, what will they do when they can't use their cell phones? When the supermarket runs out of bottled water? When they're hungry?"

"They'll tear each other to shreds." Tanya's voice was jittery, excited as if she couldn't wait to see the results of such chaos. "It makes me realize I need some protection. And supplies."

Strange that supplies were the after-thought, not protection. "Well, speaking of supplies, I need to make dinner." Michelle started back toward the house, then stopped. She turned. "What brought you to our neighborhood, anyway?"

Tanya glanced at Brian's house.

Michelle crossed her arms. She took a few steps back.

"I was, uhm … Brian had concerns. He sends a lot of

email and I wanted to address his concerns."

"How can you address any concerns?" Michelle said. "The concern is this monstrosity on the other side of the fence. You can't stop that."

"He has some smaller issues, the noise." Tanya removed the band holding her hair. Blonde hair, pale, almost white, in the growing darkness, fell across her shoulders and arms. "I should get going home." She extended her hand. "It was great talking to you, Mr. Reynes."

Michelle laughed. Surely Gerard had thought he and Tanya were peers. Now she'd made it clear she viewed him as elderly.

"Let me know how I can help. I'll email you the link to that website," Gerard said.

"Help what?" said Michelle.

"Advice on where to focus in building her security," Gerard said.

Michelle turned and walked along the sidewalk and up the front path to the house. Gerard was building a wall that would be impossible to penetrate. She'd never felt so alone.

THEY EACH SIPPED at a glass of red wine with turkey sandwiches. The glasses were still half full when they settled on the couch. Forty minutes into the movie, Michelle couldn't remember the title. She recognized the actors but had forgotten their names, or maybe she'd never known them. She'd definitely seen them before, in movies she couldn't identify.

Images and sounds wove themselves through her head like the traffic in a parking lot after a concert — no order to the flow, cars backing out and blocking others, a few aggressive drivers cutting in ahead of turn, some trying to take shortcuts. Like a shroud over the whole story, she kept seeing Tanya's face, staring at Gerard, nodding eagerly, while he babbled things he shouldn't be thinking, much less saying.

He'd betrayed her. There was no other way to look at it. It was like a wife with a cheating husband, she was the last to know — scores of people had more knowledge of her life than she had.

Her glass sat on the table, wine still glistening in the bottom. Gerard's was empty, but he didn't ask for more. They used to sit in the front room enjoying a bottle together, talking and listening to music, or sometimes just cuddling. She wanted to cry, but the tears wouldn't come, they sat at the back of her head, making her throat ache.

When the movie was over, Gerard picked up the remote and turned off the TV.

"What are you doing?" Michelle said.

"Turning off the TV."

"With that girl. Tanya."

"We started talking about survival and she was very interested in the subject."

"How did that come up?"

"She told you — my boots caught her attention."

"And how many other people know about this little project of yours?"

"Not many."

"How many?"

"A few guys at work."

"Why did you tell everyone but me?" She picked up her glass, brought it to her lips, then set it down without drinking. She could feel the migraine blossoming behind her right eye.

"I didn't tell everyone. I told a few guys."

"And Tanya."

"Tonight. I never talked to her about it before." He leaned back and put his arm around her, pulling her against his side. He pressed his face into her hair. "I should have told you. But I wasn't sure how you'd react."

That was a lie. He knew exactly how she'd react, and that's why he went through all kinds of effort to build a secret storage compartment under their deck.

"Did you tell her about the weapons?"

"Only in general terms."

"What does that mean?"

"That I was prepared to defend my home."

"Oh, Gerard."

"I'm sorry." His voice was low and because his mouth was pressed close to the top of her skull, it vibrated through her head.

She resisted the desire to pull away. He could apologize and try to blame her imagined reaction all he wanted. The truth was, he'd lied to her. And now he'd let his ego get the best of him. A total stranger knew what he was hiding.

He squeezed her shoulder. "It's nothing dangerous. I'm just prepared. I'm taking care of our family."

"It's paranoid. The people writing on that website are imagining the worst and over-reacting. The world has always had problems and we've always survived."

"Not problems like we have now. And not everyone survives. Look at a comparably small event like Hurricane Katrina. The government royally screwed that up. What if we had a real disaster? Another attack like nine-eleven. What if we had biological warfare … it would be so easy it's almost laughable."

"You're scaring me." She knew he wanted to scare her. That's how it worked, frighten everyone and they would start tossing aside their civility, every man for himself, hoarding food and stock-piling guns. She didn't even want to live in a world like that. She'd rather be dead.

"Healthy fear is good."

"How is it healthy to imagine national or global disaster, to imagine people so frantic for food and shelter that you need weapons? That's not healthy. It's sick. I feel like you've lost your mind."

"I'm not your brother."

"Don't bring him into this." She pushed his arm off her shoulder and moved a few inches away. He didn't object and didn't try to move toward her. There wasn't very much space between them, but enough that their legs were no longer touching.

"Okay. But I haven't lost my mind. The people in the forum are probably the sanest people I know. They're well-read, they keep up with politics and current events, and …"

"Get their news from right-wing extremists and violent movies and video games."

"No." He stood. "You're over-reacting."

"You're over-reacting. What are you going to do, shoot someone who tries to get our food?"

"You never know what could happen."

"The very act of having a gun, lots of guns, in your case, means you expect to kill someone. Intelligent people don't hide guns in a secret case."

He picked up his wine glass. He tipped it up to take a sip then looked into the glass, as if he was just noticing it was empty. "When you calm down, we can discuss it. I'll give you some material to read. It's not written by extremists." He picked up her glass and walked out of the room.

A moment later she heard the water running in the sink as he washed the glasses, followed by the clink as he set them on the counter. She couldn't hear the movement of the towel as he carefully wiped them clean, but she knew that's what he was doing. That's what he always did. Just like he always assumed he was right. But this time, she was right. If you bought a gun, you eventually planned to shoot someone.

Twenty-five

IT WASN'T REALLY Brian's fault that Joey had gone missing. It had taken a few days for Claire to admit that to herself. Sometimes the truth and feelings don't line up. It was similar to Greg's betrayal. He was the one at fault, he was the one that hurt her, that destroyed her family, that humiliated her by choosing to love someone else. Yet all her rage stormed at the woman she'd seen lying in her bed that warm autumn afternoon.

When she'd left for work on that final day of her marriage, she'd had a sore throat and a lump at the base of her sinuses. But she'd ignored the discomfort, hoping it was caused by dry air. The total weariness in her muscles finally got the upper hand at one o'clock. Since Joey was at day care, she would go home and sleep for a few hours before picking him up, hopefully giving her time to get some strength for the evening, before she fully succumbed to the flu, or whatever it was.

It wasn't the time of year she usually got sick, and that annoyed her. She wanted to enjoy the last days of summer, not crawl into bed feeling like a steamed dumpling.

She hadn't seen Greg's SUV. Later, she'd learned it was parked around the corner, avoiding the interested eyes of their neighbors. Although it didn't seem to have crossed his mind they might wonder why he was walking along the sidewalk in the middle of the day.

Inside the front door, she'd stepped out of her flats. She thought about making tea, but decided the liquid would wake her up once it ran through her body. She needed to sleep. Tea would be soothing after her nap, or after she picked up Joey.

She walked down the hall to their bedroom. It was strange that the door was closed. She turned the knob and pushed open the door. The comforter hung off the end of the bed, draped across the floor. She never left it like that. She stared at it, wondering why it was in such disarray. Her mind took several seconds to register why the bed was unmade and what she was looking at. It had nothing to do with the comforter at all.

Greg's dark, short hair. A woman with equally dark silky hair spread across the pillow. Claire couldn't stop staring, knowing she should turn and leave. She shouldn't be watching. She should be screaming, raking her nails across all that exposed female skin. Greg's precious little butt and those strong legs and that fine covering of hair on his chest. How could he do this in her bed, with her Egyptian cotton sheets, the bed she carefully made every morning? He'd complained repeatedly that he was under too much pressure to make love. In less time than it took for her to draw a full breath, she realized it was her that he didn't want. He wanted someone fleshier, more dramatic. This woman had a beautiful body and a beautiful face. Everything about her was smooth and silky and perfect.

Even then, Claire's initial rage was at the woman, not Greg, his face burrowed between her large breasts.

She felt weak and achy, her throat raw and bloody. She wanted to slip out of her clothes and crawl under cool sheets, but those two were in the way. They'd rumpled the sheets and made them too warm and she wouldn't get to sooth her fever-enflamed skin.

As if he smelled her pain, Greg sat up. "Oh shit."

The rest was a blur. Greg demanding to know what she was doing home, as if she'd done something wrong! The woman, Sara, wearing a smirk completely lacking in even a hint of guilt, moving slowly, without shame, as she slipped out of bed and bent over, searching for a white thong that she finally retrieved from under the fallen comforter. Greg asking Claire to give them a minute. Claire complying.

That was the part she regretted most. That she'd turned and left the room as if they deserved privacy, as if they deserved a few minutes for a final kiss.

CLAIRE DROPPED HER headset into the desk drawer and

pushed it closed. She forwarded the phone so it rang to the other receptionist and grabbed her purse.

"Are you out of here already? I thought you left at four on school nights," Gail said.

"I forgot my laptop. I have to go back home first."

Gail adjusted her headset and took a sip of water from the oversized bottle on her desk. "It better not get crazy busy. Or you'll owe me."

"Don't I already owe you?"

"Good point."

Claire undid the clasp on her purse as she walked through the patient waiting area to the stairs. She scrambled down. Her heels echoed in the stairwell. She let go of the handrail and reached into her purse. Her fingers trailed across her wallet, cell phone, pens, torn tissues, before the keys scraped her fingertips. Her mind ticked through her schedule — two minutes to the parking garage, another three or four minutes to make her way out. Race home, although racing was more a state of her heart rate than an actual measure of her progress, since traffic would dictate her speed, and El Camino Real was littered with lights that seemed oddly out of sync. At home, grab the laptop, then back to the freeway toward downtown, hope against hope the San Jose State parking garage wasn't over-flowing. It usually wasn't, if she got there early enough, but you never knew when some musical or theater event would throw everything out of whack. If there wasn't any traffic, and no parking hiccups out of the ordinary, she'd have time to grab a burger, or maybe a taco from that little place across from campus, and still make the group meeting by five.

It irked her that the group she'd been assigned to for her final project — a presentation on the long-term cultural effects of the Vietnam conflict — had three members who were under twenty-one and lived on campus, and only one other adult. That woman lived only half a mile from the school. The others agreed to meet in the student union building, not caring that Claire had a job in addition to school, not to mention a child to arrange care for. *It makes more sense for one person to drive instead of four. It's better for the environment.* How could she disagree without seeming as if she didn't care about the future of the planet? But she didn't understand why they didn't see how difficult it was for her. Couldn't they drive to her house, or a nearby coffee shop, at least once for the six or seven times they had to meet? She had a carefully orchestrated schedule, every minute mattered. To them, she was just a single mom trying to make up for lost time, or missed opportunities. She could see it in their eyes. She was almost middle-aged — twenty-eight was light years away from their world.

She needed to stop complaining to herself. Complaining didn't help her feel any affinity with the rest of the group, and they needed to do a great job on this project if she was going to get the *A* she was hoping for in the class. An *A* at which she had a very good shot.

This morning, Joey had pouted more than usual about

Brian picking him up from after school care. She wondered briefly if that's why he'd snuck out of the house. Maybe he wanted to make her angry with Brian.

She'd had to practically drag him out of bed. He'd stretched out each phase of getting ready. Simply brushing his teeth had taken fifteen minutes, as he insisted for the first time that the dental hygienist told him to floss twice a day. "I only do it *once* a day, Mom. That's not good." Claire patted herself on the back when she took time to floss two or three times a week, but it didn't make her a stellar parent if she told her son not to floss. Next, he untied and retied his shoes twice to make sure the loops weren't too long. No wonder she'd forgotten her laptop.

"Why are you stalling?" she said when he untied his shoes a third time.

"I'm sad."

"Why?"

"I don't want to stay with Brian any more."

"I thought you liked him."

"That's not true. I never liked him."

"Okay, you're right. But you didn't mind him. What changed?"

"He likes his snakes better than me."

"No he doesn't."

Joey nodded. "He does. He went in their room and stayed in there and he wouldn't let me in."

"I told him I didn't want you around the snakes. He did the

right thing. They can kill people. You understand that, don't you?" Speaking the words sent a wave of nausea through her stomach. She wasn't trading her son's safety for school, a career, her freedom from Greg, was she? She couldn't blame Brian for letting Joey out of his sight, she did it all the time. He was almost eight. He had to gradually learn some responsibility.

What was she supposed to do? It wasn't that she was putting her career ahead of Joey, she was trying to make a better life for them. A life where she wouldn't have to take child support money from a man who betrayed her, live in this house like a charity case, unable to sleep in a bedroom that felt as if it was infested with a disease. She only had a few years to pull it off. One more year at San Jose State, then apply to law school. Joey would be in junior high school before she finished. There wasn't a lot of time left. Some days she felt she'd already run out of time. Her breathing grew short and her heart tightened until she felt she was running for her life.

She had to trust Brian. He had a right to own whatever pets he chose. She couldn't look at the world and assume everyone was going to betray her, interpreting every facet as an attack directed specifically at her. It wasn't as if he had some sinister motive for keeping the snakes a secret. The subject never came up, that was all. And when had she ever heard of a python killing someone? Sure, it was possible, but did it really happen? In captivity? Brian was a nice, normal guy who had a couple of pet snakes. He doted on his students. Maybe he had a crush on her, maybe he didn't. He offered to provide childcare, he seemed to genuinely enjoy Joey's company, and he lived right across the street. All kids complained about daycare and babysitters.

Finally he'd picked up his backpack and lunch and shuffled out to the car.

It could be that he had been trying to manipulate her into letting him see the snakes. That's what this was all about. It wasn't about not going over there or Brian preferring the snakes to human companionship.

She'd smiled as she pulled onto El Camino, somewhat proud of her son's attempt to try more sophisticated tactics to get what he wanted.

Traffic was lighter than usual, and she turned onto Fairview at ten past four. She'd have time to change her clothes into something more comfortable.

A large dark blue truck was parked at the curb in front of her house. It had a full-sized bed and a silver box bolted inside, presumably to lock up expensive tools. It must belong to one of the construction workers. They weren't supposed to park on the cul-de-sac, or any surrounding streets. There was a fenced dirt lot across from the site that had been set up for parking and storing equipment. She didn't really care, but if Brian saw it, he'd shoot off another email to Tanya.

She got out of the car and cut across the lawn to the front porch. The truck door opened. She turned. It was the guy who'd found Joey.

"Hi," Doug said. He left the truck door open and walked around the front. He shoved his hands into the pockets of his jeans, powdery with dirt.

She stopped near the porch.

"How's Joe?" he said.

"He's doing great."

"He's a self-sufficient kid. Most kids would have cried and screamed all night."

"I guess so. It would have been better if he had."

"For you, sure. But you should be proud of him."

"I am."

"Anyway, I stopped by because I found this." He pulled his hand out of his left pocket and held up Joey's cell phone.

"Oh! Thanks. That's great. I'm so glad you found it."

Doug held it out. Her index finger brushed across his thumb as she took the phone from his hand. The tiny phone slid down her palm. She and Doug grabbed for it at the same time. He handed it back to her. "We figured it was gone forever."

"I guess he's a little young for a cell phone. Are you trying to turn him into a Silicon Valley executive?"

If anyone else had said that, she would have bristled. But something about his easy smile and stubbly face made him look genuine. As if the last thing he'd ever do was lob a veiled criticism of her parenting, or make fun of her son.

"I don't mean that as a criticism. He just seems young for

that BS — cell phones, computers. It amazes me that kids can sleep with all those electronic gadgets, with power lights glowing at them all night long like monsters in their bedrooms. When I was a kid, I thought there were eyes watching me. Kids now must know that for a fact."

Claire laughed. She tucked the phone in her purse. "He is young, you're right. It's more for me than for him. I know that he can text me any time he needs me. It makes me feel like I'm right there with him, even when I can't be."

"Are they allowed to send text messages in school?"

"No. But after school, when he goes somewhere with his dad or with friends. It makes me feel more secure that he can always reach me."

"I can see that." He nodded at her high heels and slacks. "You're off work early?"

"I have my study group. I go to school two nights a week. I'm trying to finish my degree so I can go to law school." She crossed her arms. Why was she telling him all this? If she didn't hurry, she'd miss dinner.

"That must be tough. Work, school, being a single mom."

"Sometimes. Do you have kids?"

He shook his head. "So how do you manage to keep it all going?"

She wasn't sure if he was trying to flatter her, or was simply curious. Somehow, the way he asked the question, made her feel like a hero, a super woman. No one ever praised her for all the things she managed to accomplish. "I like everything

I'm doing, maybe that makes it easier. I love school. I have fun hanging out with Joey. My yard might not be that great." She glanced at the bare strip of dirt that ran along the edge of the front porch, the two crusty-looking junipers, and the unadorned patch of grass. At least she'd have a row of daffodils next spring. "I guess there's some dust in the house. And the kitchen floor needs mopping." *Why* was she telling him this? He seemed easy to talk to, so insanely interested. And sympathetic. Not in a negative way, as if she evoked pity, but in an admiring way.

"There's always time to work on the yard later," he said.

"That's my thought."

"Well I should let you get ready for your class." He turned.

"I really can't thank you enough. Not just for the phone, but for finding him."

"I really didn't do anything except give him a piggy back ride."

"Why don't Joey and I take you out to dinner."

"Really, it's not that big a deal."

"For pizza or something."

"Okay. Sure."

She swallowed. She couldn't believe she'd blurted out the invitation. But like everything else with him, it leaped to the surface as if her mind had taken a back seat and her mouth was taking the lead.

"The Sunday after next?"

"That works," she said.

"I have some stuff to do. Maybe late lunch … three?"

"Okay. See you then." She went into the house. The conversation circled through her mind. She felt a little bit like she'd asked him out on a date. But it wasn't. Then, what was it? It all happened so fast, without thinking.

There was no time to change clothes now. Once again she'd look like the matron of the group. But who cared? She smiled and went into the spare room to grab her laptop off the chair in the corner. Sunday sounded more interesting than her multi-media project with a bunch of twenty-year-old kids.

Twenty-six

TANYA HAD CALLED and invited him out to dinner. The invitation caught him off guard, even though she'd been at the center of his thoughts for a week. Although she'd made it clear she adored Antony and Cleopatra, he hadn't been sure how she felt about him. He wondered if it might be a conflict of interest, but that was her problem, not his.

He didn't really want to go out to dinner. Restaurant food was dull, garnering its entire flavor from excessive quantities of sodium and over-saturation with fat. He preferred to cook for himself, and now for Tanya. The food would be healthy and taste far better. That, and he wouldn't have to sit through an entire meal, a bundle of nerves as he imagined the unwashed hands, the sneezing, the coughing, the sloughed off skin that blanketed the food in a restaurant kitchen. He had no idea why people were so anxious to eat in restaurants. They were filthy, you could see that just looking around, and he couldn't imagine the invisible things.

Tanya had been thrilled with his offer to cook dinner. Her excitement made him like her even more, if that were possible.

He unwrapped the brown paper from a half-pound of peeled shrimp and dumped it onto the ceramic cutting board. Their slippery bodies skidded toward the edge. He should have put them into the colander to rinse first. Now he'd have to scoop it all up, and then wash his hands again. He hadn't been focused on what he was doing, his mind wandering to Tanya whenever it wasn't immediately occupied with something specific. Since that day, it seemed like months ago, maybe it even seemed as if he'd known her forever, he couldn't get her out of his thoughts. He'd be standing in front of the classroom, watching the kids copy their spelling words, and if every child was quietly writing, a rare occurrence with a room full of eight-year-olds, the image of Tanya rose inside his mind as if she was uncoiling herself from his spine and sliding into this skull, circling and exploring, her tongue lashing out with quick flicks. He smiled at the image. Of course it wasn't like that, he was forcing the comparison, but he couldn't get it out of his head.

He scooped the shrimp into the colander, washed the cutting board with a soapy sponge, washed his hands, and rinsed the shrimp. From here on out, he'd pay attention to what he was doing. He was serving broiled shrimp and pasta sprinkled with goat cheese. He'd made a salad of greens and tangerine sections with vinaigrette he'd mixed himself.

Women liked wine, so he'd done some online research to try to find a white wine she might enjoy. He preferred a vodka martini, and he might have one before he sat down to dinner, but he was pretty sure most women wanted to drink wine with dinner, not martinis. Besides, he didn't want her to think he was trying to get her intoxicated.

She arrived a few minutes late, at seven past seven, an interesting time. He tried to shake the glowing digital clock on the microwave out of his head and not read anything into the auspicious numbers. It wasn't that he studied numerology or was superstitious in any way, but patterns like that sometimes jumped out and grabbed at his brain until he couldn't stop thinking about them, turning it into something symbolic by his very fixation.

They went into the living room. The drapes were closed so the room would seem cozy and warm and so he wouldn't have to look out at that spot in the backyard and worry that Jennifer was watching them. This was the first time he'd seriously paid attention to a woman since Jennifer's death. Claire didn't really count because all he'd done was think about her, and have casual conversations, mostly concerning Joey. This was very different.

"Would you like a martini? Vodka martini? Or do you prefer wine? I bought some Chardonnay."

"A martini sounds fantastic," she said. "Three olives, please."

A thrill rushed through his body, starting just behind his

ears, in that tender spot where the skull ended and his neck began. He didn't like to jinx things by leaping too far, too quickly, but he was starting to wonder whether Tanya might be his soul mate. Not that a love of pythons and martinis was the basis for a relationship, but it could be those shared affections struck a chord deep inside, suggesting a perfectly aligned view of the world. It was surprising, since they'd started off on such a bad footing.

When he turned, she started to follow him. "Go sit down. I'll serve you."

"Ooh, how nice."

He smiled. He went into the kitchen and got the martini glasses out of the cabinet. He had to wash the second one because it had a film on it from sitting unused for a year. He filled the shaker with ice and vodka and vermouth. He could already taste the sharp, clean alcohol. He preferred a twist of lime, but he'd use olives for both. Variety was a good thing.

While he shook the stainless steel container, Tanya called out from the living room, "Dinner smells terrific. It's so exciting when a man knows how to cook."

He filled the glasses and carried them slowly through the dining area. He paused at the entrance to the living room, steadying his hands as the liquid swayed close to the rims. Already an icy sheen covered the outsides of the glasses. He approached the couch and lowered the glasses to the coffee table.

Tanya leaned forward. Her hair fell over her arms. She sat

up again and pushed it behind her shoulders. Holding it back from her face with one hand, she leaned forward again and put her mouth on the glass. She took a small sip without lifting the glass. It was an unsophisticated yet elegant move. Her lips came over the rim of the glass and sucked vodka and vermouth into her mouth without making it look, or sound, like she was slurping. He thought about imitating her move, but it was likely to look awkward and mocking. He picked up the glass and raised it as carefully as he could, only leaning forward to let his mouth meet the glass at the last minute. The drink was cold and refreshing. The alcohol hit his throat and he could feel it seep quickly into his veins.

He sat next to her on the couch.

"Will I get to see Antony and Cleopatra again?"

"Of course," he said.

They sipped their martinis, looking at each other over the tops of their glasses. He wanted to touch her, put his hand on her leg, but it seemed too soon. To resist the desire that was growing more insistent with every sip of his drink, he moved away from her. It was difficult to tell whether she noticed and was offended, or if she took it as a normal shifting of position.

He asked about her job, and for a while, she told him about the parts she enjoyed — soothing ruffled feathers, helping the medical foundation become, and remain, a welcome member of the communities where they had offices. The part she didn't like so much were emails and phone calls that scared her — marriage proposals from the mentally unstable, ugly name-calling, and even threats to her life.

"I can't believe someone would threaten your life over a building project," he said. "It's easy to forget how many dangerous people there are in the world. People you might see walking through your neighborhood or shopping at the same stores."

Tanya nodded. "I know."

"But would someone actually … follow through on that?"

"I don't think it's about me. I think some types of crazies like the cloak of anonymity that email offers."

"So you don't track down the senders of crazy emails?"

"How can we? If it comes from a free account."

"Isn't there a way to find that out anyway? Through the service provider?"

"It takes a lot of effort, and they suggest I just ignore them. The crazies don't know where my office is, or who I am, so it's not like I'm terrified all the time. But it's still upsetting."

"The people in this neighborhood know who you are."

"True. My supervisor hands the serious ones over to our security department. They know how to tell if it's something to be concerned about. Whether there's genuine danger or just harmless ranting. Like the threats the president gets."

She said this without blinking and he took three quick sips of his drink to keep from smirking, or worse, chuckling. Was she comparing herself to the US President? The comparison of the threat level was ridiculous on so many levels. But then, he'd never had his life threatened, so he didn't really know what that felt like.

"And you thought I was in that category?"

"Well, you never overtly threatened me." She laughed.

Her tone was clear and relaxed, no hint of awkwardness that she'd misjudged him, or that she'd categorized him as a person to fear. She smiled, letting her lips curve slowly, revealing a glimpse of perfectly straight teeth. "What changed your mind?"

"I don't know. Maybe that Claire was friendly with you. And the snakes."

"Lots of women would interpret the snakes as a reason to increase their fear."

"I'm not most women."

He stood. "Dinner's almost ready. Do you want a glass of wine, or would you like another martini?"

She bit the last olive off her stir stick and held up the empty glass. "Do martinis go with whatever you're serving?"

"I think martinis go with just about anything." He picked up the glasses.

"Me too, so I'll have another."

He didn't know what he was going to do with the bottle of wine. He surely wouldn't drink it. Maybe Claire or Michelle would like it. He moved toward the kitchen. "So you don't think I'm scary?"

"Of course not." She stood and followed him to the dining

area. She wore a dark brown and red-flowered skirt that flared out around the middle of her thighs and navy blue high heels that wobbled a bit when she walked on the carpet. She leaned toward him and kissed his jaw.

After he arranged the shrimp and pasta on dinner plates, and the salad on smaller plates, he mixed two more martinis, slightly less full this time. He turned the dial to dim the lights. They sat at the table, raised their glasses, and tapped the rims together.

She put a piece of shrimp in her mouth. "This is delicious. You're amazing."

"Thank you."

They ate in silence for a few minutes. She set down her fork and put her hand on his wrist. It felt uncomfortable to keep eating while she had her hand on his arm, so he set his own fork on the side of the plate.

"About your email, I've come to have the opposite view," she said.

"What's that?"

"Seeing how you care for your snakes, your cooking talent. I took your excessive interest in tiny details exactly the wrong way. I think it shows how intelligent and thoughtful you are. And I think it shows that you pay a lot of attention to important things."

"Oh."

"You're a very talented man."

He thought it would seem boastful to tell her about his

sculpture. And then he remembered his last encounter with the clay — disfiguring the face and head, twisting off the appendages, the satisfaction he'd felt turning it into a monster. Still, he knew he would go back to his work. The power he had to shape clay into something real, gripped him. He'd never give it up. He'd just have to work harder. He thought he'd read somewhere that talent was passion with the stubborn refusal to give up. Something like that.

His neck and face felt hot and he couldn't decide whether it was her flattery or the vodka. "Thank you," he said, finally. She was almost too good to be true. He decided not to pursue that negative train of thought. There was no reason to think he didn't finally deserve happiness, a woman who understood him and his passions.

"I was talking to the guy who lives next door to you." She took a tiny sip of her martini.

"Gerard?"

"I think that's right."

"That's his name. Gerard. He and his wife are even more upset than I am about the construction."

"He didn't mention the construction. He was going on about some group he's in. Where they're preparing for the end of the world." She giggled. "You should have seen him. He was very worked up about it."

"That's interesting."

"They have a year's worth of food stored. And he has a bunch of guns."

"Wow."

"I don't think his wife is that into it. She seemed angry that he was telling me."

"Maybe she just didn't like him talking to a beautiful younger woman."

Tanya smiled. "I think he's freaked out about some kind of government military action against civilians."

"Really? I didn't know you were intimately involved in everyone's lives around here."

"I'm just super friendly."

"I guess so."

"Claire is kind of intense, too. I feel sorry for her. Saddled with a kid, and no guy. And she's not that cute, so it must be hard for her to find someone."

He felt something fiery inside, wanting to defend Claire, but against what? Tanya was right. Claire wasn't that cute, yet she acted so superior, pretending she didn't notice he liked her, that he wanted to ask her out. Well too late for her. He had the most perfect woman in the world eating his food and drinking martinis with him. A woman who loved snakes. He almost laughed with pleasure.

She took another sip of her drink. As she swallowed, he noticed she had a longer than average neck. It was usually partially covered, but she'd braided her hair while he was putting the food on the table, and now her neck was quite prominent, short, fine hairs clinging to the back. She wrapped a rather large portion of fettuccine around her fork and stabbed a piece of shrimp. She put it in her mouth, chewed three or four times, and swallowed hard. Her Adam's apple, more prominent than most women's, shifted up then sank down. The movement inside her throat was similar to the bulge Cleopatra and Antony got when they swallowed their prey.

It was flattering to watch her eat a second helping. Somewhere along the way, he mixed a third drink for both of them.

"You're sure we're going to spend some time with Antony and Cleopatra after dessert?"

He smiled, although he felt a little hurt. "Certainly." All this time he'd longed for a woman who would feel affectionate toward his pets, yet now he was mildly upset that she was so eager to eat his food and drink his alcohol, only to ask about the snakes. There was a sharp pain in his chest and he realized he was jealous. How could he swing so wildly from wanting a woman to admire their beauty, to resenting that she seemed to prefer spending time with them over him? He'd sort of hoped they would sit close together on the couch and see where things led after that.

The dessert was a simple dish of chocolate ice cream from a gourmet shop, but Tanya raved over it as if he'd whipped together milk and sugar and spent the afternoon hand mixing it.

He rinsed the plates and put them in the dishwasher while Tanya wandered down the hall with her drink. When he was finished, he went looking for her and found her standing outside the snakes' room. "You can't bring your drink in there," he said.

"Why not?"

"They can be dangerous, they're snakes, not hamsters."

She laughed.

"It's better to have your hands free and your wits about you."

"Okay." She set her martini on a small table in the alcove across the hall. Brian had left his barely touched drink in the kitchen.

He opened the door for her, followed her inside, and closed it behind him.

Tanya moved to the side of Cleopatra's terrarium. The snake lifted her head and looked around. She pushed her head forward and the upper portion of her body followed. She coiled around herself, moving in a casual figure eight.

"It's too bad they have to spend so much time confined to a small space," Tanya said.

"I know. I've thought about re-doing the room to give them more freedom, to make the whole place their habitat."

"Why don't you let them out the way it is?"

"Hard surfaces aren't good for their skin."

"Oh. I didn't think of that."

Without asking, he lifted Cleopatra out of her case and draped her over Tanya's shoulders. The snake lashed her tongue out, trying to adjust to the new smell. Brian held her upper body. Her muscles tightened as she moved around, dragging herself across Tanya's shoulders. "She's restless," he said.

"You should let her stay out. It won't hurt her to move around for an hour or so. That wouldn't damage her skin. Just the one time."

"I suppose not."

"Put her on the floor now."

"No."

"She seems unhappy."

"She'll be fine. Maybe I'll do that later. After you leave."

"Who says I'm leaving?"

They stood in silence. Cleopatra stretched and wound herself around Tanya's shoulders, wrapping her upper body around his arm as if she wanted to pull the two of them closer together.

Twenty-seven

MICHELLE FELT MORE REFRESHED than she had since the construction began. After two hours spent getting her hair trimmed and touched up, and another hour having her nails shaped and polished, she was ready to face Gerard and his stash of weapons, cash, and crazy ideas.

She turned into the cul-de-sac and saw the white Prius. Not again. She didn't understand how that woman could be effective in her job if she was becoming best friends with all the people in the neighborhood. Or maybe that was her strategy. Cozy up to them so they stopped complaining and she appeared to be doing her job.

A few days earlier she'd seen the Prius parked in front of Brian's house when she left for her morning walk. It was still there when she returned forty-five minutes later. She'd been curious, nosey, really, although she didn't like to think of herself that way, she was simply interested, not judgmental. She'd stayed in her front yard, plucking out some new weeds that had sprung up. A few appeared every day, so there was always a bit of weeding that could be done. And that was the way to stay on top of it, grab them when there was a tender shoot with delicate roots, easy to slide out of the moist dirt.

By the time Brian's front door opened, she had a pile of limp greenery the size of her hand. Tanya strolled down Brian's front walk, swinging her hips, her bright red and brown skirt floating around her legs. Her hair looked almost white in the sharp mid-November light. It was braided and hung over one shoulder, loose strands flying out in all directions, unwashed and uncombed. Michelle turned her back so it wouldn't be obvious she was watching. Tanya's high heels tapped the concrete, then stopped. The car alarm chirped. Michelle glanced up. The front door of the house was closed, no sign of Brian's face in the kitchen window.

Was that her game? Now that she thought about it, Tanya was chummier with the men than with Claire or Michelle. As far as she knew, Tanya had never spoken to Mrs. Bennett or Elaine.

Tanya's seductive walk down the front path, her mussed hair, and her soiled clothes twisted Michelle's thoughts toward her own bedroom. She could no longer remember how long it had been since she and Gerard had done more than hold each other, maybe an occasional slipping of his hand up under her nightgown, a little nuzzling of their faces against each other.

She straightened and stared directly through the windshield

of the Prius, not caring if Tanya saw her watching. She wiped her hands on her workout pants even though they weren't dirty.

This time, the Prius was parked in front of Michelle's house. That was bold. It seemed that Tanya didn't care whether Michelle had been watching her, wasn't worried whether Michelle judged her for spending the night with a man she hardly knew, a man who was supposed to be an adversary.

The pile driver slammed into the earth. She felt the stab of a dilated blood vessel behind her left eye, shoving against a nerve, signaling a migraine ready to blast through her skull. So much for a soothing morning of pampering. It was as if none of it had ever happened.

She closed the car window and pulled into the driveway. She hit the remote and maneuvered the Camry into the garage next to Gerard's black Escalade. It was a tight fit and she had to be careful. Sometimes she wished he'd get a smaller car. Of course, now that she knew about his *hobby*, it all made sense. No wonder he wanted a car that looked like a military transport vehicle.

After pressing the remote, she got out of the car while the garage door closed. She entered the house and walked down the hall. The office door was open and the room was empty. She went toward the great room and paused near the entrance. Through the glass doors of the dining room she could see Gerard and Tanya seated at the patio table, their backs to the door. Part of her wanted to rush out there and demand answers from him right now, another part wanted to lie down and see if she could prevent the migraine from taking hold, and a third part didn't want to spoil her styled hair and didn't want to know any more about what Gerard was up to.

She crossed the two rooms and opened the sliding door. Both of them turned. Tanya's long, narrow fingers rested on Gerard's wrist. In his hand was a very large gun. Lying on the table was a smaller gun and an open, somewhat flimsy yellow cardboard box, filled with bullets.

Tanya kept her hand on Gerard's wrist, as if she didn't care that she'd been caught in the act. Although in the act of what, Michelle wasn't quite sure.

"Michelle! You're back early," Gerard said. He placed the gun in his lap. Tanya's hand slipped off his wrist.

"No I'm not."

"I guess we lost track of time." Tanya smiled, reminding Michelle of one of those women who is famous for nothing but being famous. Michelle couldn't put her finger on the name, but maybe it didn't matter — they were all essentially the same, their names were interchangeable.

Tanya remained seated, giving the impression she was waiting for Michelle to go back inside the house and close the door. Michelle crossed her arms, taking care not to bump her freshly painted nails on the sleeves of her sweater. They were long past dry, but had an irritating habit of picking up bits of fuzz that left rough spots in the glossy finish.

Finally Gerard stood. "I guess that's enough."

Tanya took her cue and stood. She pulled her jacket off the back of the chair. "You'll send me the web links?"

"It's not hard to remember," Michelle said. "Survive now dot com."

Tanya looked at Gerard. "He already sent me that one, but the others, you'll send them my way?"

"What others?" Michelle said.

Tanya shoved her arms into her jacket. Michelle glared at Gerard. "What *others* is she talking about?"

"More stuff about supplies. And weapons," Tanya said.

Michelle took a step back. Tears seeped into her eyes. She closed them. She would not cry in front of Tanya.

"What's wrong?" Gerard said.

"Aside from what I saw when I walked through that door?"

"What did you see?"

"A silly old fart thinking a young girl is attracted to him."

Tanya smiled and sat back down.

"That's not what it is at all. And I'm not an old fart."

"In her eyes you are."

"That's not very nice," Tanya said.

Gerard looked hurt. Michelle knew that looseness in his face, the slight drooping of his lower eyelids. She didn't care. She wanted to hurt him. "Please tell me you're not stupid as well as silly."

"Of course I'm not stupid."

"So you didn't show her anything … else?"

"Why would that be stupid?"

"You didn't."

"I didn't open the box."

"But you told her it was there?" Michelle shoved her hands in her pockets. Only after they were jammed deep inside did she remember her shiny, plum-colored nails. Too late now. And too late that she was blurting all this out right in front of Tanya. She was as lacking in discretion as Gerard. Stupid. But she couldn't stop. On a barely conscious level, she knew he'd shown everything to Tanya, so it didn't really matter.

"I just pointed it out."

"So you thought it was a good idea to show a total stranger that you're hiding tens of thousands of dollars in a barely secured wooden box? Not to mention enough weapons to take down this entire neighborhood?"

Gerard leaned against the table. "I don't understand why you're so upset."

"You know nothing about her, and now she knows everything about us. And I know her type."

"What type is that?" Tanya said.

"You're the kind of girl who becomes who people want you to be."

Tanya laughed, a short abrupt sound. "How can you possibly know that?"

"I know what you said to Claire, about Brian. And I know you're sleeping with Brian. I know that you're likely not a fanatical right wing person. You drive a Prius, for God's sake." She looked at Gerard. "Why don't you think things through?"

"I don't even know where to start parsing out that leap to a conclusion," Gerard said. "First of all, I'm not a fanatical right-winger."

"In this, you are. That's what all the people on that website are. They think the government is an evil entity." The pile driver slammed into the earth. Michelle yanked her hand out of her pocket and pressed her thumb against the bridge of her nose, trying to stop the pain, trying to keep her eyes from tearing — whether the tears were over Gerard's stupidity or from the growing pain of the migraine, she wasn't sure.

"There's a lot of cause for concern." Tanya's limp fingers brushed her hair off her face.

Michelle wanted to grab those fingers and twist them like a badly formed piece of clay. She opened the door and went into the dining room. She pulled out Gerard's chair at the head of the table and sat down, leaning her head into her hands. She pressed a thumb on each side of her nose, digging them into her eyeballs as if she could drive the pain out through the soft liquid. Behind the back fence, the pile driver slammed into the ground again. She winced.

"Why are you so upset?"

She looked up. Gerard stood just inside the doorway. He pulled the door closed. Through the glass, she could see Tanya still seated at the table, running her fingers along the nose of the larger gun.

"I'm *up-set* about the threat to our privacy. And your betrayal." Her eyes were so blurred she couldn't see his face, couldn't tell if his mouth was open or closed or decipher the expression in his eyes. Her husband was an idiot.

"I didn't touch her," he said.

"That's not the betrayal I'm talking about."

"Then what?"

Tears poured down her face. She lifted her head and tilted it back, letting the tears run to the back of her jaw. She slid her fingers across her cheeks. "Everyone knows. You told everyone but me. You've had this whole secret life behind my back; you think nothing of telling her everything, yet you hid it from me for … for how long? A year? Two years? Longer?"

"She was interested, you react like this." He waved his arm over his head.

"That's not fair."

"I'm only trying to keep you safe. To protect our family."

"From what?" Her voice was hoarse and raw. She coughed, choking on the moisture flowing out of her sinuses.

"From whatever happens."

"The most likely thing that's going to happen is that girl is going to report you for hoarding weapons. Or find someone willing to break in and steal the cash and the guns."

"She wouldn't do that."

"How do you know?" She was shouting, and she wondered how much Tanya could hear through the glass door. "She's a total stranger."

He pulled out a chair and dragged it close to hers. He sat down and slipped his arm around her waist. He shifted closer and pulled her head against his shoulder, stroking her face, not really wiping away the tears, but softening the muscle that had tightened along her jaw. He moved his hand down her neck and across her collarbone. He touched her breast and stroked it gently.

Michelle shoved her chair out and stood. Her tears dried up and all she felt was the migraine, coming on full force now, a knife blade behind her eyeball. She went to the door and flung it open. She slammed it closed and strode across the deck. She grabbed the gun out from under Tanya's loving fingers. She gripped it and pointed it at Tanya.

"Hey. Careful."

"Careful?" Michelle laughed. "Gerard's not careful, you're not careful. Why should I be?"

"It's loaded. I think he released the safety."

"Let's see. I'll pull the trigger and we'll see if he's completely lost his mind, sitting around with an enormous gun, ready to fire."

Tanya giggled.

Michelle had never fired a gun, but she knew to prepare for a recoil, and she knew how to aim, she'd aimed a garden hose at the base of her flowers every other day for most of her adult life. She was so close, how could she miss? The pile driver slammed into the unyielding California clay and she pressed the trigger.

MICHELLE STARED AT Tanya's body, still seated in the chair but slumped forward, blood seeping across her scalp through her blonde hair, harsh and angry, dripping onto her dark jeans where it looked like water.

She carefully placed the gun on the table. Her position blocked Gerard's view of Tanya. He was still seated at the dining room table. He obviously didn't realize what she'd done — the pile driver had overpowered the sound of gunfire. What a mess. It felt so good to do something, when for months, maybe years, she'd done nothing, followed others, letting things simmer inside, never taking control of a situation. This still didn't solve her problem with Gerard and his paranoid plans, but at least no one else in their neighborhood would find out about them.

Blood continued to spread across Tanya's scalp. Now it was dripping on the deck. If she was honest, she was kind of impressed with herself for such excellent aim. She shivered. For a few moments, she'd been unaware of her migraine. Now it returned with a vengeance. She wouldn't be able to hide what she'd done without Gerard's help. Why had he chosen that moment, with that women sitting there, to touch her breast for the first time in months? What was wrong with him? But there was no time to think of that now. They needed to clean this up.

The construction site was silent. Work was finished for the

day. The chances of a neighbor or friend coming by were extremely low, but she couldn't leave a corpse sitting on her back deck.

She went to the sliding glass door and pulled it open. "Gerard. There's been an accident. You need to help me."

His expression was difficult to read, his voice flat. "What."

"I shot her."

He stood. "What?"

"You shouldn't leave a huge gun like that sitting around loaded and ready to fire. She laughed at me. I shot her. But unless you want me to go to prison, you need to help me figure out what to do. You have all these survival skills. Is there anything in your forums about disposing of dead bodies?"

He hurried to where she stood, pushed her out of the way, and looked at Tanya's body. He turned and stared at Michelle.

She expected him to curse, to give her a speech, maybe even cry at the loss of his protégée, or whatever she was. Instead, he went to the table and picked up the gun. He fiddled with it, presumably re-setting the safety.

"Go get a cloth to wipe this down and I'll put them away." He placed the gun on the table. "First, I'll go move her car."

"Where to?"

"Not far. Somewhere along Billings."

"What if someone sees you? What if you drop hairs or skin in the car?"

"If I'm casual, no one will notice. I'll wear my nylon jacket that has the hood. And gloves."

She sighed. Maybe he had studied disposal of bodies. His reaction was strange. But then, so was hers. She felt numb and wondered if he felt the same.

When he returned, they worked in silence, wrapping Tanya in towels and then large trash bags. Gerard said the construction site was the obvious place to leave her and Michelle wondered how they would get inside the fence. He went to the garage and returned with heavy-duty wire cutters.

When it was completely dark and they were sure the blood had stopped, they carried the body across the backyard and into the side door of the garage. They put it in the back of the Escalade. Gerard decided it was best to wait until about two-thirty. Any time after eleven or twelve p.m., they were almost guaranteed deserted streets, but it was still a huge risk. They decided that once Gerard cut a hole in the fence, Michelle would stand by the car. If anyone came by, she would double-over, feigning severe pain, hopefully with enough drama to keep a curious passerby's attention on her.

It had started to drizzle when they left the house. By the time Gerard cut the fence and dragged the body to the opening, Michelle was drenched with sweat and rain. While she waited for him, it occurred to her that she hadn't felt so connected to him, so singular in their thoughts and plans in a very long time. The thought made her cry, so that between the sweat and the rain and her tears, she felt as if her whole body was dissolving.

Twenty-eight

IT RAINED ON Sunday, making it a perfect day for a late lunch in the dimly lit pizza parlor.

After a nod from Doug that the Joey-oriented toppings were okay with him, Claire ordered a large olive and sausage pizza, coke, and a pitcher of beer. She opened her wallet.

Doug reached across her and handed two twenties to the clerk. "My treat," he said.

"This is my *thank you* for bringing Joey home."

"I already told you I don't need thanks."

If she wasn't thanking him, then why were they here? She pulled out her credit card. "I want to pay."

"Put it away."

"I'm already indebted to you, I don't want to…"

"You don't owe me anything."

She slipped her card back in her wallet, picked up Joey's soda, and went to the table. She didn't like him paying, didn't like yielding to him. It wasn't that, exactly. She didn't like adding someone else to the list of people she leaned on — Brian, Greg, now owing even more to Doug. Sure, anyone would have brought Joey home. In fact, Joey could have limped home by himself, but somehow, after all those hours of absolute terror, Doug was the face that wiped it all away and she felt indebted, even if that feeling made no sense.

Of course, eating a pizza didn't make her dependent on him. But, this wasn't a date and there was no reason for him to pay. Why did so many men think they had to pick up the check? It was a subtle assertion of authority, or maybe it wasn't. All she knew was that she didn't want to owe him anything.

It was disorienting, waiting for him to bring the pitcher of beer to the table. She was suddenly aware of how unbalanced her life was, revolving around her son, cooking only for the two of them. She rarely ate with other adults. Every month or so they visited her parents, and when she didn't have errands to run, she ate lunch with her friends at work, but most of the time it was she and Joey, seated across from each other at their kitchen table.

The pizza was hot and deliciously cheesy, the beer crisp and cold. Beer must have been invented to go perfectly with pizza, there was no other food that she really enjoyed it with, but hot, soft cheese and sausage and rich tomato sauce made her crave the penetrating chill of beer.

It took Joey all of twelve minutes to consume three slices of pizza and two glasses of coke. She held out a five-dollar bill for video games. "How many quarters will you get?"

"Twenty."

"Perfect."

"What if I run out?"

"We'll worry about that if it happens."

He took the bill and strolled to the counter. She could almost see his back and shoulders straighten as he imagined himself old enough to conduct his own financial transactions.

"He's a great kid," Doug said. "You've done an amazing job all by yourself."

"It's not all me."

"I had the impression his father wasn't around much. Joey doesn't mention him."

"No, I guess he doesn't."

Doug filled their mugs half way. After a moment he said, "Not a subject you want to discuss?"

She wrapped her hands around the mug, cooling them on the icy glass. She pulled them away — not a good way to keep her beer nicely chilled. "Have you ever been married?" she said.

"Three diamond rings, no wedding." He picked up a slice of pizza and bit off the tip. "That sounds ominous, sorry about that."

"What happened? Or is that too personal?" It wasn't really fair to pry into his past when she'd diverted him from asking about Greg, but the way he put it was almost an invitation. Or maybe it was just a practiced response.

"They couldn't deal with my sister. They knew about her, but when they had to face the reality of moving in with her, being around her every day and every night, they ran for the hills." He laughed.

It didn't sound bitter, but his laugh felt out of context. She wasn't sure if she should smile or not. "I don't understand."

"My sister was in a car accident when she was twenty. She's a quadriplegic."

"Oh. Oh, how terrible." She picked a sliced black olive off her pizza and positioned it near the tip.

"Our parents are gone, so she lives with me. I'm pretty much all she has. I have someone come in to bathe her and help with physical therapy, massage and stuff, but other than that, I take care of her. And that's how it will be. For the rest of her life."

"That must be so hard for her. Being completely helpless, depending on you for everything. I would hate that." She swallowed her beer. "I'm sorry, I shouldn't have said that, but …"

"She's pretty philosophical about it."

"How?"

"She wasn't, at first. But it's been eight years. She's come to this place where she knows she can enjoy things that other people can't, like sitting for an hour listening to the birds, or looking at the garden and not thinking about watering it or weeding it. Just being."

"I just can't imagine being so helpless." She glanced behind her. Joey stood in front of a game console, his shoulders and arms moving in perfect rhythm as he chased whatever digitized characters danced across the screen.

"You'd hate just enjoying the experience of being alive?"

She turned back to face him. "Depending on someone else for everything."

"It's not like there's anything she can do about it. I admire her for accepting it and not turning angry or bitter and making everyone else miserable."

His tone was level, as if he had also done quite a bit of accepting. It didn't sound as if he was trying to make her feel guilty for blurting out something so unfair. His eyes were kind, looking at her, not smiling but still holding a gentle glint. It was the same solid connection with her eyes that she'd noticed before, like he was really listening to her, thinking about the person he was talking to, trying to understand what she was saying. It was very unusual.

She glanced away. She knew she shouldn't make a big deal out of his sister's dependence, but she felt nauseous even thinking about it. Not being able to go anywhere on her own, never earning her own money, not even being able to eat or get into bed at night or use the bathroom without someone to help her.

"Being dependent isn't the worst thing in the world," he said.

"For me it is."

"You sound angry."

"I feel terrible for your sister." She folded her hands, pressing the bases of her fingers together, feeling the wide silver band she wore on her middle finger dig into the bone. "What's her name?"

"Susan. Why is being completely dependent on someone the worst thing in the world?"

She sipped her beer. "It just is."

The background bleep of video games and the rumble of conversation grew more distinct, then faded, until she felt like they were sitting inside a bubble of silence, all the world slipping away around them. She took another sip of beer. "I like to take care of myself."

"Depending on each other is part of life. I depend on her too."

"For what?"

"She keeps me centered. She's good company — she's funny. And smart."

"I don't like depending on people."

"You really can't live like that."

"I can."

"You don't need anyone? Not even Joey?"

"That's different. I guess you have a point."

"But that's it?"

"I depend on Brian for childcare, but I'm living for the day I don't need him anymore. My ex-husband owns the majority of my house. I hate needing him to pay the mortgage, hate taking money from him. *Hate* it. In one more year I'll be done with college and then law school. It seems like forever, but I won't be happy until I'm out from under him and can take care of myself."

"I can see that. But you can't be happy until then? That's a long time."

"I'm happy, just … anxious. I want to be self-sufficient."

"It's not really like you're depending on your ex. Joey is. You have the house for him."

"It feels like I am."

He took a long swallow of beer. "It must be hard to get close to people if you don't want to depend on anyone."

"Maybe. I'm just focused. I have goals."

"Like I said, my sister's situation scares a lot of people."

Claire looked at him. He still looked calm and self-possessed. His sister was a very lucky woman. Then she smiled at the irony of thinking that a woman confined to a chair and a bed was lucky. Completely helpless, but lucky.

THEY'D SPENT SO long talking, dusk had settled in by the time they left the restaurant. The pavement was slick and the cars were wet. A light drizzle was still falling. Claire felt as if an entire lifetime had passed while they'd eaten pizza, sipped beer, and given Joey quarters to feed into the game machines. Despite the dampness and the shadowy sky, something inside her heart felt strangely light.

They climbed into the cab of Doug's truck and drove the four blocks back to Claire's house. When she unlocked her front door, Doug touched her elbow. "I had a good time."

"Me too. And thank you so much."

He winked. "Told you ... I did nothing. Is it okay if I call you?"

She laughed.

"Really."

Claire smiled. "Do you want some coffee?"

"I'd rather go for a walk. Burn off some pizza. Clear my head of beer fuzz."

"It's raining," she said.

"Not any more."

"Can I ride my skateboard?" Joey said.

"It's too wet."

"I should get my exercise."

She and Doug laughed at the same time. Doug put his hand on Joey's shoulder. For a moment, her heart tightened. Then she let go of her breath.

Doug looked at her. His hair was damp from the drizzle, darker with the porch light shining on it. He didn't shift his gaze and as she continued to meet his eyes, she realized he knew her breath had caught in her throat for that brief moment.

"Okay," Claire said. "Just be careful. No stunts."

They walked to the corner. Joey pushed ahead, rounded the corner, then stopped. He stood on his skateboard and peered through the opening in the canvas. He backed away from the fence and propelled his skateboard along the sidewalk to the next opening. He shouted back, "When do they start building stuff?"

Doug walked to where Joey stood. Claire moved up to the spot where Joey had been a moment earlier. She looked through the opening. It was so desolate, so enormous. It made everything seem unstable, as if the surrounding houses were too fragile, easily bulldozed into nothing but splinters of wood and chunks of plaster and glass. That's what had happened to the previous building — faded wood siding, built in the 1970s, plowed into a tangle of boards and sheetrock. The total destruction had taken less than three days. The new building would be steel and glass, seemingly more permanent, but she wondered about that. It looked contemporary now, but what would be the impression in forty years? At one time, the single story complex had been viewed as a modern design.

It really didn't matter. She wouldn't be living here. In forty years, Joey would be an adult, hopefully with a child or two of his own. He'd have a wife, a career, a house. Where would she be?

She moved away from the fence and walked to where Doug stood behind Joey, explaining the next steps in the building process.

Joey climbed on his board and glided to the next viewing spot. He was silent for a few minutes. "Is that a person?" he said. His voice was low, traveling the few yards to where Doug and Claire stood, but with the quality of a whisper.

"No one's down there now," Doug said.

They walked to where Joey stood. His legs wobbled on the skateboard as he worked to keep it from rolling sideways.

"It looks like someone's legs."

"No one works on Sunday," Doug said. "It's probably a tarp covering equipment."

"You should look," Joey said.

He pushed his skateboard away from the opening. Claire stepped up to the fence.

"On the bottom. Way down in the lowest part," Joey said.

It was getting dark fast, but the sky had cleared and the moon was already out, bright and nearly full, shining across the bottom of the pit. What looked like the lower part of someone's body lay a few yards from the foot of the dirt ramp, partially hidden by a concrete post with rebar sticking out of the top, reminding her of Medusa's hair in the dim light.

She squinted. It couldn't possibly be a person. She stepped back.

Doug took her place, ducking slightly to look through the opening. "Shit." He glanced at Claire. "Sorry."

"It's okay," Joey said. "I know that word."

Doug chuckled, then stopped abruptly. "It does look like a woman's legs."

"Is she hurt?" Joey said.

Doug backed away from the fence.

"There's a hole," Joey said. "Someone cut all the wires on

the fence."

Claire and Doug walked along the sidewalk to where he stood. A large opening had been snipped in the chain link fence. The canvas mesh was cut. Doug pushed it aside and went through.

"Don't you think we should call the police?" Claire said.

"Not until we know for sure what's going on."

Joey put one foot on the skateboard and rolled it back and forth. "Maybe she's sleeping. Like I was."

"Right," Doug said. "We should check it out. Why don't you two wait here and I'll be back in a minute." He stepped over the pipe that ran along the lip of earth just inside the fence. He made his way down the slope to the edge of the pit.

"I want to look too," Joey said.

Claire squeezed his shoulder. "It's too dangerous."

"It's not dangerous. I want to see." He twisted out from her fingers and slipped through the opening.

"Joey! I don't want you to go." If it was what she thought it was, and she was almost a hundred percent sure it was a woman's body. That was not the image she wanted burned into Joey's tender brain when he was seven years old.

Joey slid down the dirt slope, scrambling to catch up with Doug. His desire to get a close look at the potentially horrific sight outweighed his usual willingness to more or less comply with most of what she told him to do, or not do. She wasn't sure whether it was Doug that had upset their usual balance.

"Your mom doesn't want you to go."

"You're going," Joey said.

He followed Doug along the perimeter to the ramp that led down to the bottom of the pit, a road, really, wide enough to accommodate an earthmover. It wasn't dangerous, and Joey was probably equally thrilled with the prospect of seeing something potentially bad as he was with the pure pleasure of getting back inside the pit he'd been staring into for the past six weeks. It was a dream come true. The fascination baffled her. Although maybe it shouldn't. There was something about that enormous hole in the earth, something that made her feel exposed, small and helpless. She didn't think about it very often, but when she was walking past, it was impossible not to look. And she'd been anesthetized by years of life. She could imagine that a child's brain would find it so intriguing, it almost seemed otherworldly.

Doug and Joey reached the bottom of the ramp and made their way past several concrete pillars to the one where the figure lay. Doug stopped about ten feet away and she knew it was what they'd thought. He held out his arm, his fingers spread, palm facing toward Joey. Her stomach collapsed as she watched him try to protect Joey. She ducked through the opening, wanting to race down the ramp and pull Joey away before he got too close, but it was too late.

There were competing demands, always, to protect her son and to expose him to life so that he absorbed its realities as he grew. The tricky part was getting the timing right. Was six too young to know a little about sex? Was four too old to tell him other children would laugh at him if he sucked his thumb? What about later? At what age would he stay home alone? Walk to school by himself? Would that ever happen? Surely he had to find his own way to school when he was sixteen or seventeen, he couldn't have his mother going with him, but when? How were you supposed to know? She was pretty sure that seeing a corpse at age seven wasn't right, but was it ever right?

Doug stepped closer to the body, his arm still outstretched. For whatever reason, despite his willful disobedience in chasing Doug through the opening and down into the pit, Joey yielded to the warning of the outstretched hand. Maybe all her questions were theoretical. It was possible children had plenty of their own instincts that helped keep them from the wrong things at the wrong time. Although if that were true, why the national epidemic of fourteen year-olds drinking alcohol and having sex?

Doug bent over the object on the ground. He moved back and took Joey's hand. He led him away from the pillar and up the ramp to where Claire waited.

"It's that lady," Joey said. "I could see. Her hair is all bloody."

Doug pulled his cell phone out of its case and pressed 9-1-1. "Maybe you should take him home."

"It's okay," she said.

After Doug described what they'd found, he ended the call

and put the phone away. They walked back to the spot where the fence had been cut. They waited in silence.

Twenty-nine

BRIAN STEPPED ONTO the swampy backyard lawn. After clearing overnight, it had rained again all day. He should have taken the day off. He'd had an impossible time focusing on the thirty-three moist faces staring at him from tiny desks.

He'd been on his way to work that morning when Claire flung open her door and ran down the front walk, her long dark curls damp and snaking around her neck, falling across her shoulders, draped around her arms, her face unnaturally pale against her dark red sweater. She darted across the street and met him in his driveway. Talking too fast, she'd told him about Tanya.

He tried to swallow while she talked, not comprehending any of her words after *dead*. He felt as if a fistful of tiny steel balls were rattling around in his heart, spilling up into his throat. He hadn't let on that Tanya was his lover. He wanted to absorb his loss in private. He'd coughed several times, trying to clear the phlegm. Finally, he'd thanked her for telling him. *Thanked* her! He had no idea why. As if she'd done him a favor. He supposed when someone gave you information they thought you should have, the natural reaction was to express gratitude. Still, his instinctive response upset him.

He'd left school the minute his classroom was emptied of children. When he'd pulled into the cul-de-sac, it was quiet. Because of the rain, the construction site was silent. Or maybe because of finding Tanya's body there. This was a perfect opportunity to spend a few hours in his pottery shed. He'd face his grief in clay. He wished he could sculpt an image of Tanya, but maybe later. He needed to stick with one thing, and right now, he planned to focus on a new piece — another attempt at a replica of Cleopatra.

He'd known immediately, while Claire was still talking, who had killed Tanya — that nut case next door. For some reason that he couldn't identify, along with his absurd *thank you*, he didn't mention his certain knowledge to Claire. It could be he wanted to share that information personally with the police. It could be he wanted to hold it inside and brood for a while. Life was cruel. To take both the women he loved. Yes, Cleopatra was the one who had taken his first love, so he couldn't blame *Life* for that. But in a way, it wasn't really Cleopatra's fault. She was simply following her nature, her desire to eat, her natural predatory behavior. Jennifer had been stupid not to recognize Cleopatra's jealousy. People acted as if snakes had no feelings. Because they were cold blooded, everyone assumed they lacked emotion, no thoughts beyond survival. They attributed all kinds of human characteristics to dogs, or cats, even rodents. Loyalty, affection, proud independence. It was wrong to assume snakes and other reptiles didn't also have those traits. If snakes weren't capable of loyalty and jealousy, then neither were German Shepherds. Cold blooded simply meant a creature that changed its nature to adapt to the environment. Why was that considered a bad thing?

It was obvious Gerard had shot her. The Reynes loathed that construction site, especially Gerard with his view that it represented a government conspiracy. Gerard was completely capable of gunning down the woman who was the focal point for all their frustration and helplessness.

When they lay in bed after the most pleasant female encounter he'd ever experienced, Tanya had giggled again about Gerard. *He was bragging about all his guns. Like I care*, she said. Her hair, silky as rabbit fur, draped across his skin. He hadn't been able to stop stroking it. Her long neck was exposed as she let her head collapse back on the pillow, plumped up under her neck, so it looked whiter and even longer, with that prominent Adam's apple stretched into something that looked incredibly vulnerable. Her voice was low and slightly rough, perhaps because of the unnatural angle of her neck. Her eyes were closed, her lids as white as the skin stretched across that bulge inside her throat.

"It was like he had a hard-on over those guns," Tanya said. "His eyes got all glassy and he was almost hopping around, describing them to me. Like he wanted to expose himself. Then his wife got suspicious and came flying out to shut him up, but I don't think she realized how much he'd already said."

"Why did he tell you?"

She was quiet for a moment. "It started out that he wanted to explain how important it was to prepare for the future, for all kinds of possibilities, but then it turned into something else."

"Into what?"

"I don't know." She sighed and moved his other hand to her belly. He let it rest there, feeling her soft flesh.

"He's preparing for Armageddon or whatever, but it's morphed into feeling powerful, like he's a real man because he has all those guns and stuff."

The memory of Tanya's skin against his wouldn't go away. He rubbed his face with both hands, as if he could squash the thoughts out of his head like he could re-form a lump of clay. The key to the shed, cupped in his right hand, scraped the corner of his eyelid. He cried out and pulled his hands from his face. Squinting from his damaged eyelid, it took several tries to get the key inserted into the lock. He pushed open the door and stepped inside.

Because of the thick layer of charcoal gray clouds covering the sky, the room was quite dark. He hadn't thought about that. Natural light from the high, narrow windows than ran around all four walls created a more peaceful, organic environment, but he'd never worked out here late on a rainy afternoon and the gloominess surprised and upset him. This was supposed to be therapeutic, life giving, not the atmosphere of a crypt. And it did feel like that, now that he thought of it, glancing around at all the half-formed figures. He thought he'd smashed it more thoroughly, but the head and the torso were still obvious, so that it looked like a half-eaten human being. He walked over and pressed on the clay to further destroy the shape. It had dried too much and resisted the pressure from the heel of his hand. He pulled off the head and used both hands to flatten it. Then he placed the lump of clay on the shelf. That was better.

He hoped this hadn't been a mistake, but he heard rain spattering on the roof, so he might as well stay. It would stop again soon and then he'd go back inside the house.

After twenty minutes or so, the shape sitting on the wood platform was disappointing. It was only a coil, nothing more than what a child would make in his first experience with a piece of clay, rolling his palms across it until it stretched out into something that had the shape, but none of the character, of a snake. The head looked nothing like the wide, slightly pentagonal shape of Cleopatra's head, lacking the beveled edges that formed her jaw. The clay itself bore no resemblance to the delicate pattern of scales covering her body. Of course, that part would come at the end anyway. Right now he had to get her head right.

He decided to form it so the mouth was partially open,

showing her teeth, with a small space where her tongue would protrude. Already he was feeling better. The act of creating, focusing on using his hands, helped ease the ache that radiated out of his heart through every pore of his body. He moistened his fingers and pushed at the clay to broaden the head. When the shape looked fairly close to what he wanted, he used the sculpting knife to dig out small sockets where he'd place her eyes.

Progress had been minimal by the time it was too dark to continue working. He stood and stepped away from the worktable. His effort would look better from a few feet away, he was too close to it. He went to the door and opened it to let in what was left of the fading light. He turned back to the sculpture and cried out as if he'd come upon Cleopatra's dead body. It looked nothing like her! It was a blob of grayish clay, the depressions made by his fingers obvious all across the head, the jaw disproportionately large on the left.

It was so wrong to think that recreating her would be easier than his unseen child's face. It was even more difficult. He would never capture her pride, her elegance. The delicate scales, the perfect markings of pale yellow and white. He couldn't even sculpt her body in a realistic fashion, he'd never be able to hint at the intelligence in her eyes, the perfect blend of predatory lust and sharp observation.

He grabbed the hammer off its hook and pounded the head. This was the second piece he'd destroyed with violence. There was something tightening inside him so he couldn't view anything with composure. He wasn't an artist at all. But as he pounded at the clay, something strange happened — it was suddenly clear that he wasn't cut out to create things. He was a lover. He knew how to give love. That was his purpose on the earth, loving his students. Loving Antony and Cleopatra, loving Claire. Even though it wasn't the love of a man and woman, he still loved her. And Joey. And Tanya, most of all. Even Jennifer. He was meant to give love but all the women he loved slipped through his fingers. He'd never hold the child that had been growing in Jennifer's womb, never be able to create a child with Tanya. Or Claire.

He walked out of the shed, the backs of his hands covered with splatters of moist clay. He left the padlock hanging loose. He wasn't sure why he'd ever kept the shed locked. No one came into the backyard, and even if they did, so what?

He opened the sliding glass door by pushing at the handle with his elbow so he didn't get clay all over it. After he washed his hands, he considered going in to spend some time with Antony and Cleopatra. The doorbell rang.

It was only dusk, but felt later because of the clouds, heavier and darker now, so black it seemed as if they'd soaked up the sky. He flicked on the hall light and went to the door. He peeked out and saw blonde hair, a face distorted by the peephole, and for half a second he thought it was Tanya. His eyes filled with tears. He looked through the peephole. The bell rang again and he opened the door.

"Brian Adams?" The blonde woman held up a leather case,

displaying a badge. "I'm Detective Burgess. Myself and another officer have been talking to everyone in the area about the death of Tanya Montgomery. May I come in?"

"What do you want to know?"

"I have a few questions. May I come in?"

Was he a suspect? Why did she want to talk to him? "What kind of questions?"

"It would be more comfortable if we could sit down."

"Why?"

"Okay then. We'll talk here. Were you aware that Ms. Montgomery's body was found at the construction site last evening?"

"Yes."

"How did you know?"

"Claire told me."

"Ms. Simpson?"

He nodded.

"Did you hear anything Saturday? See any unfamiliar vehicles on your street?"

"No."

"Where were you?"

"Home. In my office, grading papers. I'm a schoolteacher."

"What kind of relationship did you have with Ms. Montgomery?"

"What does that mean?"

"Had you ever talked to her on a personal level?"

So they didn't know about him and Tanya. How would

they? "Yes."

"Under what circumstances?"

He hesitated. He couldn't pause too long or she'd know he was weighing how much of the truth to reveal, and if he didn't reveal all of the truth, he'd be branded a liar. "We were friends."

"From before?"

"No. I emailed her some complaints, and one thing led to another and she came over for dinner."

"How did one thing lead to another?"

He didn't want to mention Antony and Cleopatra. But if he didn't, how would he explain? "I don't know. Do you have any idea who killed her?"

"That's what we're trying to find out."

Brian glanced at the house next door. Should he mention Gerard's armory? The police might find out all on their own and then he wouldn't get dragged into it. The less said the better. He'd provide a minimal amount of information and they'd leave him alone. "We were sort of dating."

"How did that come about?"

"The usual way."

"Were you jealous of Ms. Montgomery?"

"Jealous? Why would I be jealous?"

"Protective. Did you have any arguments?"

He realized his mistake. Now the officer had leaped to the idea that he was even more interesting as a candidate for her list of suspects because she'd boxed him into the cliché of jealous boyfriend, controlling and possibly violent. "No. We only started dating about a week ago."

"And was Ms. Montgomery interested in continuing the relationship? As far as you know?"

"Of course she was."

"Do you know anyone who might have had a reason to kill her?"

He glanced at the Reynes' house again. When he looked back at the detective, a thin line had formed between her brows. So. She suspected him. It was too startling and unexpected that he was dating the Disturbance Coordinator. Pointing a finger at Gerard might make it look like a nervous attempt to divert attention. Besides, once he had more time to think, maybe it would be better to punish Gerard himself. The thought calmed him. He wasn't sure why he hadn't considered it before. "Not really."

"Not really? Or a definitive no?"

"No. I don't know who killed her. I've hardly adjusted to the fact she's gone."

The detective nodded.

"Do you own any weapons?"

"No."

The detective pulled a business card out of her shirt pocket. She held out the card, waiting for him to take it.

Brian grabbed it and stuck it in his back pocket.

"I'll probably stop by again, once I've talked to the rest of your neighbors."

"Did she suffer?"

"What do you mean?"

"Tanya. Did she die instantly, or was she in pain."

"The bullet was through her forehead. I doubt she felt anything."

Brian nodded. "I hope you find the shit-head."

The officer's face remained blank. It seemed his rude comment hadn't penetrated her shield of professionalism.

When she was gone, his mind ran through all of the things she might have asked, but didn't. He wasn't sure why he worked so hard to prevent people from learning about Antony and Cleopatra. It didn't really matter what anyone thought, and it would just made him look like he had something to hide if he continued dancing around her questions, or gave vague responses. If the detective came back, when she came back, he'd tell her everything. He felt in his pocket for the card. He could call her now, tell her he'd been caught off guard and hadn't been thinking clearly. He pulled out his hand. No, better to wait.

He went down the hall to Antony and Cleopatra's room. Tanya's love for them had been so real, so pure. She wondered why he kept them trapped in such small boxes. The boxes were an appropriate size, but he could see how they looked confined, coiled back upon themselves. In honor of Tanya, he'd let them out. He could still fix up the room to better accommodate their needs, maybe create a floor-to-ceiling built-in terrarium, but there was no reason they had to stay in the glass cases while he did that. They could enjoy their freedom now. Tanya would be pleased.

He lifted both pythons out of their terrariums and placed them on the floor. He moved into the corner and slid his back down the wall until he was seated in a cross-legged position. As they began to explore, he thought about how he might punish Gerard.

Thirty

MICHELLE WATCHED THE police detective walk away from Brian's house. Her house would be next. She wiped her hands on her jeans and picked up her glass of water. She took a small sip. If she drank too much, she'd have to pee when the detective was talking to her, and that might make her too nervous, leaving in the middle of the conversation, having too much time to think about how she was coming across.

From what Michelle had been able to tell as she peered through the narrow gap in the living room curtains, the detective had spoken to Brian for less than ten minutes. Now she stood at the end of the Reynes' front path. She flipped through her notebook, although Michelle couldn't imagine what she was able to make out in the darkness. The streetlights hadn't come on yet, timed for nightfall rather than a storm.

Michelle hadn't told Gerard the detective was making the rounds of the cul-de-sac — and she had no doubt the woman dressed in sturdy shoes, slacks, a button-down shirt, and nylon jacket was a police detective. It was best if Gerard was naturally surprised so he didn't start putting on an act. She wasn't sure how good he was at lying. Men weren't usually as adept at it as women. They got too aggressive, tried too hard. They didn't have as much practice swallowing their feelings, making nice, and offering false compliments. Women were shadier characters. She laughed to herself. Of course, Gerard had been lying to her for ages, so maybe he was quite good at it.

The bell rang. She took another sip of water and walked slowly to the front hall. She stood behind the door to the count of ten, and just when she thought the detective might press the bell again, she turned the deadbolt and opened the door. She'd been right, the detective's arm was outstretched, her finger poised near the doorbell.

Detective Burgess introduced herself, displayed her badge, and explained about Tanya Montgomery's body, as if everyone didn't already know about it. She asked to come in.

Michelle had noticed Brian left the detective standing on the porch, but being friendly and polite was a better tactic. She opened the door slowly and stepped back. She gestured toward the front room.

"Is your husband home?"

"Yes, I'll go get him."

Detective Burgess held up her hand. "Why don't I ask you a few questions first."

Michelle nodded. They sat facing each other, the detective on the leather armchair and Michelle on the edge of he sofa. Her legs would get tired, sitting forward like this, but she didn't want to slide back and look too comfy. Hopefully it would go quickly. Hopefully she'd stay calm and not contradict herself or say something stupid. She wished Gerard were here.

"Did you know Ms. Montgomery?"

"Not really."

"But you'd spoken to her personally?"

"Yes."

"Under what circumstances?"

"She came around sometimes, talked to the neighbors. My husband chatted with her more than I did."

"So you had a friendly relationship with her?"

"I wouldn't say that."

"What would you say?"

"We were polite. It wasn't her fault we have to put up with this destruction of our neighborhood, but it wasn't as if she could do anything to help make things right."

"Did you see anyone unfamiliar in the area Saturday?"

Michelle shook her head.

"Did you hear any gunshots?"

"No."

"When did you learn that Ms. Montgomery's body was found in the construction site?"

"Claire told me."

"Your neighbor, Claire Simpson. And when was that?"

"This morning."

"It's surprising she didn't tell anyone last night after she spoke to us."

Michelle shrugged. It wasn't a question and she wasn't going to get lured into a chatty mood, it would be far too easy to slip up. Thank God Claire hadn't said anything last night, she surely wouldn't have been able to set the right tone of shock that quickly. She stood. "Should I get my husband?"

"Yes, please. Do you have any weapons in the house?"

Michelle swallowed. "No." Technically that was true, the guns were outside. Sticking close to the truth, no matter how misleading, made things easier. She felt her pulse was keeping a normal pace. They wouldn't have to take a lie detector test, would they? The space between her gums and her tongue was drowning in saliva. She swallowed harder, not quite able to get her muscles to contract properly. "I'll get Gerard." She hoped the detective didn't notice her voice was weak.

She hurried down the hall. The office door was closed, a habit he hadn't changed. "There's a detective here. She wants to ask you some questions about ... the body." She stepped into the room and closed the door as far as it would go without making any sound.

"Why me?"

"She already talked to me. She's going house to house."

He pushed his chair away from the desk. He lowered his voice. "What did you tell her?"

"Not now. Just stick to what we agreed."

She returned to the living room and was already seated on the couch when Gerard entered the room. He sat beside her. Although they weren't touching, she was overly aware of his body, the warmth of his skin, the smell of the oil that tended to accumulate on his scalp by the end of the day.

The detective ran through the identical list of questions, as if she was reading off a cheat sheet. Fortunately, Gerard gave similar answers. He stayed calm, and spoke boldly but not with too much volume when he was asked about the guns. It was a risk, lying about them. If there were ever a reason the police decided to search the homes in the area — their home — the lie would make them hugely suspect. But what was the likelihood of that? They needed evidence to get a warrant. As long as she and Gerard stayed calm, they were fine.

"Claire Simpson told me she saw Ms. Montgomery's car parked in front of your house Saturday. Do you have any idea why it was there?"

Michelle's confidence exploded inside her like a balloon that had been blown too large, the latex thin and impossibly taut.

"She was having some kind of relationship with the guy next door. Brian Adams," Gerard said.

Michelle smiled. She'd forgotten how smooth Gerard could be. Suddenly she was flung back thirty years. From the corner of her eye she saw the man she used to know, confident and in charge — not that guy huddled in a dark room over a computer, lurking in dangerous corners of a virtual world, or the guy losing his cool at a community meeting. This was the guy with dark hair and blue eyes, a guy that was thin and fit, with lean muscles and a charming smile. A guy who could sell ice to Eskimos, as the saying went. She put her hand on his leg. He covered her hand with his.

"Why was she parked in front of *your* house?"

The emphasis was slight, but Michelle felt a light chill run down her arms.

"Maybe Brian knows," Gerard said.

Detective Burgess stood. She tucked her notebook in her pocket and pulled her phone out of the opposite pocket. She glanced at the screen. "I'll have more questions after we've talked to everyone in the vicinity of the construction site and once I have a definite time of death."

"Any time," Gerard said. They escorted the detective to the front porch. Gerard closed the door and slid his arm around Michelle's waist. He put his chin on her head. "I think we handled that well," he said. His voice was low and soft.

She pressed against him and tried to recall each word, each change in expression on the detective's face.

The front door had been closed less than three minutes when the bell rang.

"What do you think she wants?" Michelle whispered.

Gerard squeezed her waist. He opened the door.

Brian stood on the front porch, his arms folded across his chest, his legs spread so he gave the appearance of a man imitating a police officer, but doing it badly. He smiled. His chin quivered slightly.

"How was your discussion with the detective?"

"Fine," Michelle said. "What's up?"

"Just wondering what she asked you." His chin trembled even more. His lips looked as if they were hanging off his face.

"Not much."

"Do you think someone in the neighborhood killed her?"

"That's highly unlikely," Gerard said.

"You're wrong. It's probably someone we know," Brian said.

Gerard dropped his arm from her waist. "Did you want something?"

"I want to know if you have any thoughts about her murderer."

"We're still slightly shocked," Michelle said.

Brian moved closer to the doorway. "It seems like you're not saying everything."

"Nope." Gerard pushed the door partially closed. "We just want to eat dinner."

"What's the big rush?"

"No rush, but it's dinnertime."

"You're retired. What difference does it make what time you eat, or sleep, or do anything?"

Michelle held her breath. Where was he headed? "Is there something you're trying to say?"

Tears swam in Brian's eyes. His lower lids were red, the rest of his face blanched, the skin almost transparent under the harsh porch light. She'd told Gerard not to put such high wattage bulbs out here. Yet another piece of the puzzle, the little things she'd noticed that meant nothing until she found out about his secret activities.

"Do you think they'll figure out who killed her?" Brian said.

"I hope so." It was silly of Brian to be so distraught over a woman he hardly knew. Of course, sleeping with her had made him feel there was more between them. He might not have seen Tanya for the chameleon she was. She became one person as she lured Gerard into spilling his guts, another when she poked at the concerns Claire was in denial over, and someone entirely different to persuade Brian she cared about him.

Brian was more vulnerable than she'd realized. When Jennifer left, he'd appeared to take it in stride. She'd never noticed even a whisper of grief, but now she realized he'd kept it hidden. His obvious longing for Claire, and the weight he put on his so-called relationship with Tanya, made her realize how lonely he'd been. Part of her felt sad. Still, she and Gerard were far above average in intelligence. They'd been very careful. No one would ever find out what they'd done.

"All they have to do is discover who around here owns a gun."

"There's more to it than that," Gerard said. "Her body could have been dumped there by anyone."

Brian stared at them. He no longer stood like the pseudo tough guy, arms crossed, legs spread. He looked like a child, sad and a little bit lost.

"Would you like to have dinner with us?" she said.

Gerard put his arm around her waist again, his hand tightened on her flesh. She didn't care. Brian was lost and alone, he wasn't a threat to them. In some ways, inviting him to dinner would make them appear innocent.

"No thanks. I'm not hungry." Brian turned and walked down the path.

Thirty-one

SINCE GREG WAS going out of town for an extended Thanksgiving weekend, Monday was the only night he said he could eat turkey dinner with his son. It figured that he thought Thanksgiving was only about the turkey and stuffing, but Claire agreed Joey could spend the night.

She stood on the porch and watched Greg make the u-turn around the cul-de-sac. Even though it was dark now and he probably couldn't see much, Greg's black lab, Willie, stuck his head out the partially lowered back window. His ears flapped in the breeze as Greg accelerated to the corner and turned onto Fairview without stopping. She couldn't see Joey at all, he must have ducked down to get something out of his backpack. At least Greg had come alone so Joey could sit in the front seat for once.

When Joey stayed overnight with his father, she looked forward to having time for herself. But the minute she was alone, she missed him. She'd probably make a grilled cheese sandwich for dinner, have a glass of red wine, and watch TV, but she wasn't quite hungry yet and she wasn't ready for that empty feeling, all those rooms and only herself to wander through them. The permanently closed door of the master bedroom seemed more melancholy when she was alone. One of these days she should open the door, get rid of the bed. The problem was, she couldn't afford a new one and she wasn't about to sleep in that bed.

All the lights in Brian's house were off. His fountain splashed softly in the quiet evening air. The Reynes' porch light was on and she could see the glow of interior lights through their white front room curtains. Maybe she'd invite herself over for a glass of wine. She stepped into the house, grabbed her purse, and walked back out into the chilly darkness. She locked the front door and slung her purse over her shoulder.

Michelle opened the door before Claire pressed the bell. "Oh. Hi. I thought you were Brian again."

"Was he here?"

Michelle nodded and stepped back, pulling the door open so Claire could come in. She didn't offer an explanation for why Brian had been there.

"I'm inviting myself over for a glass of wine. If you're not already eating dinner."

"I'm just starting to fix it, if you don't mind sitting at the counter. We can chat while I put things together. I think we could all use a glass of wine, after what happened."

Claire followed Michelle into the great room and over to the kitchen area. She pulled out a chair at the bar and set her purse on the granite countertop.

"Is Merlot okay?" Michelle said.

"Sure. Where's Gerard?"

"On the computer, as always." Michelle pulled the cork out of a half empty bottle sitting next to the cook top. She poured generous servings into two glasses and handed one to Claire. She lifted her glass and clicked the side of Claire's. "Happy Thanksgiving."

Something about her voice sounded uncertain, as if she wasn't even sure it was Thanksgiving.

"Are any of your boys coming home?"

Michelle shook her head gently as she sipped her wine. "Just Gerard and I this year. And you're going to your parents'?"

"Yes. Joey's with his dad tonight."

Michelle poured rice into a measuring cup and dumped it into a pot. She clamped on the lid and set the kitchen timer. "Is he okay after seeing the body?"

"He seems fine. We were with that guy who found Joey at the construction site, and he didn't let him get too close."

"Why were you with him?"

"I took him out for pizza. To thank him."

"Oh. That must have been awkward."

"Why?"

"I can't imagine you had much to talk about. Once you got

past *thanking* him."

Why did Michelle have that sour tone to her voice half the time? She managed to make it sound as if Claire had done something inappropriate.

"We talked a lot. He's a very interesting guy."

"Planning to start dating, finally?"

"I didn't say that."

"Sorry." Michelle topped off her wine. "I'm just in a bad mood."

"He talked quite a bit about his sister. She's a quadriplegic."

"Oh my."

"I can't stop thinking about her. He really admires her, I guess she's very accepting of her condition, sort of philosophical about life. But I just can't imagine. It sounds horrible, don't you think?"

"Yes, but why can't you stop thinking about it?"

"I don't know." Claire lifted her glass and sniffed the wine. She took a small sip. "All day I've been thinking about her, and you'd think my mind would be on the murder."

"I suppose," Michelle said.

"You never said why Brian was here."

Michelle opened the oven and peered inside. She closed it again. "He wanted to know what the detective asked us. He was very upset."

Claire sipped her wine. "Do you think …" Her voice sounded thin, as if she was on the verge of tears. She took another sip of wine. "Do you think he killed her?"

"Oh no."

"Why not?"

Michelle looked past her. For a moment her face lost all expression. Her lips parted slightly and her breathing was rough, picking up pace, almost as if she was gasping for air. "He was sleeping with her."

"Really? How do you know that?"

"I saw her come out of his house one morning."

"Oh." Claire moved her glass closer to the center of the counter. She didn't want to take another sip, not yet. She was drinking it too fast and already felt a mild buzz.

"Although. I guess that doesn't mean he couldn't have killed her." Michelle turned her back to Claire and lifted the lid off the rice pot. She stirred the contents with a wooden spoon and replaced the lid. "I always thought it was odd that his wife disappeared so fast."

"What do you mean?"

"She was there one day and then she was gone. We never saw her packing her car or doing anything to suggest she was leaving him."

"What are you saying?" Claire leaned her forearms on the counter but the hard surface made her bones ache. She sat up straight again.

Michelle moved away from the stove. She pulled her white cardigan sweater off her shoulders and yanked her arms out of the sleeves. She walked around the bar and placed it on the chair next to Claire. "I've always said there was something strange about him."

Claire thought about the snakes, those mysterious creatures she'd never seen. Those beasts that haunted her even when she wasn't asleep. She'd already dreamt about them twice, although in her dreams they never looked like Joey had described them — they were solid black. "Did you know he has ..."

"How long until dinner's ready?"

Claire turned. Gerard stood at the end of the bar, his hand resting on the chair where Michelle had dropped her sweater. His hair was mussed, poking out over his ears as if he'd been sleeping. His eyebrows, always somewhat unruly with a few wiry gray hairs, appeared even wilder than usual.

"Fifteen minutes," Michelle said.

As if he noticed Claire staring at him longer than necessary, he scowled. "Are you planning on staying for dinner?"

Claire took a quick sip of wine. "No. I just stopped by to say hi." She slipped off the chair and picked up her purse. "Thanks for the wine. And Happy Thanksgiving, if I don't see you before Thursday."

"Same to you," Michelle said.

"You don't have to rush out." Gerard picked up her glass and held it out to her. It still had a bit of wine in it.

"That's okay. I should get going." There was nowhere to get going to, no dinner to cook, nothing waiting at home, but since Gerard had entered the room, she felt she couldn't breathe. She felt neither of them was breathing much either.

Everyone was shaken up over the murder. She needed to turn on the TV and not think, go to bed early. "Bye." She walked to the front door and let herself out.

Brian's fountain now sounded like pebbles cascading over concrete, loud and insistent. Claire jogged across the street. Her purse slapped against her hip. She stabbed her key in the lock and opened the door. Inside, she turned off the porch light. She went into the kitchen and turned on the oven then into the hallway and adjusted the thermostat up a notch. While the oven heated, she sat down and pulled off her boots. She got out the bread and butter and cheese and a cookie sheet to toast her sandwich on.

After her sandwich was done, she poured a glass of Merlot. Drinking it by herself, getting lost in a TV drama would be soothing after the anxiety hovering around Michelle and Gerard. She wanted to forget about all of them now. And she especially wanted to stop thinking about Doug's poor sister, her useless limbs, her inability to even use the bathroom by herself. The poor girl couldn't make a grilled cheese sandwich or pour a glass of wine. Tears bubbled up in her eyes. She wiped them away with the back of her hand and felt a surge of anger. Life was so unfair.

She fell asleep on the couch and when she woke, the news was on. She turned it off quickly before there was a chance of any local updates that might mention the body at the medical center construction site. Sleeping after drinking the wine made her feel limp. She left her plate and glass on the coffee table. She didn't have the energy to pull out the hide-a-bed.

She went down the hall to Joey's room. Without turning on the light, she crossed the room and felt for the comforter. She pulled it back and slid under. The pillow smelled of Joey. She smiled and pulled the comforter up around her shoulders, turned on her side, and hugged her knees close to her stomach.

SHE WOKE SHAKING. Her stomach felt like it was filled with mud and her forehead ached. She tried to sit up, but the shaking wouldn't stop. She'd dreamt she was sleeping in the master bedroom, on top of the mattress without sheets or blankets. When she'd woken in her dream, the floor was covered with snakes — slimy black things. They had large yellow eyes and they slithered over each other as if they were searching frantically for food. Even now, she could hear them crawling, the friction of skin against skin sounded like two pieces of paper rubbed together, louder than the sound of their occasional hissing.

Sweat broke out on the back of her neck and along her spine. She felt she could still see their eyes, glaring at her in the darkness. She screeched and threw back the comforter and jumped out of bed. Her feet landed on Joey's skateboard. The force of her weight sent it sliding across the floor. She tried to jump off but her heel landed on the back edge. The board shot up in the darkness, both feet wrenched to the side, and she fell. Pain shot through her legs. She cried out, a wordless, formless plea for someone to help.

She tried to sit up, but her lower left leg wouldn't move. She rolled carefully to her right side and pushed herself onto her hip. Her right foot throbbed. Her kneecap felt like it had been hit with a hammer. She started to cry. It was so dark. At least she'd forgotten about the dream of snakes for a moment, but now the images and sounds returned in vivid detail.

She lay back down, sobbing. The first part of her dream flashed through her mind. Doug's sister. In the dream, Claire had gone to the construction site looking for Tanya. She'd wanted to register a complaint about Brian's snakes. Susan had been sitting in her motorized wheelchair at the bottom of the pit. She was singing, her voice carrying up the sides, filling the entire site. Claire felt she needed to get into the site to help her, but there was no way in. The gates were locked, and the tree Joey had climbed had been cut down. Then she was in the master bedroom, surrounded by the snakes.

Surely there was nothing permanently wrong with her legs, although she was pretty sure the left leg was broken because she couldn't move it at all. At least she had her arms.

Hoisting herself onto her right elbow, she stretched her arm in the general direction of the doorway and pulled the rest of her body forward. The carpet scraped against her jeans. The sound reminded her of the snake's bodies rubbing across each other. Had she ever had a dream where she remembered sounds? She couldn't think of one, but dreams had a way of fading into nothing. They were so sharp and insistent when you first woke, and within a few minutes they blurred. By mid-morning you'd forgotten all but a vague idea of the subject matter.

She pushed her elbow forward again and dragged herself closer to the door. A few more feet and she'd be able to see more of the light from the single lamp in the living room. She'd also left a light on in the kitchen but it wasn't visible from Joey's room or the hallway. She laid on her back for a moment and tried to remember where she'd left her phone. She'd come back from Michelle's and put her purse on the kitchen table while she made her sandwich. She thought she'd brought her cell phone into the living room while she watched TV, just in case Joey texted. It was what she usually did, but she couldn't specifically remember doing it this time. Hopefully once she managed to drag herself to the living room doorway, she'd be able to see from there whether it was on the table. Already her elbow and the bone of her forearm ached. By the time she reached her phone, her arm might be in the same shape as her right ankle and kneecap. She was more aware of that leg than the one she couldn't move.

She pulled and dragged herself out of Joey's room into the hallway. Turning sideways, she continued the movements down the hall to the living room. The phone was on the floor in front of the couch. She pulled herself across the room. She reached out her hand and covered her phone, then collapsed on her side and allowed herself to cry for a few minutes.

The point of everything was finishing college, going to law school, getting free of Greg's house and Greg's support payments. But so far, she wasn't free of anything. She was dependent on everyone — Greg, Brian, Michelle. Right now, it seemed as if she couldn't do anything for herself. She was heading in the opposite direction of where she'd planned.

The tears flowed faster, cascading down her cheeks. A sob swelled in her chest. She opened her mouth and cried with gasping breaths, letting the deep sounds turn into wails of self-pity. She was aware of herself crying, aware of how pitiful she sounded, but she couldn't stop.

It wasn't that she wanted to be alone forever. She just couldn't see her life beyond what it was now. If she was honest, she wasn't even sure she could see herself as an attorney. There was nothing but a blurry image when she tried to picture her future. All she knew was what she didn't want — depending on Greg and his girlfriend for shelter and part of her livelihood, feeling their smug superiority. If she was really, truly honest, she did want someone to love, someone to love her back. She pressed her hands to her face and felt the sharp bones of her cheeks, the cartilage of her nose. Her fingers crept up to her brow and her hairline. Right now, her whole body felt like sharp, splintered bones. She was okay looking. And she had a great smile, and beautiful hair. It shouldn't all be about her appearance anyway. What about the rest of her? That slippery, impossible-to-define thing called a human being. She didn't want to spend her life alone.

After a while, she wiped her sleeve across her face. Her nose was stuffed but she didn't have the energy to drag herself to the kitchen for a tissue. She inched forward a few feet and reached onto the table where the napkin from her dinner lay on the plate. She wiped her nose and blew hard into the scratchy paper.

Would Michelle and Gerard be able to carry her to the car? She picked up her phone and pressed 9-1-1. It was easier that way. She didn't want to need Michelle's help.

Thirty-two

BRIAN COULDN'T FORGET the pity in Michelle's eyes. When he saw it, he'd known without a doubt what he had to do. On Tuesday he called in sick. In all the years he'd worked at Hickam Elementary, he'd only called in sick three times, so there was no problem having them believe he'd succumbed to a flu bug. Everyone did, eventually. Not even the upcoming five-day weekend made them doubt his word.

He glanced out the kitchen window to check whether Michelle was in her front yard. He filled the coffee maker with Columbian Roast and poured filtered water into the receptacle. He set two mugs on the counter, a white one for Michelle and a handcrafted one glazed with blue and green for himself. The room was gloomy from the thick covering of clouds, but they weren't dark enough to hint at rain. He turned on the light to brighten things up.

The boards under the hallway carpet creaked as he walked toward the pythons' room. Construction still hadn't started up again waiting for technicians to finish combing the building site and surrounding area for evidence from Tanya's murder. The extraordinary silence was probably half in his mind, disoriented from being home on a weekday morning. There was nothing profoundly different from a Saturday or Sunday, but molded into the crevices of his brain, after years of routine, was a sense that something wasn't quite right.

He opened the door to their room. They were coiled in opposite corners. Cleopatra flicked her tongue and started to move toward the door, but he closed it quickly. They hadn't eaten in nearly a week.

It was close to nine-thirty. He could count on Michelle working in her yard nearly every day, plucking out a stray weed or two. She watched that yard with even greater vigilance than he gave to his property, and he was aware that he was overly fussy. He didn't think he'd ever seen a weed growing in the Reynes' yard, aside from the times he'd stood right next to her, watching as she plucked out the shoots with her fingertips. If it weren't raining, she would be out there, kneeling in the dirt. He was counting on it. The clouds had softened and were more white than gray now. There definitely wouldn't be any rain this morning.

He turned on the coffee maker and went out the front door. The Reynes' yard was empty, the garage door closed. That wasn't good. He stood on the front path. Water trickled out of the statue's upended vase into the bowl of the fountain. He watched it for a moment, trying to decide whether he should go knock on their door. But that would make it too formal, too contrived. He crossed the lawn and put his fingers under the stream of water. He touched the concrete form. Water and an invisible film of algae forming on the statue caused his fingers to slide down her skirt. He yanked his hand away and wiped it on his pants.

The Reynes' garage door opened. A moment later, Michelle stepped out onto the driveway with a bucket and her weeding tool, although why she needed a tool for digging out such small plants, he had no idea.

He walked down the front path and along the sidewalk, stopping near the small gully filled with river rock that separated the two yards.

"What are you doing home?" Michelle said.

"I couldn't face the kids today. I'm not in a good place with my grief."

"It must be difficult for you." She knelt by the rocky border and poked the iron tool between the rocks. She nudged one out of the way and reached down. She pulled out a long blade of grass and dropped it in the bucket.

"I was thinking you might like to see my sculpture. You're always asking, and now seems like a good time."

She sat back on her heels. "You said you didn't show your work to anyone. Why the sudden change?"

"I feel kind of lost right now. It would be nice to …"

Her face softened. She moved her lips as if she was going to smile, but didn't.

As he'd hoped, her pity was over-riding any mild distrust over why, after all these years of living right next door, he was inviting her into his home.

She stood and dropped the tool into the bucket. It clattered and the bucket tipped over. She straightened it and wiped her hands on her jeans, although he couldn't see how they'd be dirty. Her nails were clipped short, painted with a purplish color. There was a large chip in the polish on her right index finger.

"I would like to see it. Thank you for trusting me."

He wanted to laugh, but he gave her a tender smile and said nothing.

Inside his house, Michelle glanced into the kitchen. "It smells like fresh coffee."

"I just made some." He didn't offer any. "My studio is out this way." He led her into the living room and across to the sliding glass door. He unlocked it and pulled it open, stepping back so she could go out first.

She looked across the yard. "How lucky that you have a studio. Did you build it?"

"I did." He stepped outside and crossed the patio. How could she not have known he'd built it? She must have heard him sawing and hammering. Sometimes the human capacity for self-absorption astounded him. He walked along the gravel path.

"Aren't you going to close the door?"

"No, it's fine. Some fresh air in the house will be good."

She looked over her shoulder as if she couldn't bear the thought of leaving the door open. She stood rooted to the spot and he could tell she wanted to close it despite his wishes, but he needed it left open.

"Tanya told me your husband is nervous about the future, over-prepared for disasters … or war."

She laced her fingers through her hair and pressed them hard against her skull. Her knuckles turned white from the effort.

"You didn't know?"

"I knew. She shouldn't have mentioned it to you."

"Why not? She told me everything."

She laughed. "Really."

"Yes. I know about the guns."

She pulled on her hair, yanking it back from her face. The follicles were visible where the hair strained away from her skin. "I don't want to discuss it."

"I can understand that."

"I don't think you can."

"It's funny that Tanya was shot and you're the only people I know who have guns. Are the police aware of that?"

She turned toward the house and stepped off the path, starting across the yard in the direction of the patio.

"Don't you want to see my work?"

She stopped. "Please don't talk about Gerard's supplies. He's a little paranoid and he's just gotten mixed up with the wrong people. That's all. I don't think he even knows how to fire a gun."

"It's not difficult," Brian said.

"Maybe not, but he's never done it, that's what I meant."

He nodded. Her voice was firm, steady — she sounded truthful. Maybe *she'd* pulled the trigger. He'd never considered that. Even better. He put his key in the padlock and turned it. He opened the door, remaining on the path while she stepped inside and looked at the shelves. "Oh! You've … why did you smash it? I told you not to be so hard on yourself."

"It looked horrible."

She looked up at the shelves. "Are these your students?"

"No. I was trying to sculpt my son."

"I didn't know you had a son. Do you see him much?" She turned slowly, scanning the shelves. She still had her arms lifted, her fingers buried beneath her hair. "Why did you invite me here if you destroyed the project you're working on?"

He stepped into the shed. Her failure to comment on the quality of his other work created a vacuum in the small space. "I've also been trying to sculpt one of my pets." He lifted the hammer off the rack and gestured toward the other set of shelves.

She turned slightly. He raised the hammer and swung it, landing a solid hit at her solar plexus. She made a strange, guttural sound and collapsed.

He dropped the hammer and ran back to the house. He raced through the living room and down the short hallway.

He opened the door to the snakes' room and went to the corner where Cleopatra had stretched herself out, pressing her body against the baseboard. Placing one hand about eighteen inches below her head and the other a few feet away so that his arms were outstretched, he bent his knees slightly and lifted her off the floor. He placed her mid-section across his shoulders. Slowly, he backed out of the room. He left the door open, knowing Antony would find his way out, searching for food. Antony's absence was important, so that Brian would be able to tell a plausible story to Gerard, the police … to Claire and Joey.

Construction had started up again today after all. He'd been too focused on Michelle's position and how he might best slam the hammer into the right spot to notice. Now he was fully aware of the rumble of trucks and the occasional shouted instruction. He hoped the noise didn't frighten Cleopatra, but she seemed relatively calm, mostly interested in whether she was finally going to get a meal.

He stepped into the shed and placed her on the floor. Michelle had moved slightly. Her eyes weren't fully closed. The flicker of her eyeballs beneath her lashes unnerved him. Cleopatra moved toward Michelle, her body gliding silently, her tongue stabbing at the air. She crept over Michelle's legs and wound her way up until her head was near Michelle's neck.

As interested as he was in watching Cleopatra, he felt queasy. Michelle had been a friendly neighbor for quite a few years. Until she, or Gerard, murdered Tanya, he'd been fond of both of them. But now, Gerard had to share the endless despair of grief. Still, he couldn't watch. He stepped out of the shed, closed the door, and inserted the padlock. He snapped it closed. He'd check back in an hour or so.

WHEN BRIAN KNOCKED on Gerard's door to deliver the awful news, he was crying. In the short time it had taken to carry Cleopatra to the pottery studio and leave her alone with Michelle, Antony had gone missing. Brian felt sick knowing the snake might have been sacrificed to satisfy Brian's rage, as if he was some kind of god the snakes had to appease. That, plus seeing Michelle, bruised and lifeless. Her eyes had been wide open, the whites visible all the way around the iris — whether that was caused by suffocation or horror, he wasn't sure.

Cleopatra hadn't tried to swallow Michelle's body. He'd known she probably wouldn't. Michelle was a tiny woman, and Cleopatra certainly started in the direction of eating her for dinner, but clearly found her too difficult after all. When Brian had opened the studio door, Cleopatra had her mouth around a mouse. It must have come over from the construction site, disturbed by the digging. Or maybe there were always mice in the yard, it just took Cleopatra's instinct to find them.

Gerard opened the door. "What is it?"

"Something terrible happened." He resisted the urge to add

a polite *I'm so sorry.* He was not sorry and he wouldn't say it simply to make his message more complete.

Gerard lifted his eyebrows, forcing the wiry gray hairs to stand out from his forehead.

"Michelle came over to see my sculpture."

Gerard's eyebrows plunged so that his eyes looked like small stones, buried in the skin around them. He thrust his head forward.

"I have snakes."

Gerard stepped back. His mouth was partially open. He grabbed the doorframe. "So what? You're not making any sense. Where's Michelle?"

"Let me explain." Brian wiped his hand across his face. "I have two snakes. Burmese Pythons. They're quite large. I was so upset about Tanya, I forgot to close the door to their room. They got out and I didn't realize it and I went into the house to make some coffee and then I received a phone call. When I hung up, I realized my snakes had escaped from their room. I was hunting all over the house. I didn't realize one of them had managed to find her way outside. I'm so sorry."

"What the hell are you talking about? What are you trying to say?"

"My python got into the pottery studio and I don't know if Michelle was scared, or what happened, but the python attacked her." His tears evaporated. He cleared his throat. "She's dead."

Gerard stepped onto the porch and shoved Brian to the

side. He fell against a ceramic pot that contained a small orange tree. The branches scratched at his face.

"Where is she? Did you call 9-1-1?"

"It's too late."

Gerard pulled his phone out of his pocket and stabbed at the screen.

He ran across the lawn, past Brian's fountain, and up onto Brian's porch.

Brian felt in his pocket. The padlock and key were there. He pulled himself up and walked to the edge of the cul-de-sac and around the corner. He dropped the padlock and key down the drainage opening.

He was walking back to his house when he heard a scream, deep, bellowing. It continued for nearly a minute — far longer than he thought someone would have the breath to cry out.

Thirty-three

CLAIRE LET HER shoulders and upper back collapse onto the pads of her crutches. She waited while Joey brushed and flossed his teeth. After thirty-six hours of ice and rest, she could manage quite a few steps on her sprained right ankle. Joey would help her across the street and over to the construction site so he could take one last look at the pit. Already it looked less shocking, filled with perfectly spaced concrete pillars. In another week or so, the hole would be lined with the skeleton of the underground parking garage.

She leaned against the porch post to relieve the pressure against her armpits. Her left foot was so heavy, encased in plaster almost to her kneecap, she felt like she'd doubled her body weight. Luckily it was the left foot that was completely useless, but she still wouldn't be driving for several more days. Hopefully by the time the long Thanksgiving weekend was over, she'd be semi-mobile.

She looked across the cul-de-sac at Brian's house. Water

splashed in his fountain, the grass was clipped short, the border of agapanthus perfectly groomed, as always. The blinds were closed. Nothing about the house said that two deadly pythons used to live there. She'd been so stupid to ignore her fears. It wasn't a simple phobia. Her single-minded ambition had put her son in real danger. She blinked several times. She didn't want Joey to see her crying.

Of course, the snakes were gone now.

Yesterday, two detectives had explained what happened and asked her a long list of questions about Gerard, Michelle, and Brian.

After the van from the morgue left with Michelle's body, animal control had pulled into the cul-de-sac. They arrived so quickly, Claire wondered if they'd been parked around the corner. The enclosed back of the truck had vents on the sides and thick doors with heavy-duty latches that looked like they belonged to a commercial freezer. There was no visibility to the interior. A pick-up truck followed the larger vehicle. A man and woman dressed in coveralls got out of the primary truck, and two other men, similarly dressed, emerged from the pick-up.

Part of her didn't want to watch them remove the snakes, but then she decided to follow Brian's suggestion that she face her fears — from the safe distance of her front porch. She'd been glad Joey was still with his father. She hadn't been prepared yet to answer his questions.

The animal control officers rang the bell multiple times

before Brian answered. They went inside, leaving the door open. It was quite a while before the woman stepped onto the front porch.

Claire gasped. Of course she'd realized that a twelve-foot snake was nearly double Brian's height, but seeing the elongated body gradually emerge as three people carried the creature out of the house caused her fingers to tremble on the handles of her crutches. She wanted to close her eyes but forced herself to keep watching. The handlers had their arms spread about three feet apart, gripping the snake's body, contracted muscles visible beneath sleeves rolled up to their elbows. The snake was pale yellow and white. From where she stood, the eyes weren't visible, but she imagined them, staring at her, most likely still hungry. Fortunately, the mouth was closed.

The weakness in her fingers was the only physical reaction. She was amazed that thinking of the snake had caused her to shudder and seeing it did nothing. It was almost unreal.

When the second, brown and black snake was carried out, Brian stepped onto his front porch. His eyes also weren't visible from across the street, but his distorted face told her he was crying.

"I don't understand!" His voice was shrill, near hysteria. "It's not right. He didn't do anything."

No one from animal control even glanced in his direction.

"He's innocent," Brian screamed. "He never hurt anyone."

He fell to his knees. Claire winced at the sound of bone

smacking concrete.

Brian grabbed his hair, pulling it, howling like a starving coyote.

It was beyond horrifying that Michelle had been killed so brutally, murdered, really. Had she been murdered? The detailed questions they'd asked about Brian made her think that was the direction the investigation was headed.

As scared as Claire had been of the snakes, picturing them in her mind as enormous monsters, powerful enough to take whatever prey they wanted and squeeze the breath out of it, she realized it had been a vague fear, a fear of their shape, their non-human-like form, and their unfamiliarity, more than a conscious expectation they would actually kill a human being. Despite her new-found bravery as she watched them get locked up and taken away, she knew the creatures would haunt her dreams for a long time. No wonder cold blooded had become embedded in language as a description for someone with no heart, someone who could kill without thinking.

But didn't other wild animals kill with the same ferocity? From time to time, when the Bay Area experienced drought, mountain lions came into the foothills and sometimes down to the valley floor, looking for food. They would kill a human being just as easily, and with as little remorse. Meaning no remorse whatsoever. So why the *cold-blooded* label taken from snakes and alligators? She'd have to look into that sometime. It would be useful information for an attorney to have.

Of course, her career plans were stalled, and maybe that was a good thing. Maybe she needed to take her eyes off the goal and pay attention to the scenery of her life, racing past. She was angry at herself for ignoring every small twist in her stomach, every vague complaint from Joey about the atmosphere in Brian's house. That beast could have killed Joey far more easily than it squeezed the life out of Michelle.

Everything was on hold. No more school for now. In a few years, Joey might be able to stay with a friend in the evenings, then she'd start over. Being dependent on her ex-husband wasn't the worst thing in the world after all. Look at Doug's sister — utterly dependent. Helpless. Yet she hadn't defined her life around her neediness. She accepted it and went on living.

Brian would still be right across the street, and avoiding him would be difficult. It was unclear how Michelle had ended up alone in his pottery studio. And it wasn't clear how the snake had found its way outside or whether Brian knew it was in the studio. You'd think he would have looked, since he'd insisted he was frantically searching for both snakes. The police would sort it out. Maybe Brian wouldn't be around much longer. It was all too horrifying, and it made her wonder what had really happened to Jennifer. Did she pack up and leave in the middle of the night? Without a car? Simply vanished?

Claire felt as if the neighborhood was emptying around her — Elaine and her family abandoning their home to a fantasy remodel, Michelle's body removed. The weapons carried out of Gerard's house while he watched with a bitter scowl. In some ways, the sharp gray hairs, his eyebrows knitted together in a single line, frightened her more than the presence of all those guns and grenades. After the weapons were removed, including the gun that was suspected of killing Tanya, Gerard himself was taken away for further questioning.

They all thought the threat to their lives was in the pit that yawned just beyond the fence. Soon the three-story structure would rise up and the pit would be nothing but a memory. All the danger had been right inside their own homes, lurking in their bedrooms. Gerard, preparing for some sort of apocalypse, hovering over the computer keyboard in his son's discarded bedroom. Brian, harboring pythons in his spare bedroom. The devastation in her own life had emerged from her bedroom, the place that was supposed to be a refuge where you made love and created new life, rested and dreamt.

She shivered again and pulled the sides of her jacket closer. She fumbled with the zipper, but she couldn't maintain her balance while hooking the two sides together. She'd ask Joey to help. She heard him thumping toward the front door.

She hoped his interest in the pit was still the innocent, child-like fascination with a large hole in the ground, not a morbid desire to re-live finding Tanya's body spread across the wet dirt. Looking into that unfriendly cavern and seeing a woman's body exposed to passers-by, to crows, and the cold, was something she wanted wiped out of her memory. And even though she hadn't actually seen it, she wanted to be rid of the imagined memory of that pale yellow and white snake coiling around Michelle, tightening its grip until she was dead.

Was that what happened as you got older? There were just more and more things you wanted to erase from your mind, trying to forget you'd ever seen them? The image of Greg, naked with another woman flashed behind her eyes. What she really needed were some beautiful images to replace those. Right now, she was as empty as that hole in the ground.

Joey didn't seem bothered by memories of a dead woman. Aside from a hummingbird they once found on the front porch, and worms that crawled out onto the pavement when it was raining, but failed to return to the soil in time so they shriveled and died, Joey had never witnessed death. They hadn't discussed the subject much. It bothered her that Tanya's body was his first encounter with the brutality of life, and its end. More troubling was his lack of emotion. Was that something to worry about? Or had he not fully absorbed what it meant?

Joey flung open the front door. "Ready."

"Will you zip my jacket for me?"

He poked the metal tab into the socket and pulled it halfway up. "Is that good?"

"Yes. Thanks."

Joey raced to the curb. She hobbled behind him. When he reached the center of the street, he moved effortlessly into a forward flip.

"Joey! Not on the pavement."

He stopped and waited for her to catch up. "We should have brought the camera."

"We don't need a picture."

"I'll never see a hole that big again."

"You will. Maybe we'll plan a vacation to the Grand Canyon."

"It would be fun to have a picture of it. And the tree I climbed."

Claire didn't speak.

"Can we go get the camera? Or can you take it with your phone?"

"I don't want a picture."

"I do."

They walked up to the fence. The construction workers were just arriving. The gates on the opposite side, nearly two blocks away, were open. A dump truck rumbled up the curb and into the site.

"There's Doug," Joey said.

Doug stood on a concrete block, looking out across the pit. He was at the bottom, appearing small from where she stood, as if he was twenty miles away, a dot on the horizon. It amazed her how the pit distorted everything.

While she was lost in her observation of proportion and the size of the hole, Joey had climbed partway up the fence. He strained to reach his arm past the top, waving frantically. "Doug!"

"Shh. Get down."

"I see Doug."

"I know. But you can't shout at him."

"Why not?"

"He's working."

Joey moved higher, appearing to defy the law of gravity. Maybe it was a lack of fear.

"Doug!"

Doug turned in their direction and looked up. Claire couldn't see his face, couldn't tell whether it was a casual turn or if he'd heard Joey's shouts.

"Get down," she said.

"I want to say hi to Doug."

"He's not going to come over here. He has to work. We're interfering."

"You're not interfering, just me."

She laughed.

Joey shouted again.

Doug stepped off the concrete block. His work boots hit the ground with sure footing and he walked in their direction. Claire felt her face grow unnaturally warm. It was forty-six degrees when she'd checked the weather that morning, there had been a sheen of frost on her neighbors' roofs, but the temperature of her skin, the warmth spreading from her face, down her neck, and across her chest, made her want to unzip her jacket. Was it her imagination that the truck had stopped moving when Doug looked in their direction? Were they all watching his progress across the bottom of the pit, the lengthening of his stride as he climbed the grade?

He stopped a few feet from the fence.

"Hi," Joey said. "How much longer will the hole be here?"

"We'll be filling it in soon."

"For the parking garage?"

Doug nodded. "What happened to your leg?"

Joey looked down. "I left my skateboard out and she tripped on it."

Claire tapped Joey's leg with the tip of her crutch and he looked up at her. She smiled. "It's not your fault. It was an accident."

Joey turned back to Doug. "We might have to move."

"Why's that?"

"So we can be closer to my grandma and grandpa. So they can watch me when mom's in school. Brian can't watch me any more."

Joey's voice was giddy. It sounded like he had his own plans for their future, unaware that they were essentially trapped in the house she and Greg owned. She couldn't move further away from work, and she couldn't afford to rent a place on her own.

"I guess I won't be seeing you around?" Doug said. He looked at her with that same steady gaze she'd noticed before.

"I didn't say we *are* moving, we might," Joey said.

Below them, the dump truck started moving again. The engine roared and for a moment, it took away the need to fill the air with conversation.

"Or you could watch me." Joey rattled the fence.

"No," she said.

Doug took a step back. She thought he might slip on the sloped ground behind him, but he remained steady.

"Why not?" Joey said.

"We don't even know him." There was a thickness in her throat that made it difficult to swallow.

Doug moved closer to the fence. His breath came out in a puff of vapor that came up to the chain link but dissipated before it passed through. "You could get to know me better."

Joey released his grip on the fence. "You can come over for dinner. My mom makes really good lasagna."

Claire felt she was being railroaded. Yet possibly, she wanted to be railroaded. She was too mistrustful of her own judgment. So she'd made a few mistakes. It didn't mean her entire view of life was off base. She had excellent judgment with Joey. And the people she'd misjudged had lied to her. Even Brian. It wasn't as if she was a mind reader. A cheating husband and a creepy neighbor didn't make her a failure at judging character. In fact, the longer she thought about it, the more she realized that it was more a matter of ignoring her instincts. She'd known Greg never had enough of anything. She'd known that from their first date when he ordered two desserts and told her he wouldn't be happy until he proved to all his college buddies that he was the best, that he'd be the top earner in their class. And there'd never been any question that Brian was a bit unusual. Her problem hadn't been misjudging him, it had been using him because she was desperate.

She was no longer desperate.

"I love lasagna," Doug said.

"Hers is better than any you've ever tasted." Joey darted behind her and jumped to grab the low-hanging branch. He swung his legs up and around the branch.

Claire laughed. She was pretty sure Joey had never tasted anyone else's lasagna, yet he spoke with the authority of broad experience. "I'd like to make lasagna for you."

She looked at Doug. His eyes, dark brown, looked warm and patient, if eyes could look patient. Her hair blew across her face.

Doug poked his finger through the fence and moved the long wavy strand away from her mouth.

She turned. "Get down Joey. We should go."

"What about lasagna?"

She turned back. Doug had moved away from the fence, but she could still see his eyes and they still looked like they were filled with something infinite.

"Friday?" she said.

"I'll bring a bottle of wine."

"See you then."

Joey let go of the branch and dropped to the ground. They walked back to the cul-de-sac without speaking. This time, Joey kept pace with her and she had a brief glimpse of the man she was raising. She was proud of what she'd accomplished so far.

THE END

About The Author

CATHRYN GRANT IS the author of Suburban Noir novels, ghost stories, and short fiction. Her writing has been described as "making the mundane menacing".

Cathryn's fiction has appeared in *Alfred Hitchcock* and *Ellery Queen Mystery Magazines*, *The Shroud Quarterly Journal*, and *The Best of Every Day Fiction*. Her short story "I Was Young Once" received an honorable mention in the 2007 *Zoetrope All-story* Short Fiction contest.

When she's not writing, Cathryn reads fiction, eavesdrops, and plays very high handicap golf. She lives on the Central California coast with her husband and two cats. Visit her website at SuburbanNoir.com or email her at Cathryn@SuburbanNoir.com

Made in the USA
San Bernardino, CA
08 June 2016